More Than a Touch

A Snowberry Creek Novel

Alexis Morgan

A SIGNET ECLIPSE BOOK

SIGNET ECLIPSE
Published by the Penguin Group
Penguin Group (USA) LLC, 375 Hudson Street,
New York, New York 10014

USA | Canada | UK | Ireland | Australia | New Zealand | India | South Africa | China
penguin.com
A Penguin Random House Company

First published by Signet Eclipse, an imprint of New American Library,
a division of Penguin Group (USA) LLC

First Printing, January 2014

ISBN 978-0-451-41772-5

Printed in the United States of America
10 9 8 7 6 5 4 3 2 1

This book is dedicated to all the brave men and women in our armed forces to whom we owe such an enormous debt of gratitude. Thank you and your families for your service to our country.

ACKNOWLEDGMENTS

Snowberry Creek continues to be a whole new adventure for me, and I couldn't do it without help from so many people. So my heartfelt thanks goes out to:

Susan Mallery for your friendship and encouragement. I hope you know how much it means to me.

Janice Kay Johnson for being my friend for longer than either of us wants to admit and for all of our brainstorming lunches, which help keep my stories on track.

Michelle Grajkowski, the best agent ever! Your friendship is a gift in my life. (And a special thank-you to your resident expert on the subject for answering all of my questions.)

Kerry Donovan for being such an amazing editor and for bringing out the best in me and my writing.

To all the behind-the-scenes people at New American Library for sharing your talent and hard work on each of my books.

Chapter 1

The crunch of tires on the gravel driveway out front announced the arrival of the first guests. Leif glanced out the front door to see if he recognized anybody before heading off to the kitchen to let Callie know it was showtime.

"Gage and his daughter just pulled in, and there's a pair of pickups right behind him."

He made the announcement from the safety of the dining room door. The kitchen had been declared off-limits to him, Nick, and even Mooch. Since right after breakfast, Callie and Bridey had been preparing for the potluck dinner they were hosting for the crew of volunteers Nick had recruited for the afternoon.

She had just taken a huge tray out of the oven. The scent of fresh brownies wafting through the air made Leif's mouth water, but Callie knew him well enough to keep the pan safely out of his reach. She smiled at him. "Can you let Nick know, too?"

"Will do."

The last time Leif had seen Nick, his former sergeant when they were deployed together, he'd been heading around to the backyard to set up the tables and chairs that Callie had borrowed from a local church. The shortest route was through the kitchen, but he knew better than to try to go that way. Instead, he did an about-face and went back through the dining room toward the front door. On the way, he whistled for Mooch. The dog came running but skidded to a stop when he spotted the leash Leif had snagged off the table.

When the dog tried to avoid capture, Leif lost patience. "Damn it, Mooch, hold still. There are too many cars pulling in right now for you to be outside without the leash. Otherwise I'll have to lock you in the den for the day."

Not that he would do any such thing, but it did the trick. Finally, Mooch slunk over to lie down at Leif's feet, looking pitiful. Yeah, right—he had it cushy here in Snowberry Creek, and they both knew it. After clipping the leash onto Mooch's collar, Leif patted his furry friend on the head. "Okay, boy, let's go greet our guests."

Outside, Sydney had her father by the hand and was towing him across the yard. "Come on, Dad. Mooch is waiting for me."

"Slow down, Syd. There's no reason to run."

Even so, Gage made no real effort to stop his daughter's headlong rush toward the porch. In his role as chief of police for the town of Snowberry Creek, the former Army Ranger was as tough as they came. But when it came to his daughter, he was pretty much a pushover. Leif liked that about him. He stepped out onto the porch with Mooch hot on his trail. As soon as the mutt spotted Syd, he yipped happily and wagged his tail like crazy.

"Hi, Gage. Hi, Sydney. Mooch has been watching for you."

That much was true. The dog had spent most of the morning lying on the back of the couch, which afforded him a clear view of the driveway out front. Leif eased his way down the steps to join Gage and his daughter in the front yard.

Before handing off the dog's leash, Leif set the ground rules. "Syd, I know you're really good with him, and I don't have to worry about Mooch when he's with you. But until everyone has arrived, I don't want him running loose. Too many moving cars. I've already told him that it's either the leash or he's locked in the den. So if he tries telling you otherwise, ignore him. Okay?"

The nine-year-old giggled at the notion but nodded vigorously as she took control of the leash. "Come on, Mooch. We can still have fun."

They took off running, carefree and happy in the way only children and their four-legged friends could be. Leif called after them, "Syd, can you tell Nick that people are arriving? He's out back."

She nodded as they dashed around the far end of the house. Gage stood next to Leif and watched until the pair was out of sight. "Thanks for letting me bring Syd with me. My folks offered to watch her today since this is supposed to be a work party, but she was so excited about the chance to play with her buddy."

"Not a problem. Callie brought over a couple of her favorite Disney DVDs in case Sydney gets bored and wants to watch a movie. "

Gage looked pleased. "I'll let her know. Meanwhile, I'll grab my toolbox and head around to see what Nick has planned for us."

When Gage went off to get his gear, Leif crossed to where the other new arrivals were unloading stuff from their cars. Two of them were strangers, but he recognized

Clarence Reed, the owner of the local hardware store. Normally the older man wore neatly pressed khakis with a plaid shirt and a sweater vest, all topped off with a flashy bow tie. Today he was dressed in a chambray shirt, jeans, and sturdy work boots. The change in style looked good on him.

"Mr. Reed, it's good to see you again!"

"Hi, Leif." After they shook hands, Mr. Reed introduced his companions. "These are my sons, Jacob and Joshua. And that plastic container there in the backseat has two of my wife's blueberry pies in it. Just a fair warning: Neither of my boys can be trusted within ten miles of anything she bakes, so I'll take them inside for safekeeping. While I do that, do me a favor and tell Nick to put my boys to work as soon as possible. It's the only way these two will stay out of trouble."

His sons, both of whom towered over their father, just laughed. Leif made a point of eyeing the pies when Clarence got them out of the car. "If I slip you a few bucks, would you hide one of those in the den? Even half of one would be good."

Jacob, who looked to be in his late teens, was already shaking his head. "We already tried bribery and got nowhere. I figure if Dad said no to his own flesh and blood, he's gotta say no to you, too. It's only fair."

Joshua joined in. "Dad said the only way we could earn a piece of Mom's pie was to work as hard as we could this afternoon."

If that was the going price for a piece of Mrs. Reed's pie, Leif could pretty much kiss any chance of tasting one good-bye. Considering the shape his leg was in these days, there was no way he could keep up with Mr. Reed, a man twice his age and half his size, much less his two able-bodied sons. On the other hand, Callie's friend Bridey had brought along two of her cheesecakes, and she was a soft touch.

"You guys should find Nick in the backyard somewhere. I'll be along as soon as everyone else arrives. Nick will assign jobs, but I think Callie has told him he has to make a speech first. That should be fun. There's nothing Sarge hates more than public speaking."

After another fifteen minutes of directing traffic and parking, Leif finally joined the rest of the small crowd gathered in the backyard. He caught Nick's eye to signal that the last of the scheduled crew had arrived. Nick immediately ducked inside the house, no doubt wanting Callie by his side when he kicked off the afternoon's festivities. While everyone waited, Leif pulled one of the lawn chairs closer to the porch where he'd have an unobstructed view of the proceedings. Trying not to wince, he lowered himself onto the seat and stretched his legs out.

He'd skipped his morning dose of painkillers because they made him too sluggish to work around power tools safely. Right now he regretted that decision. Damn, his leg hurt, but he was determined to ignore the throbbing pain that dogged his every step. There was no way he'd let it rule his life. Not now, not ever.

The sound of the back door opening snapped him back to the moment at hand. Bridey walked out ahead of Callie and Nick; she headed right for him with a can of pop. When she handed him the drink, she also slipped him a couple of pills. "Nick thought you might need these about now."

Was it that obvious? Leif glanced at the pills and was relieved to see they were just aspirin. They wouldn't knock out the pain completely, but maybe they'd at least blunt its sharp edges.

"Thanks, Bridey."

She patted him on the shoulder as they waited for Nick to get the show on the road. The sergeant looked a bit twitchy up there on the porch, but he finally cleared his throat and started speaking. "I want to thank everyone for coming today. I promise not to work you all too hard, and it means a lot that you all volunteered."

One of Clarence's boys called out, "Or in our case, got volunteered!"

Clarence shot his son a dirty look but then grinned. "His mother begged me to bring them with me. Something about wanting an afternoon off from having to worry about what the pair of them were up to."

Someone from the back shouted, "Can't say as I blame her."

Everyone laughed, including Jacob and Joshua. It had been a long time since Leif had been around the kind of humor that arose from everyone knowing everyone else's business in a close-knit community like Snowberry Creek. As a teenager he'd hated it and was only too glad to leave his hometown behind when he'd enlisted. Odd to realize now that he'd actually been missing this kind of camaraderie after all these years. Meanwhile, Nick picked up where he'd left off.

"Well, however you came to be here, Callie and I both appreciate it." He paused to take her hand, his smile fading a bit. "As you all know, Callie inherited this place from our good friend Corporal Spencer Lang."

At the mention of Wheelman's name, everyone in the crowd grew silent. They'd all lost one of their own. Thank God Nick kept the pause too short for Leif to lose himself in the past for long. "In Spence's memory, we're not just going to restore the house and the grounds to their former glory. As of today, we're making it official that we'll be converting the place into a bed-and-breakfast and naming it Rose Blossom Place, after his mother's favorite kind of flower."

Everyone clapped as Nick and Callie hugged each other, looking so damned pleased to be sharing their future plans with so many friends. Leif might have been jealous under different circumstances, but Sarge deserved to be happy. Besides, maybe now the couple would stop feeling guilty about having inherited the place and just be glad for the gift Spence had given them.

As the applause died away, Callie left Nick's side long enough to pick up the surprise she'd had Leif stow in the back corner of the porch earlier in the day. She held up the brightly wrapped package. "There's one more thing. As most of you know, Nick's going to have to leave soon to finish out his tour in the army. Once he's back, he'll open his own remodeling business here in Snowberry Creek."

After another round of applause, she handed Nick the package. "Go ahead and open it."

He shot Leif a WTF look before tearing into the paper. When he had it unwrapped, he studied the certificate that Callie had had framed for him. His eyes were blinking like crazy as he turned it around and held it up to show everyone else.

"It's my business license. As of right now, I guess Jenkins Renovations is officially up and running." Nick swallowed hard and once again pegged Leif with a long look. "And just so you know, Leif, I left room for your name if you ever decide you want to throw in with me. We'll hold that spot open until you're ready, regardless of how long it takes."

When Nick jumped down off the porch, Leif pushed himself up to his feet. What could he say? They both knew his current goal was to resume his army career. But looking around at the people scattered across the backyard, it hit him that there were worse places to end up than here in Snowberry Creek.

He and Nick exchanged one of those awkward man hugs that never felt comfortable but still meant so much. "Thanks, Sarge. That means a lot. No promises, though."

His friend nodded. "I understand. I just wanted you to know that you've got options."

Leif's throat clogged up with the volatile mix of emotions that seemed to be his constant companion these days. The look in Nick's eyes made it clear he was having the same problem, but he once again spoke to the crowd. "It's time to kick off the work on Rose Blossom Place. The goal today is to move all the furniture from the third-floor bedrooms down to one of the spare rooms on the second floor. Once everything is out of the way, we'll start knocking down walls and ripping up carpet! First of all, though, Leif and I will take a couple of ceremonial swings with the sledgehammer to get things started off right!"

While everyone else gathered up their tools and got their assignments, Leif headed inside to start the trek upstairs. It was a long haul to the top, but damned if he'd miss seeing Nick take out that first chunk of plaster. Right now, the plan was to turn the third floor into a private apartment for Nick and Callie.

Nick had confided that he'd also drawn up plans to convert the large attic on the fourth level into a master bedroom and bath combination so that there would be more room if they expanded their family. It was hard for Leif to get his head around the idea of Nick already thinking about kids, but good for him.

He reached the third floor just as the rest of the crew came pounding up the steps. Earlier, he and Nick had shoved all of the furniture in the first bedroom to one side. Everyone crowded into the small room, lining the walls as they waited for Nick to take that first ceremonial swing. Using the camera on his cell phone, Leif prepared to preserve the moment. He loved that Sarge made a production of it, pretending to spit on his hands and taking two practice swings with the sledgehammer. Then he threw all his strength behind the first blow to connect with the old plaster-and-lathe construction. Dust and wood splinters flew.

"Damn, Sarge! Nice job."

Nick grinned and traded Leif the tool for the camera. "Your turn."

He hefted the sledgehammer, liking the heavy feel of it in his hands. Like Nick, he took a couple of trial runs before finally really cutting loose. The impact sent a jolt screaming up his arms, but it felt good. Kind of like hitting a home run back when he played baseball in high school.

All the other men hooted and hollered while Nick stood next to him and grinned. "I've always known you had a real talent for wrecking things, Corporal!"

Leif handed back the sledgehammer and clapped his friend on the shoulder. "I learned from the best, Sarge."

Nick looked around the room at the other men. "We probably shouldn't bash up any more walls until we get the rest of the furniture out of the way and the carpet ripped up."

He handed Leif a clipboard and a mechanical pencil along with a pair of screwdrivers. "Here's the list of jobs that I'm hoping we can get through today. I've already told everyone where they should start and to check in with you when they're finished."

Next, Nick pointed at a separate list on the second

piece of paper. "I put you down for taking a bunch of stuff off the walls, including light switch covers and the like. There are boxes and packing tape in the closet over there to put it all in. That should keep your lazy ass busy when you're not playing supervisor. Any questions?"

"Yeah, one. As supervisor, does that mean I get to tell you what to do?"

His friend smiled and shook his head. "You can try, but you might want to remember which one of us has the sledgehammer."

Laughing, Leif hung the clipboard on a nail that was sticking out of the wall. "Good point, Sarge. Guess I'll get started on those light switches now."

"You do that, Corporal."

Zoe parked at Callie's parents' house and cut through the woods to deliver the pan of lasagna she'd promised to bring to the potluck dinner. From what she understood, the gathering was in honor of Callie and her fiancé kicking off two new business ventures. Interesting that Callie had decided to stop flitting about the country to stay in Snowberry Creek and turn the old Lang place into a bed-and-breakfast. That should make her parents happy. Nick was going to oversee the necessary renovations to bring the old house up to code and then open his own remodeling business.

Although Zoe was several years older than Callie, they'd known each other back in high school and had become reacquainted since they'd both moved back to Snowberry Creek. When they'd run into each other at Something's Brewing earlier in the week, and Callie had mentioned the work party they had planned for today, Zoe had offered to donate a casserole to the cause.

tonight." Callie held out her hands. "Why don't you let me take that for you? Grab a drink and relax. We'll be eating as soon as we finish reheating the last few casseroles."

Zoe surrendered the lasagna. "Careful. I took it out of the oven just before I left, so it's still hot."

While Callie found a spot for the pan on the table, Leif appeared at Zoe's side with her drink. "I hope you like amber ale; this is one of my favorites. Ever since we got here, Nick and I have been working our way through all of the local microbrews."

"This is fine. Thank you." She took a sip and looked around the yard. "That gazebo looks new. Was that part of the plan for the B and B?"

"Right on both counts."

A catch in his voice hinted that there was more to the story, but she didn't press for details. Still, it did make her curious. "Mind if I take a closer look?"

"No, go ahead."

He looked hesitant about following her, but then Callie called his name, which settled the matter. Zoe stopped a few feet away from the gazebo to admire the gentle curves of the roof and the lacy look of the latticework that formed the sides of the structure. The design was simple but elegant. She stepped inside and immediately wished it was hers. For sure, Callie's future guests would love it.

As she turned back to see if Callie could use a helping hand, she noticed some writing on the back wall. Stepping closer, she read the words written there in black paint. As soon as she did, she almost wished she hadn't. Leif and Nick had built the place as a memorial for their friend and fellow soldier Spence Lang. It was a lovely gesture, one that also explained the odd note she'd heard in Leif's voice when she'd asked about it. It was tempting to find the man and give him a big hug.

Soldiers were a tough lot, but she knew firsthand how much they suffered when they lost a friend in battle. She immediately took a mental step back from the sign and the painful memories it triggered. Now wasn't the time for any dark thoughts. It was an evening for celebrations. She stepped out of the gazebo just as Callie picked up a pan and banged it with a wooden spoon to summon the hungry crowd.

They came pouring around from the front yard, pushing and jostling one another like a bunch of kids. The women immediately took refuge on the far side of the table. Zoe thought that showed good sense and joined them. Picking up a serving spoon, she began dishing out the food as the line filed by.

When it was Leif's turn, he smiled at her. "Can I save you a seat?"

"I'd appreciate it. I'll be along as soon as the line dies down."

"Want another ale?"

"That would be great."

A pair of teenagers right behind Leif grew restless. "Leif, get a move on. We're hungry. Besides, we want to get in the dessert line early to make sure we get some of Mom's pie."

Leif rolled his eyes. "I don't want to hear about it. You two get to eat her pie all the time. Do the decent thing and let the rest of us have first dibs."

Bridey joined the conversation. "Leif, I'm disappointed. Here I made a point of bringing my strawberry cheesecake because you like it so much."

He gave her a guilty look. "Aw, come on, Bridey. We're

talking blueberry pie here! Besides, I planned on having a piece of your cheesecake, too."

Looking disappointed, Bridey shook her head. "Sorry. Too late."

Although Zoe was sure Bridey was kidding, she intervened on Leif's behalf. "Can't he have both? I'm sure he's put in a long day doing all kinds of manly things."

Leif looked hopeful. "That's right, I have. I personally took down at least a dozen light switch covers and knocked a big hole in the wall. I also checked things off a list."

The other woman wasn't buying it. "Seriously? You think checking things off a list warrants a piece of my cheesecake AND a piece of pie?"

The Reed brothers complained again. "Quit holding up the line, Leif. Flirt on your own time."

Leif shot his younger companions a dirty look. "Hush, children. To answer your question, Bridey, maybe I don't deserve both, but I have been known to carry out a strategic raid when the objective is worth the risk. Stealing a piece of your cheesecake definitely falls into that category."

Then he winked at Zoe. "I'll save you that spot."

After he continued on down the line, Zoe realized Bridey was giving her an odd look. "What?"

Bridey whispered, "What do you think of Leif? He's cute, isn't he?"

Zoe's first instinct was to deny that there was any kind of attraction going on. "I just met the man a few minutes ago!"

Then it occurred to her that she might be treading on someone else's territory. "Sorry, Bridey. I didn't know you were—"

Realizing that their conversation wasn't exactly private, she lowered her voice, too. "Interested in him."

"I'm not, I'm sad to say. He's a great guy and a real cutie, but that's as far as it goes. For one thing, I don't know how long he'll be here. No use in getting involved with someone who's not going to stick around."

Bridey immediately turned her attention back to serving the next guy in line. As Zoe waited for him to reach her station, she followed Leif's slow progress across to where he'd staked out two lawn chairs. Bridey was right. He was a cutie, but Zoe wasn't one for short-term flings, either.

Surely one evening of good food and conversation wouldn't hurt anything, though. With that in mind, she served the last few people in line and then fixed her own plate. As she loaded it up with a variety of salads, Bridey stopped her. "Tell him I'll cut him pieces of both the cheesecake and the pie and hide the plate in the cabinet over the stove. Never could resist a pair of puppy dog eyes like his."

Zoe laughed. "I'll tell him—well, except for the puppy-dog-eyes part. No use in letting him know we're both suckers for that kind of thing."

She picked up her plate and headed over to deliver the good news.

The potluck turned into a real party as wives and girlfriends joined the men who'd helped kick off the renovations. Leif had been prepared to spend the evening alone in the crowd, but his luck had changed the minute he'd spotted Zoe standing at the edge of the woods. She seemed content to sit next to him rather than mingling with the others. He should feel guilty about hogging her company, but he didn't. Not really. Besides, other than him, most of the other men were too old, too young, or taken.

Besides, it felt damn good to spend time laughing and talking with a pretty woman. Zoe's eyes, which were the exact shade of blue as the sky on a hot summer afternoon, were never still as she watched the shifting crowd in front of them. She wore her dark hair twisted up in the back and held in place with some kind of stick, making him wonder just how long her hair actually was. It was tempting to tug the pin out to find out.

Callie had dragged out Spence's old boom box and put on music. As soon as the first song started, Sarge grabbed her by the hand and pulled her out into the center of the yard to start dancing. Funny, Leif didn't remember Nick being much of a dancer, but the couple looked pretty good out there. Maybe the three bottles of ale he'd had were affecting his vision. More likely, it was just one more side effect of the couple being so in tune with each other.

A movement off to the left caught Leif's attention. One of the Reed boys was sidling up to Zoe. What was the little jerk up to now?

"Zoe, wanna dance?"

What was the idiot thinking? The boy had to be a good ten years too young for her. Leif waited to see what she'd say. He'd like to tell Jacob to get lost, but it wasn't as if Leif had any claim on the woman's time. She seemed reluctant, but she finally set her drink down on the ground.

"Okay, but just one song." Before walking away, she glanced back at Leif. "I'm saving the next dance for you."

She was? Had she somehow missed seeing the boot on his left leg, the one that pretty much guaranteed he wouldn't be able to do more than shuffle his feet, especially on an uneven surface like the grass? Maybe that was her way of discouraging Jacob, not to mention his brother, who was lurking nearby. Regardless, Leif would give it his best shot. At least with Jacob keeping her occupied, Leif would have time to push himself back up to his feet and make his way over to where Sydney was playing deejay.

He shuffled through the stack of CDs that Callie had brought out and settled on a slow ballad by one of his favorite country singers. "Syd, play the third song on this one next for me, and then the fifth one."

She wrinkled her nose. "You actually like that kind of music?"

He tugged on her braid. "I do, and I'll owe you big-time. How about a chance to play with Mooch at the park?"

Syd gave him a narrowed-eyed look. "And an ice-cream cone."

He didn't even hesitate. "It's a deal."

The current song was winding down. Leif propped his cane against the table and made his way through the crowd, moving slowly to keep his balance. Jacob had just said something to Zoe that had her laughing. Before he could ask what it was, the song he'd asked Syd to put on started playing. He held out his hand and was glad when Zoe didn't hesitate.

"I apologize if I mainly stand in one spot and sway. You might have noticed that my boot isn't exactly made for dancing."

"That's all right." She smiled up at him. "Isn't that what slow dances are all about?"

Who was he to argue? Especially when everything was going his way. His pain was at a manageable level, and he had a pretty woman willing to dance with him.

As soon as the first song ended, Syd started the second one. Zoe paused to give him a suspicious look. "How did you get her to play two slow songs in a row?"

Leif did his best to give Zoe a quick spin and then twirled her right back into his arms. "It would be wrong to bribe a young child."

"But you did."

"I hate it when my nefarious plots are uncovered. Don't tell her dad. He carries a gun and handcuffs."

Zoe laughed and rested her head against his chest. "Your secret is safe with me, but it's going to cost you some of that pie that Bridey saved for you."

Leif thought about protesting, but all things considered, a piece of pie was a pretty cheap price for two dances with Zoe. "You drive a hard bargain, lady, but it's a deal."

When the song finally ended, Leif retrieved his cane and headed back to his chair while Zoe went inside to get the secret stash Bridey had left for him. She returned with one plate and two forks. That was okay. He liked the idea of sharing his favorite desserts with her. They battled good-naturedly over who was hogging the goodies. When they were down to the last two bites, Zoe set her fork down on the plate.

"You finish it."

"Are you sure?"

"Yeah. I'm already going to have to put in some extra hours in the gym to make up for everything I've eaten tonight. Besides, I need to get going."

Just that quickly, the pie and cheesecake lost their appeal. He set the plate on the ground and started to stand up. "I'll walk you back to your car."

For the first time all night, Zoe gave his leg a pointed look. "There's no need, Leif. My car is right next door."

Which was a hike along a rough path through the trees. The smart thing was to take the out she was offering him, but pride had him insisting on providing escort at least part of the way. Taking a header in the woods wouldn't help his leg or impress Zoe. "I'll walk you as far as the trees."

At least she didn't argue. "Okay. I'll let Callie know I'm leaving."

When she came back, they walked in companionable silence across the yard to the start of the trees. "I had a good time tonight. Maybe we can get together again while I'm still in town."

Zoe studied him for a few seconds before slowly nodding. "Callie's got my number."

Then she was gone, but not before she pressed a soft kiss to his cheek. It seemed like things were finally starting to look up for him. His good mood didn't fade until he was stretched out in bed and his pain pills sent him over the edge into a deep sleep.

Chapter 2

For a soldier, the mission was everything. Leif knew that and had lived by that creed for his entire army career. At twenty, he'd signed up to serve his country and ended up being deployed three times to fight in a pair of down-and-dirty wars on the other side of the world. Experience was a bitch of a teacher, but he'd learned damn near everything there was to know about combat in the dust, dirt, and bloody sand of Iraq and Afghanistan.

Which was why his current surroundings had him a bit freaked. He glanced out at the neatly trimmed grass and towering firs scattered around the gently rolling hillside. This wasn't where he was supposed to be—that was for damn sure. He should be holding a gun, not a cane. At least he felt more at home in his ACUs than he would've in jeans and a golf shirt even if his desert camouflage uniform did stand out like crazy in the midst of all this Pacific Northwest greenery.

By the time Leif reached his friend's side, he was breathing hard. A pain pill sounded good about now, but they'd become even more of a crutch than his cane. Besides, he needed his wits about him to get through the next few minutes.

"Well, Wheelman, sorry it took me so long to stop by, but that guy Murphy had it right about everything that can go wrong will go wrong."

He smiled and shook his head. If anybody knew about the role Murphy's Law played in the life of a soldier, it was Spence.

"Anyway, I brought the beer." He held up the six-pack in his right hand. "You always did say that conversation was thirsty work, and I've got a few things to say. I figure you won't mind if I do all the talking."

He popped the caps off a pair of bottles of the Wheelman's favorite microbrew, one for himself and one for Spence. Leif took a long swig to let the smooth chill of the beer clear out the last bit of fear.

As tempting as it was to stare up at the blue sky, Leif forced himself to look at his friend head-on. "I've only been back in the States for a few weeks, Spence. That last mission landed my ass in the hospital in Germany. Well, not my ass, exactly."

He reached down to knock his beer bottle against the plastic contraption that encased the lower half of his left leg. "My ankle got busted up pretty bad on that last mission. The army surgeons did a bang-up job of screwing the bits and pieces of my bones back together. That's the good news. The bad news is that they tell me it's going to be a long haul to get it back to full strength.

"I haven't told the sergeant this next part, Spence. He already feels guilty. No use in making it worse for him." Leif paused for another long drink. "The docs insist on telling me the prognosis is good, but I'm not buying it. Maybe it would be easier to believe them if even one of the bastards could look me in the eye for a second while he said it."

But that hadn't happened yet. Hell, he knew he was damn lucky to have a leg left at all. All things considered, he didn't have much to complain about.

"Anyway, they've fixed me up with someone at a civilian clinic and a physical therapist right here in Snowberry Creek. I'm supposed to meet up with them this morning."

He shook his head. "That's another thing you should know, Wheels. Nick and I, well, we somehow ended up hanging out here in your hometown, and it looks like we'll be staying a while. How weird is that?"

The words kept coming. "You see, Nick drove all the way out here from Ohio to see if Callie would give Mooch a home. That was his excuse, anyway. Mostly, he needed to put some space between himself and his folks. You know how hard it is to adjust to being stateside again."

Leif rolled his shoulders, hoping he could get the rest of it out before he ran out of beer or courage. "This is a real nice town, Spence, and the people are sure friendly. Sarge has decided to stay here in Snowberry Creek permanently. I know you had thoughts about coming back here to Callie, what with the two of you being so close and all. I don't know how serious you were about that, but she and Nick have hooked up big-time. Hell, they're planning on getting married."

There. He'd managed to get the worst part out. "Not only that, but Nick's starting his own remodeling business here in Snowberry Creek once he gets clear of the army, starting with your house. He wants me to think about throwing in with him on it. For sure, he's not going to reenlist, and I'm not sure the army will want me back with this leg. Maybe they'd offer me some kind of desk job, but you know how much I'd hate that."

The alarm on his cell phone chimed, reminding him he had places to be, other people to see.

"I think I've covered the high points of what we've got going on these days. Guess I'd better head over to the medical clinic now, Wheels. I'll stop by again soon. I'll leave the beer for you."

Leif set the rest of the six-pack next to Spence's headstone before reaching out to trace his friend's name, carved into the polished granite. The stone was surprisingly warm, but then Spence had always run hot, charging through life at full bore.

"Damn it, Wheels, I miss you so fucking much. We all do." Leif took a step back. "It hurts so damn much knowing that you died on that street so Nick could drag my worthless ass to safety. He and I are both having a hard time learning to live with that, but maybe we'll figure it out eventually. I'm not much for the mushy stuff, Wheels, but it was an honor to know you and serve at your side."

Leif straightened up, ignoring the fresh stab of pain in his leg. Blinking hard to hold back the sting of tears, he could have sworn he could hear the ghostly strains of "Taps" echoing through the nearby woods. Maybe he was only imagining how it had been the day his friend had been laid to rest here next to his parents on this Washington hillside. Real or not, it didn't matter. Throwing back his shoulders, Leif stood at attention until the last note died away.

Clutching his cane in his left hand, he executed a perfect salute, did an about-face, and marched away.

Chapter 3

❧❧

"Hey, Zoe, your next appointment is here."

"I'll be with you in a second, Brandi. I need to finish this before I lose my train of thought."

Her medical assistant nodded and leaned against the doorframe while Zoe finished typing an e-mail. She scanned it one last time and hit SEND before looking up. "Now you've got my undivided attention."

Brandi held out a clipboard and a stack of paperwork. "His name is Corporal Leif Brevik. He's a soldier who needs physical therapy for his leg."

Leif? Zoe stared at the forms he'd filled out. How had she missed seeing his name on her patient list for the day?

Brandi kept talking. "He's a real cute guy, by the way, if a bit too clean-cut for my tastes."

"And how is that last part pertinent to his medical care?"

Totally unrepentant, her assistant just grinned. "I wanted to make sure you noticed that he is totally drool-worthy. You have a tendency to miss important details like that."

If Brandi figured out that she and Leif had not only met but had shared drinks and slow dances, Zoe would never hear the end of it. She gave an exaggerated sigh. "He's a patient, Brandi, which means what he looks like is completely irrelevant."

She pointed her finger at the top of the form. "Besides, according to this, he's three years younger than I am."

"Your point being?" Brandi popped her gum and gave Zoe her best wide-eyed–innocent look. Somehow, she managed to pull it off despite her black lipstick, nose ring, and white spiked hair, which was tipped with green this week.

"He's too young for me, so you can quit playing matchmaker. I'm not interested."

Especially now that he was a patient. The trouble was that she wasn't interested in anyone else, either, a situation that her young assistant seemed determined to change. Good luck with that.

Zoe slipped her lab coat on and settled her stethoscope around her neck. "While I talk to Corporal Brevik, can you give Isaac a heads-up that I'd like him to pop in to meet his new patient?"

She glanced at her watch. "Tell him we should be ready for him in about twenty minutes."

"Will do."

Zoe waited until Brandi was gone before making her way down the hall to the examination room. Before knocking on the door, she paused for a few more seconds to finish reading through Leif's answers to the questions on the form.

Typical guy, he'd ignored the entire section on mental health and had answered the rest of the questions with one- or two-word responses: yes, no, not applicable. That was all right. Zoe knew enough to fill in the gaps. After serving three tours of duty, of course he was having a few issues. At the very least, she doubted he'd slept through the night in months. And if she were to toss something through the door with no warning, she'd bet her last dollar he'd be diving for cover. It took more than a few weeks to overcome the effects of living on the edge for months at a time.

Considering the amount of hardware the surgeons had used to reconstruct Leif's lower leg, he had to be hurting. On a scale of one to ten, he'd put his pain level at one. Yeah, right.

Well, upon careful review and all things considered, she decided Leif rated an eight, maybe even a nine, on her own personal bullshit-o-meter. Not that it mattered. She'd spent years learning how to deal with tough guys and hard-asses like him when she was in the army. She and Corporal Brevik might knock heads over his care, at least at first, but eventually they would come to terms.

For his sake, she'd make damn sure of it.

Zoe rapped on the door of the examination room before walking in. Most patients looked up as soon as she stepped into the room, but not Leif. Instead, he kept his back turned toward her, his stance rigid with tension and his left hand grasping his cane in a white-knuckled grip.

"Corporal Brevik. We meet again."

While she waited for a response, she studied the man standing in front of her. Judging by the fit of his uniform, she'd been right about him needing to put on a few pounds. He'd lost quite a bit of weight since he'd been injured. No surprise there, but he still managed to fill up a lot more space than most men his size usually did.

Something to do with those broad shoulders and that military bearing. He didn't need that uniform to prove he was in the army. She would've recognized him as a soldier even without it.

When he still didn't respond, she tried again. "Corporal? Do we need to check your hearing, too?"

He finally turned to face her, and it was all she could do to hold her ground. His dark eyes, which had been warm and welcoming last night, were now rock hard and cold.

Leif finally acknowledged her with a quick nod. "You never mentioned you were a doctor."

"I'm a nurse practitioner, Leif, not a doctor. You can still call me Zoe. Ms. Phillips works, too, if you'd rather."

Time to get down to business. She gave his leg a pointed look. "Although we're a family practice clinic, you're not the first referral I've had for a soldier rehabbing in this area, and our physical therapist is one of the best. Like me, Isaac is former military himself, although he was in the navy. I've learned to overlook that particular failing on his part, because his other gifts more than make up for it. Almost, anyway."

She grinned at Leif, hoping the small joke about interservice rivalries might break through his control. Sure enough, the grim slash of Leif's mouth quirked up at the corners, if only briefly. It was the first crack in his icy demeanor. Good. The two of them didn't need to be best friends, but they did need to find some common ground. A patient's trust was imperative if they were to work together as a team.

"Why don't you have a seat, and we'll get started."

He eyed the examination table with obvious reluctance. Realizing that climbing up there would be problematic for him, she pointed toward the bench in the corner.

"Would you mind sitting there? That way, we'll be at eye level while we talk."

As she spoke, she sat down on the rolling stool that had been tucked under the counter. "To tell the truth, my neck gets tired after a day spent staring up at people on the exam table."

Whether or not he believed her explanation was beside the point. The small lie gave him the excuse to accept her offer without having to admit to any weakness on his part. There was no mistaking the flash of relief when he lowered himself to sit on the bench, his leg stretched out in front of him.

Zoe frowned. Had she caught a whiff of alcohol on his breath as he passed by her? Maybe, but he was now too far away for her to know for sure. It was awfully early in the day to be drinking. That was something she'd have to keep an eye on.

Meanwhile, he leaned back and closed his eyes, his body language making it clear that he'd rather be anywhere else right now. She wanted to smack him upside the head to get his attention.

"I've read through your file. The doctors want you to start a course of therapy designed to improve both strength and mobility in your leg."

No response.

"I see you've been given a prescription for a pretty powerful painkiller. How much of that last refill do you have left?"

Those dark eyes popped open to glare at her again. "Some."

God, she hated guessing games. "How often are you

taking them? Do you wait until you're hurting or do you take them more often than that?"

"If you're asking if I'm addicted to them, the answer is no." He sat up straighter, wincing as he did so. "I don't like taking the damn things at all. They leave me thick-headed, and I hate that feeling."

Leif shifted again, as if still trying to find that one magical position that didn't hurt. "I do take them at night. I sleep better that way."

Another lie or at least an exaggeration. People who were sleeping well didn't have those dark circles under their eyes. She made a couple of notes on his chart before moving on to another hard question.

"Are you self-medicating with anything else, like alcohol or recreational drugs?" She softened the question with a small smile. "I'm not talking about an occasional beer with friends, Leif. We all need those once in a while."

How odd. For a second there he'd looked a bit sheepish. At least now he was answering in more than monosyllables.

"Yes, as you well know, I do drink beer, but I don't take the pain pills when I do. The medics warned me that mixing the two wasn't smart. And for the record, I don't do street drugs. Never have and never will. That's a damn good way to get yourself killed in combat."

His response was vehement enough to convince her that he was telling the truth. He was still talking, the bite of temper ringing clear in each word. "I didn't take a pill this morning because I knew I was going to have a beer with a friend. That's why I'm hurting worse than usual right now. Satisfied?"

She put a little more starch in her own response. "Yes, I am, Leif. I also understand these questions are making you angry, but I will ask them anyway. I can't help you if I don't know the truth of your situation."

Leif flexed his hands several times, clearly trying to find a safe outlet for his frustration. "Fine. Ask away."

They ran through the rest of the list in short order. Toward the end, he was even offering up more information than she'd asked for. That was progress.

"I've asked our physical therapist to stop in. Before he gets here, I'd like to take a look at your leg. If you'll come with me, the exam table in the next room is lower, which should make it easier for both of us. My assistant would've put you in there to begin with, but it was in use at the time."

Okay, that was another lie, but she wanted to protect Leif's pride as much as possible. She wasn't about to point out that she doubted very much that he could make it up onto the exam table without causing himself a lot of pain right now.

"I'll open the other room for you and then rejoin you in a minute or two. I need to check in with my assistant to see if Isaac will be able to stop in soon. Boot and pants off, by the way."

She offered him a smile and walked out. Experience had taught her that despite their wounds, soldiers were still soldiers. He might cut himself some slack when no one was watching, but he wouldn't appreciate an audience as he struggled to stand up, much less getting out of his boot and pants.

It didn't help that she was feeling a bit off her game having him as a patient. At the party, they had flirted and laughed. She could still remember how it felt when he held her close as they danced. They could have been friends or even something more. Now, because he'd come under her professional care, an unexpected chasm had opened between them that she wasn't sure how to bridge or if she should even try. No, her gut instinct said they'd both be better served if she maintained a professional distance.

With that in mind, she opened the room next door and then made herself scarce.

An hour later, Leif made it out of the clinic in one piece. Barely. Right now his leg ached, his head throbbed, and his pride was shredded.

Yeah, he appreciated Zoe's efforts to make things easier for him by moving him to the room with the lower table. But damn, did she really think he wouldn't notice the room was decorated for kids? It was hard to miss all those cutesy zoo animals painted on the walls and the box of toys in the corner.

He hoped he hadn't been too much of a jerk. It was hardly Zoe's fault that he was in pain. Hiking his ass all over the cemetery earlier when he was scheduled to see her and that huge guy who was going to be his physical therapist hadn't been smart. The long overdue talk with Spence had left him emotionally drained and hurting before he even got to the clinic. Then having her and the therapist twist and turn his ankle like it was a fucking pretzel hadn't helped much either.

He was supposed to come back in two days to see both Zoe and Isaac again. They'd promised that by then they'd come up with a plan of attack to start rebuilding the strength in his leg. Good luck with that. He wasn't holding out much hope that anyone could put his Humpty Dumpty leg together again.

It was time to kick it into gear and head back to the house. Nick had loaned Leif his truck for the day, but he didn't want to abuse the privilege. He checked the time.

Maybe he could squeeze in one more stop along the way. Now that he was stuck here in Snowberry Creek for a while, he needed to buy his own set of wheels.

As soon as he pulled into the parking lot of the small dealership on the outskirts of town, he knew he'd made a tactical error. He needed something practical, not flashy. The smart thing to do would be to drive right back out of the parking lot, but evidently he was stuck in dumb mode. Before he could stop himself, he was out of Nick's pickup and headed straight for temptation itself.

The truck wasn't new, but somebody had taken damn good care of it. The finish was a bright red, polished to a fault. The interior was absolutely pristine. He slowly walked around the truck in hopes that he'd find something that turned him off. No such luck. Right now he knew what a fish felt like, nibbling at the worm while doing its best to ignore the danger.

Approaching footsteps warned him the local angler had noticed Leif's interest in the truck. The salesman came trolling by, hoping to set the hook good and proper.

"Good afternoon, Corporal. I see you picked out the best vehicle on the lot."

Leif wouldn't know. He hadn't bothered to look at any of the others. He peeled his eyes away from the truck long enough to glance around. The salesman wasn't exaggerating. Everything else looked faded and shopworn by comparison. That was probably an unfair assessment, but then, he'd always been a sucker for red trucks and cars.

"How much?"

If it was way out of his price range, there wasn't any reason to even take the truck out for a quick spin. That didn't keep him from opening the door to the cab to take a better look at the interior, though. Meanwhile, the salesman prattled on about everything but the price: one owner, well maintained, blah, blah, blah.

Finally, Leif pegged the man with a hard stare. "I repeat, how much?"

The price didn't exactly send Leif into sticker shock, but it was a close call. He immediately stepped away and headed back toward Nick's truck.

"Thanks. That's all I needed to hear. No use in wasting any more of my time or yours. I'll be going now."

He hid a smile as the salesman trotted after him, sputtering. "Look, Corporal, I should have made it clear that was the price before we apply the military discount. Why don't you come inside and have a seat? I'll get us each a cup of coffee and then see what other discounts we can offer you."

Leif made a point of looking at the time. "I suppose I have a few minutes. But I've got to tell you"—he leaned closer to read the man's name tag—"Chuck, you'd have to come way off that price for me to even consider buying that truck. Way off."

Chuck looked relieved. Maybe sales hadn't been so good lately, which could work in Leif's favor. As he followed the salesman into his office, Leif couldn't help but wonder which one of them was about to hook a big one.

An hour later, Leif walked out of the dealership twirling the keys on his finger. He'd already called to see if Nick could come get his own truck so Leif could drive his new purchase home. Luckily, Callie had errands in town and could drop Nick off at the dealership.

They should be pulling into the parking lot at any second. While he waited, Leif circled the truck with a big grin on his face. If he'd had any doubts about the wisdom of buying the first truck he'd looked at, they'd been vanquished by the test drive. The truck hummed with power and handled like a dream.

He'd just finished his second lap, admiring all its attributes, when Callie pulled into the parking lot. She and Nick joined him in staring at the truck. Why didn't either of them say anything?

"Well?"

Nick let out a low whistle. "Hot damn, Corporal, she's a beauty. I can see why you bought her. Hell, I'd have been tempted myself."

Callie joined in. "You know, I'm pretty sure I know who used to own this truck. If I'm right about that, you can rest assured it was well maintained. Mr. Wolfe takes good care of everything he owns."

"That's the name the salesman told me. He was surprised I wasn't familiar with it. Sounds like the previous owner is one of the big fish in this little pond."

"That's true. His family actually founded the town." Callie trailed her fingers along the fender. "Well, congrats on the truck, Leif, but I'd better get going. See you both at dinner."

She paused to give the sergeant a quick kiss before heading back to her car. Both men watched in silence until she was gone. It was nice to see his friend smiling more often. Meanwhile, he handed Nick back his keys. "Thanks both for the loan and for coming so I could drive this baby home."

"No problem."

Nick kept his eyes firmly on the truck, but he definitely had something on his mind. Leif figured it was one of two things. Either he wanted to know what was up with Leif's leg or if buying the truck meant Leif was going to stick around Snowberry Creek.

He bet it was the prognosis for his leg that had the

man tied up in knots. "Sarge, you're about to choke on whatever it is you're trying to hold back, so just ask me. Either it'll piss me off or it won't. Besides, the suspense is killing me."

"Okay, fine." Nick released the breath he'd been holding. "So how did it go at the clinic today?"

Score one for Leif. "It turns out that Zoe Phillips, that woman who brought lasagna to the potluck, is the nurse practitioner in charge of my case. I go back in two days to find out what specific form of torture she and the therapist have in mind for me."

Nick knelt down to study the front tire on Leif's truck, staring at it as if the tread depth was the most fascinating thing he'd ever seen. "Are you going to do what they say?"

What choice did he have? None, not if he didn't want to be tied to this fucking cane the rest of his life. "I'd be scared not to, considering the size of the guy in charge of my PT. I don't know what Isaac did in the navy, but he could have bench-pressed a submarine."

"How about Zoe? What did you think of her?"

"She's nice enough. She's also former army, so she's had experience working with injuries like mine."

Looking back, he bet she'd seen far worse, too. Something about the expression in her eyes had hinted that she'd had her fill of mangled limbs and bodies.

"That's not what I meant, and you know it. I didn't miss the fact you were dancing with her at the party."

What was he supposed to say? Yeah, he liked her, especially at the potluck. Today she was all business. That didn't make her any less attractive, although her features were a little too strong to be merely pretty. The word "striking" came to mind, especially with the contrast between her nearly black hair and bright blue eyes. He had to say something, though. The last thing he wanted to do was give Nick the idea he'd been attracted to Zoe.

"Look, I was too busy trying not to punch somebody while they messed with my leg."

Nick had moved on to poking around under the hood. "So, does this mean you're going to stay in town long enough to help me rehab Spence's house for Callie?"

"Yeah, for now anyway."

It wasn't like Leif had anywhere else he needed to be. Unlike Nick, he wasn't particularly close to his family, something he'd had in common with Spence. Part of the reason he'd enlisted in the first place was to get away from his folks. They weren't bad people, but they'd separated about the time he'd started high school. Overnight everything he'd ever known was gone, sort of like the way the beautiful symmetry of a spiderweb could be destroyed by the touch of a careless hand.

They had each remarried shortly after the divorce was finalized and started second families. That had left Leif the only one bouncing back and forth between two households, neither of which ever really felt like home.

Oh, he knew his folks had loved him and still did. He'd never doubted that much about them, but that didn't mean he fit in with their new lives. Everyone, him included, was more comfortable with the occasional short visit between deployments. They wouldn't know what to do with him if he showed up on their doorstep needing a long-term place to crash.

He could get his own crib, of course, but living in his hometown held no appeal. It had been years since he'd had any contact with the crowd he'd hung out with in high school. Sitting on his ass by himself night after night? No, he didn't think so.

"I'm glad to hear it, Leif. There'll be enough to keep

both of us busy for a long time to come." Nick put the hood back down. "I have to report back to get processed out, but I shouldn't be gone all that long. I'll sleep easier knowing you're here to keep an eye on Mooch and the house. Callie will appreciate the company, too."

Nick had already been waffling about reenlisting when he'd arrived in Snowberry Creek looking for a home for Mooch, the dog their unit had adopted in Afghanistan. Soon afterward, he'd sent for Leif, hoping to use him as a buffer between himself and Callie. Yeah, like that had worked.

It had been obvious from the get-go that the man had been fighting some pretty strong feelings for her. Well, that battle had been waged and won. Now it would take a crowbar and dynamite to pry Nick out of Snowberry Creek.

Leif didn't blame him. Nick had served his time and his country. God knows the man deserved a little happy in his life. Leif hoped his decision also meant that Nick had shed the shitload of guilt he'd been carrying ever since an IED had changed both of their lives forever.

"I'll feed the mutt and keep the lawn mowed." He started to take a step, but as soon as he shifted his weight, his bum leg almost gave out on him. It was definitely time to get back to the house and take one of his pills. Maybe two.

He ignored Nick's look of concern and opened the door of the truck. As he climbed up, gritting his teeth against the pain, he cautioned his friend, "But all bets are off if Callie starts sending all of the cookies she bakes to you."

Nick laughed. "I'll make sure she holds a few back for you."

"A few, my ass, Sarge. I'd better get my fair share, especially if you want me to talk you up to Callie's parents when they get back. After all, you managed to get engaged to their daughter without them ever having met you."

His friend swallowed hard. "It's a deal."

Leif laughed at the sick expression on Nick's face. Her parents were coming back from their summer in the sun in another two weeks. They'd wanted to come sooner, but their departure had been delayed when her father threw his back out golfing. Now Nick would be gone before they returned.

Leif turned the key in the ignition, once again taking pleasure in the smooth rumble of the engine. "See you back at the house."

And if he burned a little rubber driving out of the parking lot, who could blame him? A man was entitled to have a little fun with a new toy.

Chapter 4

✣ ✣

It was Zoe's turn to man the clinic's booth before the high school football game. Her boss, Dr. Tenberg, hoped to have someone at every home game to offer free blood pressure checks and answer questions about the medical services available in the area. She'd done a steady business since people had started arriving for the game.

As she replenished the stack of brochures, she noticed Gage Logan, the chief of police, hovering nearby. He sidled a bit closer to her table, all the while scanning the area as if watching for someone, or maybe for trouble. Finally, he headed straight for her.

"Hi, Zoe! Got time for one more?"

As he spoke, he kept his eyes on the surrounding crowd. What was going on? She didn't see anything out of the ordinary.

"Always, Gage. Have a seat and slip your arm out of your jacket sleeve."

When he was settled in the chair, she put the cuff in place and started pumping the bulb. It didn't take long to take his vitals and then record them on the small card that he'd pulled out of his wallet. Despite his obvious tension, his readings were good. "Not bad, Gage. One-twenty-five over seventy."

His relief was obvious as he abruptly stood up and shoved his arm back into his jacket sleeve. "Great, Zoe. Thanks."

"Is everything okay, Gage? You're acting pretty jumpy."

Now he looked guilty. "My daughter's here, and I didn't want her to see me getting my blood pressure checked. Sydney has turned into an awful nag lately. They've been studying health at school, and now she watches every bite I eat and crabs at me to exercise more."

Okay, that was funny, although Zoe was careful not to let Gage see that she found the big, tough lawman's predicament entertaining. Evidently her efforts were less than successful, judging by the rueful look he gave her.

"Yeah, it's cute to hear her spouting all the facts and figures on cholesterol and the effects of job-related stress. But then this morning she lectured me on how dangerous it is for older men to become too sedentary. Hell, I'm only thirty-eight, but to hear her talk, I'm closer to a hundred."

Zoe gave up on holding in her laughter. "Well, your blood pressure is great. I'd be glad to tell her that personally if you'd like."

"It may come to that." His smile faded. "Seriously, I don't mind her nagging, but what if it's because she's afraid she'll lose me like she did her mother? I don't like the idea of her worrying so much. Well, I'd better get back. I promised I'd sit with her during the game."

"The offer stands, Gage. Just let me know."

As he disappeared back into the crowd, another familiar figure made his way toward Zoe's table. Her smile tightened, although she felt guilty for feeling less welcoming toward this visitor. It wasn't the man himself, but what he represented to her.

"Pastor Haliday. Have a seat."

The minister held out his arm, watching her with those pale gray eyes that always saw too much. "How are you doing, Zoe?"

"Fine."

She wrapped the cuff around the Army Ranger tattoo on his arm and pretended her terse answer was due to the need to concentrate on getting an accurate reading on his blood pressure. While that was true, it wasn't the only reason. He'd been after her to get involved with his veterans' support group for some time. She hadn't been interested the first time he'd asked and she wasn't interested now.

After jotting down his results, she handed him his card back. "There you go. Hope you enjoy the game."

Before he could respond, the band struck up a spirited march, making it nearly impossible to carry on a conversation. However, the good pastor was nothing if not determined. He leaned in close enough to make himself heard.

"I was wondering if you'd be willing to do a presentation on the services available for veterans in our area."

How could she refuse? Maybe by asking someone who already had all of that information at her fingertips. "I have a friend who works at the VA hospital who talks to veterans all the time about that sort of thing. I'll give her a call and ask her to meet with your group."

Pastor Haliday sighed, clearly disappointed. "That would be great, Zoe."

"I'll let you know what she says."

She ignored the twinge of guilt over not reaching out to the group herself, but she couldn't. Just couldn't. She fought the urge to apologize, even though the sympathy in the former soldier's eyes made it clear that he understood exactly what was going on in her head.

"If my friend can't fit it into her schedule, I'll ask her to send me all the information for you."

She didn't know how old Jack Haliday was for sure, but she guessed he was in his early fifties. There were times he looked much older, and tonight was one of them. "Most of our members are doing all right, but there are a few who need help whether they realize it or not."

Could he be talking about her? She hoped not. There was a roar in the grandstands. "Sounds like the game's started."

Just that quickly, the minister's demeanor changed. "Should be a good one."

He wandered away, his attention now on the teenagers out on the field as they formed up for the next play. Zoe took several calming breaths and packed up her equipment. The chances of anyone else stopping by before halftime were pretty slim. For now, she would join the people ranged along the sidelines to watch the game.

The home team was already ahead by seven points and was moving steadily down the field again. It looked like tonight's game would continue the great start to their season. Lately, there'd been quite a buzz about the mayor's son, Colby, being an up-and-coming star. Only a sophomore, he'd made the varsity team as a wide receiver. Rumor had it that several colleges were already taking notice.

The quarterback sent the ball sailing high in the air right into heavy coverage, but Colby made an over-the-shoulder catch that had the crowd going crazy.

Two men standing somewhere behind her struck up a conversation. "That was a helluva catch."

"Bet you ten bucks they go with the same play again."

"That's a sucker bet, Nick. He's obviously the best player on the field, but the other team knows that. They'll double-team him, which will open up room on the other side for the other receiver."

Zoe glanced back over her shoulder to see who had spoken, because the second speaker sounded all too familiar. Leif spotted her at the same time.

"Zoe?"

Ignoring how her pulse kicked up a notch just hearing him say her name, she aimed for sounding casual. "Hi, Leif. Enjoying the game?"

"Yeah, so far."

His friend gave Leif a questioning look and shifted to nudge him, shoulder to shoulder. Leif rolled his eyes but dutifully performed the necessary introductions. "Nick, this is Zoe Phillips, the nurse practitioner who will be overseeing my rehab here in Snowberry Creek. Zoe, this is Sergeant Nick Jenkins."

She smiled and held out her hand. "We haven't officially been introduced, Nick, but I've heard a lot about you from Callie. We didn't get a chance to talk at the party the other night, so it's nice to finally meet you." She would've also recognized Nick as another soldier even without Leif mentioning his rank. It was there in his hypervigilant eyes and that stance that meant he was ready to spring into action if the situation warranted it.

"Same here. So, Zoe, you going to take good care of my boy here?"

"I plan to."

"Good. I'm glad to hear it."

He softened the short statement with a fleeting smile, making eye contact briefly before once again scanning the crowd. Leif was doing the same thing. She bet both of them were struggling with the press of the crowd, coupled with all the noise. A few seconds later, Callie appeared at Nick's side.

"Hi, Zoe! Looks like half the town turned out for the game tonight."

"Yeah, it's nice they've been winning so many games. The mayor's son is sure fun to watch."

While they talked, Nick wrapped his arm around Callie's shoulders. Maybe others wouldn't have noticed, but it was clear to Zoe that Callie's presence helped anchor him in the moment, immediately reducing his tension level. She also noticed that Leif was watching the small interaction with what looked like a touch of envy. She didn't blame him. It was hard for anyone to readjust to life after living in a combat zone. Doing it alone was doubly hard.

She had firsthand experience with that herself. And it was time to get moving.

"It was nice seeing you all again. I'm going to wander down to the refreshment stand and grab a hot dog before the line gets too long."

Leif stepped away from his friends. "I'll come with you."

She couldn't refuse his company without coming across as churlish. "All right. Then I'll have to get back to work. It's my night to take blood pressures and hand out brochures about local medical care."

Leif nodded but didn't say anything. His attention was on maneuvering across the rough stretch of ground they

were crossing. When they reached the paved area outside the gym, his speed picked up a bit. They got in line
at the refreshment stand.

Leif looked around, his dark eyes probably not missing a thing. "I'm guessing high school football is a big
deal around here."

"It is. I would've come to the game even if I hadn't
had to be here for other reasons. A fair number of the
kids on the team are patients of mine, as are their parents. I like to show my support when I can."

He nodded. "It was the same where I grew up."

They'd reached the front of the line. "How many hot
dogs do you want, Zoe?"

"Just one, but I'll get my own."

Leif eyed the handwritten menu as he pulled out his
wallet. "I'm ordering for Nick and Callie, too. One more
won't break me. Besides, I'll need help carrying it all
back to where Callie and Nick are waiting. Consider it
payment for services rendered."

Good point. Rather than stand there and squabble
over a two-dollar hot dog, she gave in. "If you're sure. I'd
like a diet cola, too."

On the way back, he balanced the cardboard tray with
the hot dogs while she carried the drinks. His friends had
staked out some seats on the second row in the bleach-
ers. She delivered the drinks to Callie and waited to
make sure Leif managed to reach his seat without mis-
hap, while trying not to be obvious about it.

After he handed out the hot dogs, she thanked him
again. Before she could walk away, the home team
scored again. The percussion section of the marching
band exploded in a loud, rumbling celebration. Both
Nick and Leif ducked, almost sending their hot dogs flying. Luckily, Callie managed to save the drinks.

Leif let loose with a string of curse words, echoed by his friend. Zoe met Callie's worried gaze and shrugged. Here in public neither man would appreciate the two women acknowledging what had just happened.

"Enjoy the game, guys. Callie, we'll have to meet up at Bridey's place again soon."

Then she turned her attention to Leif. "Thanks again for the hot dog, and I'll see you at the clinic tomorrow."

Leif nodded, his expression totally blank, his emotions carefully banked. He couldn't quite hide the slight tremble in his hands, though. "I'll be there."

Zoe made herself walk away. As much as she wanted to stay and help Leif deal with the crush of people and noise, she had other obligations tonight. That was her excuse, and she was sticking to it, but her heart hurt for him.

Chapter 5

꙰ ꙰

What was it about the clock that was suddenly so fascinating today? Every few minutes Zoe found herself glancing at the time in the lower corner of her computer screen or watching the wagging tail on the black cat clock as it ticked off the minutes. It wasn't like there weren't better things to do, patients to see, not to mention the endless paperwork that flowed across her desk. She managed to chip away at the stack of files in front of her, but she definitely wasn't working at her usual speed. Finally she gave up and headed for the small break room. Maybe an early lunch would give her the boost of energy she'd need to get through the afternoon.

The patient schedule wasn't as full as it could've been, but that didn't necessarily translate into an easy day. She'd deliberately blocked out the last ninety minutes of the day for one patient: Leif. He was scheduled to meet with her and Isaac to begin his therapy. They would go over everything together, and then he and Isaac would get started. She planned to hang around and watch how it went.

After seeing him last night at the football game, she was even more worried about him. As a healer, she didn't like to see anyone suffer. Finding a cure for someone's illness was a balm to her soul, but some things couldn't be fixed. Some people, too. At best, they could be patched back together with a hope and a prayer that the makeshift repairs would hold.

Zoe had personal experience with that, but right now her focus was on Leif's problems, not her own. His left leg was a mess of scars and shattered bones screwed back together with metal plates. Her own shin had ached in sympathy for hours after he'd limped out of her office.

From the anger in his parting look, he had realized the examination room had been designed for munchkins, not men who'd almost died in combat. Maybe she should've offered him the choice of using that room or seeing if he could make it up onto the regular table with help. But then again, probably not. No matter which option he chose, he would hate anyone acknowledging his weakness.

Zoe made quick work of her salad. With luck, maybe she could knock out those last few charts before the first of her afternoon patients came in. There really wasn't any hurry; certainly paperwork could wait until after office hours. But if Leif's appointment was as emotionally tense as she expected it to be, she was going to want to go straight home afterward.

Brandi came charging into the room looking flustered, something that rarely happened. "Thank God I found you! I was afraid you'd gone out to lunch. Mrs. Wolfe just brought in her husband, who is having chest pains. He claims he only came in to humor his wife, but he looks bad to me. Clammy and pale, for sure. I would've sent them over to the walk-in clinic side, but Dr. Tenberg is in the middle of stitching up a nasty gash in some guy's leg. He said he'd be over to assist as soon as he finishes."

Zoe followed Brandi out of the room at a run. She'd learned early on to trust her assistant's judgment. If she said Mr. Wolfe looked bad, he did.

Brandi was still talking. "I put him into room one, but I haven't taken his vitals yet. I thought I should find you first."

"Not a problem, Brandi. You did good. I'll take his blood pressure myself while you let Dr. Tenberg know where we'll be."

They separated at the door to the examination room. Inside, Zoe took one look at Mr. Wolfe's labored breathing and gray skin tone and stepped back out in the hall. "Brandi, call the EMTs and tell them we'll need a patient transported to the hospital STAT."

"Will do."

Crossing her fingers that the emergency med techs from the fire department weren't already out on a call, Zoe returned to her patient and his wife.

"So, Mr. Wolfe, how long have you been having these chest pains?"

Following Isaac's advice, Leif had dressed in a T-shirt and loose-fitting shorts. He approached the clinic with a load of dread and determination in his gut. He so didn't want to do this, but that was a stupid mind-set. Each step forward took him that much closer to getting control of his life back.

What that life would look like depended on how much effort he put into the course of action that Zoe and Isaac had planned out for him. That's what he wanted to believe, anyway. He stepped through the front door of the clinic, only to be hit with the slightly stale smell of air conditioning tainted with that same funky medicinal stink that all hospitals and doctors' offices had.

The receptionist looked up with a smile as he approached the counter. "Hi, Corporal Brevik. Zoe asked that you fill out this questionnaire while you wait."

"Thanks."

The lobby was deserted, giving him his choice of seats. He headed over to the far corner toward a row of chairs that were higher than normal. He suspected they were designed to make it easier for people like him to get back up.

After getting situated, he studied the questions Zoe had left for him. It was the same stupid list he'd answered two days ago. Rate his pain? What activities hurt the worst? What would help ease any discomfort he might have? All kinds of smart-ass answers crossed his mind on that last one. Somehow he doubted Zoe would appreciate some of the suggestions that came to mind. It was tempting to find out, though.

Especially if he admitted that ever since the night they'd danced he'd enjoyed a few late-night fantasies that had involved the two of them. And at the game last night, he'd even pretended that they'd been two regular people, still checking each other out, and maybe on the verge of hooking up for more than a hot dog.

Instead, he was sitting there staring at a stupid piece of paper. He carefully considered the first question and then rated his pain at a five, figuring that was closer to the truth than the number he'd marked two days ago. On Wednesday, Isaac had waited until they were alone to get all up in Leif's face about screwing around like that. The big man made it damn clear he wouldn't waste his time on an effing idiot who didn't want to get better. He'd used a lot of colorful expressions and some physically impossible suggestions to make his point. Bottom line: Zoe wouldn't have asked the questions if the answers weren't important.

"Corporal, you can come on back now."

It was the same spike-haired blonde who had taken him back before. Her name niggled at his memory. Candy? No, Brandi.

"Be there in a sec, Brandi." He flashed a smile in her direction while he gathered up his things. "And call me Leif. 'Corporal' sounds a bit formal since it looks like I'll be hanging out here a lot for a while."

She looked pleased that he'd remembered her name. They bypassed the examination rooms to end up in a small office at the end of a short hall.

"Have a seat. Zoe and Isaac will be with you soon. Can I get you some coffee or a bottle of water while you wait?"

"Water would be nice. Thank you."

Brandi disappeared out the door, leaving Leif alone with his thoughts. Patience had never been his strong suit, but all this waiting around made him crazy. The army had been his life for years, dictating where he lived and what he should be doing pretty much twenty-four-seven. But now, until he knew how much could be done to restore the use of his leg, he was stuck in limbo, spinning his wheels and unable to move on with his life.

Twenty minutes later, his frustration had about reached the boiling point when he heard a noise out in the hall. He cocked his head to the side to listen. Someone was headed his way. Two someones, in fact. It was damn well about time. He straightened up taller and did his best to get his game face back in place.

Zoe was the first one through the door, followed closely by Isaac. She tossed him the bottle of water Brandi had promised him. The therapist perched on top of a low filing cabinet, taking up a great deal of space, but it was Zoe who captured all of Leif's attention.

Before he could stop himself, he blurted out, "You look like hell."

She flinched as if he'd slapped her as she rounded her desk to drop into her chair. Well, damn, that wasn't what he'd meant to say, even if it was true. Her blue eyes were dull and faded, almost as if someone had extinguished the light that had sparkled in them just last night. Something bad had happened. That much was clear.

He held up his hands. "Sorry. I didn't mean that the way it sounded."

She quirked an eyebrow. "If you were aiming to compliment me on my looks, soldier, you need to hone your skills."

Okay, so there was enough life left in her to spark a bit of temper. He gave apologizing another try.

"I meant to ask if you were feeling all right. You look a bit under the weather."

The physical therapist's muffled snicker signaled that Leif was only digging himself in deeper. "Never mind. I'll just shut up now."

Isaac leaned over to clap Leif on the shoulder. "I would've thought it would be hard to talk with that size twelve wedged in your mouth, but you seem to have a real talent for it, soldier boy."

"Stuff it, squid."

"Gentlemen."

Zoe put enough oomph into the single word to have both men slamming their mouths shut. Isaac actually snapped to attention briefly before remembering he wasn't in the navy anymore. Leif couldn't have jumped to his feet if he'd wanted to, but he still threw his shoulders back and sat up straighter.

For the first time since she'd walked into the room, Zoe looked more like herself. She gave each of them a superior look. "It's nice to know that officers training crap still comes in handy once in a while."

Her expression softened a bit when she met Leif's gaze. "To answer your question, I'm fine, but it's been a tough afternoon around here."

Evidently, Isaac took that as his cue to enter the conversation. He picked up a file he'd brought in with him. "I've put together two sets of exercises for you, Leif. You'll be working on the first bunch here at the clinic. The other ones will be your homework."

Zoe pulled out two more sheets of paper and slid them across the desk. "I shouldn't have to remind you that adequate sleep and proper nutrition also play a big role in a patient's recovery. I want you to take a multivitamin and extra calcium. That top sheet will give you some recommendations about your daily diet and what you should look for in a vitamin to make sure you get the right dosage."

Her eyes narrowed a bit. "The second sheet is a prescription for a different painkiller. It's not as strong as the one you've been on, but it's also not as addictive. You okay with that?"

He knew what she was really asking. "I'd rather not take them at all. I'm using them less all the time."

"Good, although after Isaac gets done with you today, you may want to rethink that."

Leaning back in her chair, she continued talking. "Ideally, we'd like to see you in here for an hour appointment three times a week. Isaac will keep me apprised of your progress. In turn, I'll keep the army doctors in the loop. I've also scheduled you for a follow-up evaluation with me in two weeks. If everything is going well at that point, you'll only need to check in with me every four weeks."

Isaac rejoined the conversation. "I've already reserved my first appointment of the day for you on Monday, Wednesday, and Friday for the next two weeks. We can change the time if you want, but I figured you'd rather get it over with and have the rest of your day free."

"Sounds good."

It wasn't as if he had anything better to do with his time, but he had promised Nick to help him get a little more work done on Spence's house. He gave the two pages a quick look before sticking them in the small backpack he'd brought with him.

"Do you have any questions for either of us?"

Yeah, but they weren't the kind anyone could answer yet. How long would he have to keep coming here? Would his leg ever be normal again? He settled for pulling out the paperwork he'd completed in the lobby. "No questions, but here's the form you wanted filled out."

Zoe read over it before handing it to Isaac. "I have one for you. You marked your pain level at five today. Is it really that much worse than it was two days ago or just a more accurate assessment?"

He shifted in his seat, his face flushing hot. She'd left him no wiggle room. "More accurate."

Instead of giving him grief over it, she smiled. "That's great. Now we have a baseline to work from. I've no doubt you're going to hurt worse for a while, but that's normal. I promise you'll eventually start to see improvement."

Her brief surge of energy seemed to fade as quickly

as it had come. Despite her assurance that she was fine, there was definitely something going on with her. Isaac looked worried about her, too. Maybe the big man would clue him in once they were alone.

Zoe was still talking. "So if you don't have any more questions for me, how about the two of you get started? I've got a few things to deal with that can't wait, but I'll stop by to see how you're doing on my way out."

"Sounds good."

Leif pushed himself up out of the chair, glad that he managed to do so without wobbling. A man had his pride, especially in front of an attractive woman. After looping the strap of his backpack over his shoulder, he followed Isaac out of the office, pausing briefly in the doorway.

"I'm sorry, Zoe."

She looked up from the file she was studying. "For what?"

"For whatever happened this afternoon that knocked the wind out of your sails."

At first she just stared at him, her mouth open but with no words coming out. Finally, she sighed. "Thanks, Leif, but it's nothing I can't handle."

"That doesn't mean it isn't tough."

She looked up again from her paperwork, her expression stark and sad. "No, it sure doesn't."

Two hours later, Leif turned into the driveway and slowed the truck down to a crawl to avoid throwing up any gravel that could chip the paint job. When the front wheel hit a pothole with a hard lurch, he cursed. Damn, he hoped that fixing the heavily rutted driveway was near the top on Callie's list of things to do to Spence's house. The place wasn't exactly home, but it was the closest thing to it that Leif had these days.

Right now, he would've settled for a foxhole as long as he could stretch out and not have to move for the rest of the day. At least he'd have the weekend to recover before having to do it all again.

He parked next to Nick's truck and tried to muster up enough energy to climb down out of the cab. Damn, his leg hurt so badly right now that he would've had to pencil in a few extra numbers on Zoe's pain scale to come close to how it felt. The only thing that had him opening the driver's-side door was the knowledge that once he got inside the house he could take one of his pain pills and veg out on the couch until the throbbing subsided.

Leif slid down to the ground. Hell, when had the truck gotten so high? He hit the ground with a jolt, setting off another string of curses. Rather than give in to the pain, he concentrated on making it as far as the sidewalk in front of the porch.

Mission accomplished. The steps presented the next obstacle. Bracing himself with the cane, he counted them off as he hauled his ass upward and onward: one, two, three. Objective achieved. Now all that stood between him and comfort was the distance from the front door to the kitchen and then back to the couch.

As soon as the screen door slammed shut behind him, Nick stepped out of the kitchen with a pill bottle in one hand and a can of root beer in the other. "Get yourself settled on the couch, soldier, and I'll bring you something to eat."

Damn, there were times Leif really loved that man. Any other day, he might have growled about being fussed over, but right now all he felt was grateful. He changed directions and hobbled straight for the couch. Mooch trailed after him but hung back far enough to avoid getting in Leif's way.

As soon as he was settled in with his leg propped up on a pillow, the dog jumped up on the couch and carefully maneuvered until he was stretched out next to Leif, his head within easy petting distance.

Leif obliged him.

Mooch had saved all their asses one night in Afghanistan when he inexplicably joined their patrol in time to sound the alarm that they were about to walk into an ambush. The mutt had taken one for the team that night. Spence had been the one who insisted that they make Mooch an unofficial member of their squad, but in truth the dog had actually adopted all of them.

Whenever they'd come back in from a tough day, he'd be waiting with a friendly wag of the tail and doggy kisses for anyone who needed them. If anyone ever bottled the restorative power of canine love, he'd be a rich man overnight.

Nick popped the top on the soft drink and handed it to Leif. "How many pills do you want?"

"The whole damn bottle," Leif muttered as he held out his hand, "but I'll settle for one. No, make it two."

"It was that bad, huh?"

"Worse." Leif swallowed the pills and washed them down with half the can of root beer. "My leg hurts like hell, but Isaac and Zoe both warned me I wouldn't feel like going out clubbing tonight. And here I was going to dazzle you and Callie with all my best moves."

Nick plunked down in the closest chair. "Well, that is disappointing, especially considering I don't remember ever seeing you do anything out on the dance floor that could be described as dazzling. Bizarre, maybe. Definitely herky-jerky, but never dazzling."

Leif held up his middle finger in salute. "Liar. I have mad skills, or at least I did. You're the one who always hid in the middle of a crowd so none of us could see what a crap dancer you are and make fun of you."

Nick dragged the ottoman closer to the chair and put his feet up, clearly settling in for a while. "Not true. I didn't want to make the rest of you look bad. Especially Spence."

That was true. "I'll concede that he was the worst of the bunch. After a couple of beers, he'd ask some poor woman to dance. There he'd be, arms and legs flying every which way like a marionette being operated by a drunken puppeteer."

They both chuckled at the memory, which felt good. Wheels's death had torn both of them up pretty badly, but Spence wouldn't have wanted either of them to wallow in their grief. He'd want to be remembered with laughter, not tears.

Or guilt, for that matter, but too bad. Leif was alive only because Spence was dead. That was a fact. Maybe time would eventually soften the edges of Leif's regret, kind of like the way the pills he'd taken didn't actually make the pain disappear, but made it bearable. He hoped so.

Nick dragged Leif's attention back to the present. "So how did it go today? And don't try to bullshit me. I want the truth."

Leif shifted so that his head rested on the arm of the couch. The narcotic was definitely kicking in, enough to make it hard to stay awake.

"Isaac showed no mercy, but I shouldn't complain."

Nick laughed. "Since when has that stopped you?"

"True enough, but at least I got to keep my leg. He's working with a couple of guys who weren't that lucky."

Rather than dwell on how close he'd come to joining that particular club, though, Leif kept talking. "Starting Monday, I'll be seeing him three times a week for a while. I've also got a list of god-awful exercises to do here at the house the rest of the time. Mostly stretches for now."

"You don't sound excited."

Leif pried one eye open to glare at his friend. "That's because I'm not. I'm also pretty sure that in a prior life Isaac honed his skills working for the Spanish Inquisition."

"Sounds as if I'd like the man. But, Corporal, if you slack off on what he tells you to do, I'll kick your ass for you. Repeatedly."

Now that was the Nick Leif knew and loved. "That's some motivational speech, Sarge. Seriously, I think you should embroider that on a pillow or some such shit."

His friend took a different tack. "I could always put a chart on the fridge and give you a gold star every day you do them. Maybe buy you an ice-cream cone when you've earned a few. Does that work better for you?"

Leif stared up at the ceiling and pretended to give the matter some hard thought. "Yeah, all things considered, it does. Or maybe instead of ice cream, you could spring for a steak dinner when I've earned a month's worth."

"Whatever works, Leif. I want to help."

He didn't have to look at Nick to know he suffered from the same guilt that plagued Leif, but his was two-fold. Nick had been in charge the day their M-ATV had hit an IED. Nick had a nasty scar on his arm to show for his efforts, but they both knew he'd gotten off light. All things considered, so had Leif. He'd come out of it with a fucked-up leg; Spence had died that day.

"I love you, too, Sarge. Now go away and let me sleep."

Mooch, ever sensitive to his people's moods, jumped down off the couch and followed Nick out of the room. Leif missed the warm press of the dog against his leg, but right now Nick needed Mooch more than Leif did.

He hated the way the pain pill fogged up his mind, but he didn't try to fight it this time; he just let sleep claim him.

Chapter 6

✽ ✽

Zoe dumped her purse and keys on the kitchen counter. What a bitch of a day. It had started off all right but had gone to pieces by the end of the afternoon. She hated—HATED—losing a patient. Granted, Mr. Wolfe hadn't actually been one of her usual clients. He preferred to see the "real" doctor instead of a nurse practitioner even for something as simple as a sinus infection. She never took it personally. Not much, anyway.

At least Dr. Tenberg had been there within minutes of Mr. Wolfe's arrival. Zoe had finished taking the man's vitals and was only too glad to step aside and let the doctor take over. The EMTs had arrived in less than ten minutes to whisk Mr. Wolfe off to the hospital.

He'd gone into full cardiac arrest on the way, dying shortly after they'd arrived at the emergency room. Maybe he would've survived if his wife had taken him straight to the hospital, but maybe not. Second-guessing anyone's actions at this point wouldn't change a thing.

For certain, the man's death would have far-reaching

implications for the town. After all, his company was the single biggest employer in the immediate area. And yet she was far more concerned about Mrs. Wolfe. How was she taking the loss of her husband? She had to be devastated. After all, they had to have been married for thirty-plus years.

While they'd been waiting for her husband to be transported to the hospital, the woman had hovered in the corner. She'd looked so darn fragile, as if the slightest touch would shatter her. The couple had a daughter, but Melanie no longer lived in Snowberry Creek. There was no telling how soon she would arrive to help her mother deal with everything.

Again, not Zoe's crisis to solve. She and the Wolfe family had never moved in the same social circles, and it had been years since she'd seen Melanie. Right after high school, Zoe had gotten her nursing degree and then joined the army, returning to Snowberry Creek only after her enlistment was up.

She was proud of her service to her country, but those years had definitely left their mark. Without warning, memories of Iraq would come flooding back. So much blood. Wounds that no amount of nursing care could ever heal.

She shivered. The small movement snapped her out of the past. Looking around, she realized she'd been standing in the middle of the kitchen floor for nearly ten minutes. Damn, she hated losing chunks of time like that. She'd been doing so much better lately, but every so often something happened that triggered another episode.

It didn't help that her day had ended watching Leif Brevik struggle to do even the simplest of the exercises that Isaac had asked him to try. By the end of the session, Leif's shirt had been soaked through with sweat, and he'd been panting as if he'd been running a marathon instead of dragging himself up a few steps.

He hadn't appreciated her being there, either. Once, when he stumbled a bit, she'd rushed to help steady his footsteps. Leif had snarled and jerked his arm out of her grasp, making it very clear he didn't want her assistance. He obviously didn't have the same issue with Isaac propping him up, so it had to be something about her.

Right after that, she'd left. The stubborn idiot! She'd only wanted to help. Of course, some guys had that macho jerk thing going where they couldn't appear weak in front of a woman. How stupid was that? She was there as a medical professional, not someone he was interested in impressing.

Well, for the time being she'd leave him to Isaac's tender mercies. The therapist would keep her posted on Leif's progress or if there were any problems with his treatment plan. Still, it was a crappy ending to an even crappier day.

She opened the freezer and picked out a frozen dinner at random and read the label: frozen mystery meat with frozen vegetables smothered with some unidentifiable sauce. Yum. She couldn't wait. Maybe she should've accepted Brandi's invitation to go out for pizza, but it was too late now.

After programming the right time into the microwave, she punched the START button and headed for her bedroom to strip off her clothes. Tonight was definitely a time for the comfort of her favorite flannel pajama bottoms and oversized T-shirt.

After shoving her feet into her bunny slippers, she shuffled back to the kitchen just as the bell pinged, announcing that her dinner was ready. As tempting as it was to stand over the sink and eat it right out of the container, she took the time to set a place for herself at the table. After dumping the steaming mess onto her plate, she opened the fridge and considered which wine went best with a frozen dinner.

She settled on the red simply because it was sitting in front and easy to reach. At least she had enough class left to drink it from a wineglass instead of straight from the bottle. After all, a woman had to have some standards, didn't she?

Before taking a bite, she lifted her wineglass and offered a toast in memory of Mr. Wolfe and his family. "May he rest in peace."

Then as an afterthought, she added, "And Leif, I hope you can see past the pain to the possibilities."

Because if he could, maybe—just maybe—she could do the same.

Monday morning rolled around all too quickly. Making good on his threat, Nick had posted a hand-drawn chart on the front of the fridge. The squares were a bit crooked and the writing nearly impossible to read, thanks to Sarge's illegible scrawl, but the important part was that Leif had earned four gold stars over the weekend.

Right after dinner last night, Sarge had produced the chart and then added the four stars to it with great ceremony and a speech that was supposed to be inspirational. To top it off, Callie had presented Leif with a bowl filled with two huge scoops of ice cream with all the fixings.

Even now, the memory made Leif grin. He would've been happier with just the ice cream and no hoopla, but he appreciated the fact that Nick and Callie had made the effort. It had been tempting to bring the chart to his appointment with Isaac, figuring the other man might get a kick out of it.

Zoe would, too, but Leif wasn't supposed to see her today. He'd been a bit of a jerk to her on Friday. He regretted his actions, but he'd reacted instinctively. It was hard enough having Isaac hovering nearby.

Besides, he didn't want Zoe to think of him as damaged goods. Stupid, he knew, but he was getting sick and tired of even total strangers staring at him with pity and curiosity as he hobbled around.

He pulled into the clinic parking lot and drove around back, to the door of the physical therapy department. Since he wasn't seeing Zoe today, he didn't need to check in with the front desk.

Isaac looked up and waved as soon as Leif walked in. "Stow your gear and hop up on that table over there. I'll get Mitch here situated and be right with you."

As soon as Leif got himself settled on the table, one of the assistants joined him. After helping him remove his boot, she put some heat on his leg to get the muscles warmed up.

"Do you want some magazines to read?"

Leif smiled at the young woman. "Thanks, but I brought a book this time."

She left him to read in peace while she moved on to another patient. The place was busier today than it had been on Friday afternoon. Leif tried to focus on his mystery, but all the activity was too much of a distraction. He finally gave up and marked his place.

Isaac was still sitting with the same patient. Whatever the two men were talking about had to be some serious shit. Maybe Isaac was giving another rendition of his patented "get serious or don't waste my time" lecture.

For sure, the other guy's body language reeked of resentment, with a touch of "fuck off" thrown in for good measure. Isaac, on the other hand, wasn't putting up with it any more than he had with Leif. His deep voice rang out across the room.

"Fine, Mitchell, sit here and do nothing if that's what makes you happy. When you decide you're ready to get to work, let me know. Until then, I'm going to be over there with my man Corporal Brevik."

Isaac stalked away, leaving the other patient glaring at his back in frustration. Embarrassed for the other man, Leif opened his book again and pretended an interest he certainly didn't feel. While he stared at the page, it dawned on him that the other man looked familiar for some reason. Maybe he'd seen him around town.

Before he could place him, Isaac appeared at his side. "So, Corporal, how did you do with your exercises over the weekend?"

Leif sat up taller. "I'm bunking with my sergeant here in Snowberry Creek. The jerk made me a chart and gave me a gold star for each time I did them."

Then he added proudly, "I earned a bowl of ice cream for all my hard work."

Isaac's deep laugh rang out and his mood brightened considerably. "Seriously? That's some great stuff."

Then he raised his voice enough that it carried across the room. "At least some of my patients are smart enough to take responsibility for their own rehab, unlike some lazy-assed people I could mention."

Leif couldn't help but look to see how the other patient reacted to Isaac's comment. His embarrassment was obvious, but so was his anger. His hands coiled into tight fists, and if his eyes could have shot bullets, Isaac would've been dead. Leif jerked his focus back to his therapist, figuring the other patient didn't need everyone staring at him. It was hard, though, until Isaac's big hands started digging into the painful knots in Leif's leg.

"Son of a bitch, Isaac, that hurts."

Isaac didn't ease up on his efforts. "Yeah, Leif, I know. Doesn't mean it isn't good for you, but let me know if it gets to be too much."

Leif nodded and bit his lip. Holding on to the sides of the table, he tried to resist the need to cuss loud and long. He might have given in to the urge if it had been just Isaac and him in the room, but Leif's mother had raised him better than that, especially when there were women present.

Isaac's dark eyes were sympathetic. "I know this hurts, but the muscles are actually not as tight as they were on Friday."

It sure as hell didn't feel like it, but Leif gritted his teeth and didn't complain. Not out loud, anyway. After a few more minutes of legalized torture, Isaac stopped. He flexed his hands as he looked around the room.

"Think you can handle a little time on the exercise bike over there? I'm thinking low resistance and going slow, aiming to stretch things out a bit more but without putting too much stress on the leg."

"You're the boss."

Leif slung his legs over the side of the table and gingerly eased down to the floor. He hadn't done much walking without the boot's support, so he held his breath and waited to see if his leg would hold up under his weight. It was dicey at first, but the first step was the hardest. After that, he managed to find his balance as he slowly shuffled across the short distance.

Isaac matched his steps to Leif's, staying close enough to rescue him if necessary. A slug could've crawled across the floor faster, but at least Leif reached the bike on his own. Wow, what a victory. With considerable effort, Leif hoisted himself up onto the seat while Isaac set the controls for ten minutes and the lowest resistance the bike offered.

"If it gets to be too much, stop. The idea is to push yourself a little further each time but not so much as to cause more damage. Got that, Corporal?"

Isaac put enough growl in the question to have Leif grinning. "I've got it."

He pushed down on the pedal, wincing when his muscles protested a bit at being stretched beyond their comfort zone. After a few repetitions, though, it became easier and he picked up some speed.

"Slow it down, Leif."

He should've known Isaac would be keeping an eye on him. The man must be attuned to the whir of the bike, because right now he had his back to him. Evidently that other guy had finally decided to cooperate. Good for him.

Leif pulled his MP3 player out of his pocket and lost himself in his music for a while. It gave him something else to think about while he kept spinning the bike pedals. Slow, fast, it didn't matter. Regardless of the speed, he wasn't getting anywhere fast, and if that wasn't a metaphor for his life right now, he didn't know what was.

Mitch knew he was being a total jackass, but he couldn't seem to help himself these days. For sure he owed Isaac an apology. He was lucky the big man hadn't flattened him for a few of the things he'd said.

Luckily, the two of them went way back together, so hopefully the man would cut Mitch some slack. He automatically fell into the same rhythm on his stationary bike as the guy next to him. Isaac had referred to him as Corporal something or another. At the time, Mitch had been too pissed about his own situation to pay much attention to anyone else.

He risked a quick peek at the soldier's left leg and winced. Damn, the poor bastard's lower calf looked as if someone had carved a road map in it using scar tissue. That had to have hurt.

At least the new scars on his own right knee were tidier. The surgeons had told him he was damn lucky they managed to repair the damage this time. One more hit like that last one and he could be looking at a total knee replacement.

Where was the luck in that? Sure, he didn't want to be walking around with a hunk of metal where he used to have bone. But either way, the surgery had shoved Mitch down a road he didn't want to travel. Not yet, anyway. He could have done his rehab with the team's trainers, but they had their hands full with the guys who had a better chance of returning to the playing field this season.

Besides, there was nothing Mitch hated worse than the pity he saw reflected in the eyes of his teammates. There'd usually been a glint of fear mixed in with it, too. No doubt his potentially career-ending injury served as a vivid reminder of how tenuous their highly paid jobs were. One wrong move, and the money and all the bells and whistles that went along with the job description were gone for good.

So instead of being on a jet flying to the next away game, Mitch was back in his hometown licking his wounds and wondering what to do next.

The timer on the soldier's bike pinged, jarring Mitch out of his one-man pity party. He watched as the man eased himself off the bike, grabbing a cane to support himself. Isaac saw him moving around and yelled across the room, "Hang tight, Leif. I'll be right there."

Leif froze, but he clearly wasn't happy about it. Mitch

surprised himself by trying to distract the guy. "So what happened? Motorcycle accident in the rain?"

A pair of rock-hard brown eyes glared straight at Mitch briefly before looking away. "No. An IED in Afghanistan."

The answer was delivered in a monotone as if the guy had somehow distanced himself from the incident. The expression in his gaze was equally as flat. Clearly no further questions on the subject would be appreciated.

Instead, he asked, "And you?"

Mitch automatically reached down to rub his knee, remembering the sound of the bone crunching and the waves of pain that had left him writhing on the ground on national television. "Linebacker tackled me, and I landed with my knee twisted in a direction nature never meant it to bend."

Instead of looking sympathetic, the soldier's face immediately lit up. "Damn, no wonder you looked familiar. You're Mitch Calder! I love watching you play. You have a hell of an arm."

And worthless knees. Before Mitch could respond, Leif's grin widened. "Although you did cost me fifty bucks in that play-off game last year. My buddy Spence crowed about it for a week afterward. Said he knew you'd pull it off."

Now there was a name from the past. "You served with Spence Lang? I haven't seen him in years. How is he doing?"

"Actually, not so good." Leif's smile bled away. "He died in Afghanistan instead of me."

Then he turned his back and limped away.

Chapter 7

✌ ✌

Okay, that had been the pain speaking. It wasn't Mitch Calder's fault that he'd accidentally stomped right on the detonator of Leif's temper. Clearly Mitch hadn't heard the news. That he'd obviously known and liked Spence only made the brutally blunt announcement worse.

Leif coasted to a stop halfway across the busy room. Fuck, if his leg had been up for a quick sprint, he would've bolted out the door. On second thought, it was more than his bum leg that kept him from giving it his best shot. He needed to man up and apologize.

It was a long, slow shuffle back to where Mitch sat in stunned silence. "Look, I'm sorry. I didn't mean—"

Mitch wasn't having any of it and cut him off. "Didn't mean what? To be a total asshole? I've known Spence my whole damn life."

He dragged himself off the bike to get right up in Leif's face. "Do us both a favor and don't talk to me right now. My leg might be screwed up, but there's nothing wrong with my fists."

He had several inches on Leif and at least thirty pounds in pure bulk. Fine, but Leif knew more about down-and-dirty fighting than Mitch did.

"You want to dance? Fine, but let's take this outside."

Unfortunately Isaac had a different opinion on the subject. He shoved his way in between them, turning his back to the football player. "Stop this shit right now, both of you. You're scaring the other patients."

Leif didn't bother to look around. The uneasy silence surrounding them spoke volumes. So did the quiet movement around the edges of the room as Isaac's staff evacuated the rest of the patients. At this point, he and Mitch would be lucky if someone didn't call the police.

"I said stand down, damn it!"

Isaac's voice was little better than a growl. Leif broke off the stare-down contest he had going with Mitch but stood his ground until Mitch backed up a step. Evidently satisfied that the two of them would listen to reason, Isaac gave them some breathing room.

"In my office. Now."

Mitch started to speak. "But—"

Isaac crossed his arms over his chest and planted his feet wide. "Argue with me and the next call I make will be to the cops. If that's how you want this to play out, fine."

He paused long enough to give each of them a hard look. "But know this. If that's what happens, you'll both be looking for another therapist."

Mitch frowned. "You're the only one in town."

Isaac's smile was nasty. "That's not my problem. So what's it going to be? My office or do I call in the cops to throw both of you jackasses out of here?"

Leif didn't trust what might come out of his mouth at the moment, so he let his actions speak for him. He started for Isaac's office. When he stumbled a bit, the big man reached out to steady him, his touch gentle despite his obvious anger.

When Leif reached the small cubicle in the corner, Mitch was right behind him. Leif took the chair in the far corner and left the closer one for the football player.

To his surprise, Mitch gave him a rueful smile as he looked around the small room. "It's been a while since I got sent to the principal's office, but some things never change. I'm just hoping he doesn't phone my folks."

Okay, that was cute. Leif couldn't help but chuckle. "Yeah, I had my fair share of those calls, too."

Isaac had hung back long enough to talk to his staff. When he marched into his office, he slammed the door behind him.

Parking his ass on the edge of his desk, he gave them each one of those looks that said he wasn't going to put up with any more bullshit from either of them. "Which of you idiots wants to tell me what the hell happened out there?"

The two of them hung their heads, not in shame, but to hide their growing need to laugh. Maybe it was time to give Isaac a break.

"It was my fault, and I apologize to you both. Isaac, I'll understand if you want to kick my ass to the curb."

"As tempting as that is at the moment, Corporal, I don't have the time to fill out the paperwork required to ship said ass back up to the military hospital."

Then he rounded on the football player. "I don't give a rat's rear end what he said to you, Mitch. My schedule was already full when you called, but I made room because we were friends once upon a time. Lose the attitude or you're out of here. Got that?"

Mitch no longer looked as if he was fighting the urge

to laugh. "Yeah, I've got it. I'm sorry I've put you in this position, Isaac."

"Okay, then. Both of you get back out there. Your time's up, so we'll ice your legs for a few minutes before you hit the road."

Leif started to push himself back up to his feet. Isaac opened the door for him. "I've got you both on the books at the same time on Wednesday. Let me know if that is going to be a problem, and I'll change it around."

Leif looked past him to where Mitch was sitting. "It won't be a problem for me. Can't speak for him."

Mitch had made it back up to his feet, too. "I can stand it if he can."

"Go on out there, both of you. And I don't want to hear any bitching about how cold the ice is. It's supposed to be that way."

Leif got his book out of his pack and settled back to endure the cold burn of the ice pack on his leg. After the first few minutes, his leg grew blessedly numb enough to mask the pain. If only it had the same effect on his memories.

Zoe set a steaming mug of herbal tea down in front of Isaac. "I hear you had quite the morning."

He was usually a coffee drinker, but when either of them had a particularly rough day, Zoe broke out the soothing blend of tea that she purchased from Something's Brewing, the coffee and tea shop in town. Her friend stared at the cup as if trying to decide if the day had been bad enough to warrant drinking it.

When she added one of the blackberry muffins she'd also bought, his expression lightened up considerably. "It wasn't anything I couldn't handle."

He took a big bite out of the muffin before continuing. "Your soldier boy and Mitch Calder almost came to blows, and I had to evacuate the other patients. I came this close"—he held up his thumb and forefinger indicating a space of about a quarter of an inch—"to calling the cops on them. I don't need that kind of shit going on in my clinic."

Zoe's stomach tightened into a knot. Mitch Calder wasn't her patient, but everyone in town knew who he was. He'd been the star athlete at the local high school before moving on to college and then the pros. But her real concern was for the other man in the equation. If Isaac refused to treat Leif, he'd have to go all the way to Tacoma for his therapy. Chances were he wouldn't stay in Snowberry Creek if that happened. All things considered, she'd really hate that for him, especially because he would need the emotional support of his friends to get through all of this.

"How about Leif? Is he doing all right?"

Isaac took a big sip of the tea. "I think so. As far as I could tell, they exchanged some heated words and glared at each other. I got there before it escalated beyond that point."

"What were they fighting about?"

Isaac had finished his muffin and was eyeing the remaining half of hers. She pushed it across the table to him. She was no longer hungry.

"They didn't say, and I didn't press for answers. I suspect it had something to do with the incident in Afghanistan that ripped up Leif's leg, but I could be wrong. The biggest problem is that both of them have hair-trigger tempers right now. They're hurting, frustrated, and pissed off in general."

He paused for another bite of muffin. "However, they seemed to have made peace on their own. By the time I got ready to lay down the law, they looked more sheepish than mad. Anyway, they both promised to be back same time, same place on Wednesday. If they act up again, I'll change their appointments around."

She felt marginally better about the situation. "Let me know how it goes. If there are any more problems, I'd be glad to have a heartfelt talk with Leif."

Isaac grinned at her. "I just might take you up on that offer, lady. Hell, the last time you had one of those talks with one of my troublesome patients, the jerk behaved himself for weeks afterward. My size and color make some folks nervous, but little do they know I'm the pussycat around here. You're the real badass."

That much was true, a fact Zoe took no little pride in. "Keep me posted. No use in letting things get out of hand."

"Will do." He finished the muffin down to the last few crumbs. "Now we'd better get back to work."

She stayed right where she was. "Not me, my friend. I have the afternoon off because I traded shifts with Dr. Tenberg. Saturday afternoon, I'm covering the walk-in clinic for him so he can attend Mr. Wolfe's funeral."

He scooped the wrappers from the muffins into his hand and stuffed them into his empty cup. "Enjoy your afternoon, Zoe. It's Friday, so do something fun. You've been putting in some long hours lately."

"Don't worry. I've got plans."

Her friend nodded his head in approval. "Good. It's about time."

She didn't bother telling him those plans consisted of catching up on her laundry, washing her car, and paying the bills. If she got all of that done, she might treat herself to dinner at the Creek Café. There were other restaurants in the area, but there was something about a

Creekburger and sweet potato fries that sounded good today.

If she also got the apartment vacuumed and dusted, she might even throw caution to the wind and have a big piece of Frannie's banana cream pie. Eating that woman's cooking full-time would clog her arteries and add on the pounds, but some sins were worth the cost. Besides, if Zoe did succumb to temptation, she could always do penance on the exercise equipment at the clinic tomorrow.

Her work at the office done and her plans made, Zoe gathered up her things and headed out into the bright sunshine.

Leif wanted to gag. If he had to watch Nick and Callie making goo-goo eyes at each other much longer, he might just toss his cookies. Although neither of the pair ever made Leif feel like a fifth wheel, that's what he was. Now that Nick had gotten over his reluctance to get involved with Callie, thinking she'd belonged to Spence, they no longer needed Leif to play chaperone.

Besides, the sergeant was leaving in a few days to finish cutting his final ties with the army. The couple would appreciate some time alone even if they were too damn noble to ask for it. Leif figured he'd grab dinner in town and then hunt down the bar that Nick had discovered recently. According to him, it was nothing fancy, but the place had decent pool tables and an array of local microbrews.

Apparently the only things that identified it as a bar at all were a parking lot full of motorcycles and a flashing neon sign that simply said BEER. Leif was definitely looking forward to tossing back a couple of cold ones while he knocked a few balls around.

He waited until he had his keys in hand before announcing, "I'm out of here, guys. Don't wait up."

He was out the front door before Nick could do more than sputter a protest. But thanks to the snail's pace at which Leif moved these days, Nick caught up with him before he'd made it off the front porch.

"Where are you headed?"

Leif rolled his eyes and kept going. "Aw, Dad, I'm a big boy now. I'll be back by curfew."

Nick planted his size thirteens right in front of the driver's-side door of Leif's truck, his arms crossed over his chest. "Don't be a jackass. I just thought you might like some company."

Yeah, he would, but Nick needed the time with Callie more than he needed to shoot pool with Leif. "I plan on grabbing a burger someplace and then maybe hang out at BEER for a couple of hours. I'll be all right on my own."

He softened the refusal with a wicked smile. "Considering Callie's folks could potentially arrive any day now, I'd think you'd want as much alone time with her as you can get. You don't really think they're going to let her invite you to a sleepover at their house, do you?"

The look on Nick's face was priceless. Seriously, had that never occurred to the man?

His friend gave him a disgusted look. "Did anyone ever point out that you have a mean streak a mile wide, Leif? Besides, I'm only worried about you being out on your own because you could barely walk when you got home from your therapy this morning."

That much was true, but Leif wasn't about to give in to the weakness now. "Sarge, I'm fine. My leg hurts, but no more than usual. Now get out of my way and enjoy your lady's company while I go hunt down some dinner."

Once Nick moved out of the way, Leif unlocked the door and climbed into the driver's seat. He started the engine but rolled the window down to reassure his friend. "Seriously, Nick, if I'm going to spend time here in Snowberry Creek, I need to get to know some of the locals for myself."

Nick finally nodded. "Okay, but if you get bored, call me. It's been a long time since I've had a chance to remind you which one of us is better at pool."

Like Leif needed the reminder; he was the one who always ended up buying the next round when they played. The memories were good ones, though, so he smiled. "Which is exactly why I want a chance to sharpen my skills without you breathing down my neck. Now get back before I run over your foot just for spite."

Nick did as ordered as Leif pulled away slowly to avoid sending up a spray of gravel. At the top of the driveway, he turned left toward town. Isaac had told him the Creek Café was the best place to eat. He cruised down Main Street until he spotted the diner just past city hall.

The place looked packed. Clearly he wasn't the only one in town who needed to get out of the house tonight. Luckily a spot opened up near the front just as he pulled into the parking lot. On his way in, he paused to read the menu posted in the window by the door.

Home-style cooking and fresh pie. Definitely his kind of place. He stepped inside and met a solid wall of noise. The sign said to seat himself, but as far as he could tell there wasn't an empty table or booth in sight. Should he wait or give up and look for some other place to eat?

The question was answered for him when he spotted a familiar face across the crowded room. His mood brightened immediately. Zoe was sitting at a small booth

tucked in the back corner. It was designed for two people, and the other seat was empty. She was already looking at a menu, so maybe that meant she wasn't meeting
anyone else for dinner.

As if sensing his gaze, she looked up. When she spotted him, she smiled and waved. Never let it be said that
Leif was slow to react when an opportunity presented
itself. He started right for her, weaving his way through
the crowded room.

By the time he reached her booth, she'd put the menu
down and sat back with a slightly puzzled look on her
face. She angled her head as if looking to see if he was
dragging anyone along in his wake.

Leif coasted to a stop by her table. "Hi, Zoe. I see I'm
not the only one who didn't feel like cooking."

"Yeah, I couldn't face slaving over the microwave
again tonight. Seems like half the town had the same
idea."

Once again she looked beyond him. "Are you by
yourself, too?"

He shrugged. "I thought I'd give Nick and Callie a
break from my company tonight. He has to report back
in a few days, not to mention that her parents are coming
home soon. That will definitely interfere with any quality
alone time they might have left."

Zoe grinned. "Yeah, parental units can put a real
damper on things sometimes."

"So true."

He needed to make his move before another table
opened up. "Look, I don't mean to intrude on your privacy, Zoe, and if you'd rather eat alone, that's fine. I was
wondering if you would mind if I shared your booth?
The place is full right now."

Her expressive eyes filled with sympathy as she stared

at his cane. "Of course, Leif. I should've realized. Please have a seat."

Damn it, he wanted to sit with her because she was an attractive woman, not because she felt sorry for him.

"Never mind. I can wait until something opens up."

Or, better yet, he could just leave.

Zoe caught his wrist before he could move. "No, don't go. To tell the truth, I'd appreciate the company."

He still hesitated. "Are you sure?"

"Yes, I am. Although don't expect much in the way of conversation when the food comes. Frannie, the owner, gets testy if people don't pay the proper respect to her cooking."

She winked at him and offered him the menu when he finally got settled in the booth. After he read over it, he asked, "What do you recommend?"

"Personally, I stick with the classics: a Creekburger and sweet potato fries, but everything here is good. Just make sure you save room for pie. I've been dreaming about her banana cream all day long."

His sweet tooth kicked into action. "It's that good?"

"Way better than good." Her expression turned deadly serious. "And just so we're clear up front, I don't share, so order your own if you want some."

Before he could respond, an older woman with a halo of red hair in a color that couldn't possibly be natural appeared at the table. She gave Leif a heated look that had him blushing. "Zoe, who's your handsome friend here?"

"His name is Corporal Leif Brevik." Zoe's eyes twinkled with mischief. "He's handsome enough, but a bit on the young side, Frannie. I'm guessing he might be able to keep up with you, with an emphasis on *might*."

The redhead wiggled her eyebrows and slapped Leif

on the back hard enough to rattle his teeth. "Think so, Corporal? I've always had a weakness for a man in a uniform, or better yet, out of one."

Okay, if that's how they wanted to play this, it was time to join in. He grabbed Frannie's fingers and pressed a soft kiss on the back of her age-spotted hand. "And I've always had a weakness for wicked redheads who can bake a mean pie."

Frannie threw back her head and laughed loud enough to draw the attention of all the people seated around them. She patted him on the shoulder this time.

"You'll do, Corporal, you'll do. In fact, you remind me of a few soldiers I've known in the past, and for that the pie is on me tonight. Zoe, take good care of our friend here."

"Don't worry. I will."

Frannie pulled out her order pad. "So what will it be?"

Zoe handed her the menu. "I'll have a Creekburger, sweet potato fries, and banana cream pie. Iced tea to drink."

"And you, Leif?"

"I'll have the same."

"Sounds good. It shouldn't be long."

After she walked away, Leif let out a deep breath and wiped the back of his hand across his forehead. "Whew, for a minute there I thought I might be on her own personal menu for tonight."

Zoe waited until Frannie was out of hearing before speaking again. "Heart of gold and all of that, but there's no telling what that woman will say or do. Frannie is definitely a law unto herself. I hope we didn't embarrass you too much."

"I'm a combat-hardened veteran, Zoe. I'm pretty sure I can handle whatever you want to dish out."

Then he let a little heat show in the look he gave her as he leaned closer over the small table. "Especially if you're going to go around telling people you think I'm handsome."

He sat back feeling smug and grinning big-time as Zoe's cheeks flushed a nice rosy red.

Chapter 8

It was definitely time to turn the discussion to a more neutral subject. She was curious about what had caused the confrontation between Leif and Mitch earlier, but that was hardly suitable dinnertime conversation.

She settled for the one thing she and Leif had in common. "So why choose the army?"

Leif immediately looked away, staring past her at something only he could see. "It seemed like the logical choice after I finished two years at the community college. I was never that great of a student, so any more college didn't make sense at the time. However, for the past couple of years, I've been taking classes as time allows, hoping eventually to finish a degree in business."

His stark gaze shifted back to her. "I also grew up listening to both of my grandfathers talk about what it was like fighting in the Big One."

He held up two fingers on each hand as if they were quotation marks as he repeated the last few words. "Yep, the Big One. That's what they always called World War

II, as if the words were capitalized to show that what they did back then really counted for something. Guess I soaked up some of that same desire to serve our country, because once I donned the uniform it felt as if I was part of something bigger than myself, something I could be proud of."

He gave her a lopsided grin. "Okay, that sounds like a recruiting poster. That doesn't mean it isn't true, though." Then Leif lobbed the ball back into her court. "And you? How did you end up as an army nurse?"

"In my case, it was my grandmother. She served as a nurse during the Big One." The memory made her smile. "By the way, that's what she called it, too. She was stationed in North Africa and then Italy, which is where she met my grandfather. He was one of her patients. Grandpa always showed off the bullet scar on his shoulder with pride, saying he would've taken a dozen just like it to be with her. I guess it all sounded romantic to me."

But combat medicine was anything but romantic. Luckily, she was saved from having to say any more by the arrival of their food. Leif's eyes widened at the sight, and he gave a low whistle.

"Damn, Zoe, you didn't tell me the burger was half a cow, and we'd each get half a bushel of sweet potatoes on the side."

She cut her own burger in half. "I never come here unless I've worked up a big appetite. Wait until you see the size of the piece of pie, especially since Frannie has taken a liking to you. For now, I'd concentrate on eating before she gets the idea you'd rather just look at your food."

"Yes, ma'am."

He meant no disrespect, but being called "ma'am" by Leif made Zoe feel like she and Frannie were contemporaries. That was so not true. She knew for a fact that she was only three years older than Leif; that was hardly any difference at all, despite what she'd told Brandi that first day. Not that she was interested in him except as a patient, no matter how good-looking he was or how much she liked his smile. Maybe she'd even believe that if she kept repeating it often enough, but memories of the good time they'd had at the potluck together didn't help.

"Do I have mustard on my chin or something?"

She blinked and then frowned at her dinner companion. "Pardon?"

"I asked if I had mustard on my face," Leif repeated, that twinkle back in his eyes. "After all the talk about chowing down on our food, I couldn't help but notice you've yet to take a single bite."

He looked as if he was fighting the urge to grin when he added, "Not to mention you've been staring at me with this big frown on your face."

Great. This must be her night for blushing. "Sorry. I was trying to remember if I signed off on a couple of charts before I left work today. I didn't mean to stare."

To prevent the need to say more, she took a big bite of her hamburger. She suspected that Leif didn't completely buy her explanation, but at least he didn't call her on it. She'd never been any good at lying anyway, but she wasn't about to admit the truth.

At least the food kept the two of them busy for the next few minutes. She was making serious inroads in the enormous pile of fries on her plate when Frannie reappeared with their pie. The expression on Leif's face was priceless when he caught sight of the huge wedge of pie with several inches of whipped cream piled on top.

Leif dropped the fry he'd just picked up. The look he gave the older woman was positively reverent. "Frannie, my love, if this damn boot didn't prevent me from getting down on my knees, I swear I'd be bowing at your feet right this second."

The older woman's expression softened when she stared down at the device that protected Leif's leg. "No need to go to that extreme, Corporal. I just want to do my part to fatten you up a bit."

She set the pieces of pie down on the table and then slapped the bill down next to them. "I'll bring refills on your tea in a minute, but just holler if there's anything else you need."

She left in a cloud of perfume and smiles for her other customers. Leif watched her walk away. "Like I said earlier, there's just something about a redhead—"

"Who makes a mean pie," Zoe finished for him.

Leif scooped up a bite of whipped cream with his finger. Before popping it in his mouth, he gave Zoe a hot look and said, "What can I say? I'm easy."

There was nothing safe she could say to that, so she settled for issuing an order. "Get busy eating, soldier. Frannie's headed this way, and she won't be happy if you don't do that dessert justice."

The crowd in the diner had started to thin out, but the line at the register was still pretty long. Zoe and Leif made small talk as they shuffled along, and she waved and nodded at several acquaintances and patients she recognized from the clinic.

The chief of police walked into the diner with his daughter, Sydney, in tow. He stopped to talk to Leif while Syd skipped on by to take a seat at the counter. By the time Gage walked away, Zoe and Leif were at the counter. When she reached for her wallet, Leif stopped her.

"No, it's my treat. You were nice enough to share your

booth." Then he leaned in closer to whisper, "Not to mention saving me from Frannie."

He handed the high school girl who was manning the register several bills and turned away without waiting for the change. Zoe considered protesting, but figured it would be a losing battle.

"Thank you, Leif. This is the second time you've bought me dinner. The next time will be on me."

The offer surprised her as much as it did him. When had she decided that there would even be a next time?

When they were outside, Leif looked around. "Where's your car?"

She pointed down the street. "At home. I knew I'd never be able to resist that pie, so I staged a preventive attack and worked off some of the calories in advance by walking here."

"A smart way to get ahead of the curve." He shifted his weight off his injured leg. "Would you like a ride home? I've got my truck right over there."

Part of her wanted to accept, but the strength of that desire had her refusing. The more time she spent in Leif's company, the harder it was to remember that he was a patient, nothing more.

"No, that's all right. It's not all that far, and the walk will do me good. Thanks again for dinner. I enjoyed it."

When she started to walk away, Leif fell into step beside her. "Leif, I thought you said your truck was that way."

He kept walking. "It is, but I thought I might keep you company. I don't have any place I need to be, and it's a nice night for a stroll."

Yes, it was, but it wasn't the weather she was concerned about. "Look, while I don't mind the company, I live over a mile from here. Are you sure your leg is up to walking that far and then all the way back here?"

Nothing like throwing a match on a puddle of gas. He went from affable companion to pissed-off soldier in a heartbeat.

"Damn it, Zoe, I have a mother and I don't want or need another one. Why don't you let me decide what I can handle?"

He crowded close to her and spoke in a cold monotone but with absolute fury coating every word he uttered. Her first reaction was to apologize, but her concern was legitimate. If she backed down now, he might never respect her opinion again. With her hands on her hips, she crowded him right back.

"Back off, soldier! If you want to walk me home, fine. I won't stop you. But you know, I'm surprised you can walk at all considering the weight of that boulder-sized chip you've got parked on your shoulder."

She threw her hands up in the air. "I just wanted to make sure you knew how far it was to my place. But God knows, if you want to risk screwing your leg up even worse, who am I to stop you?"

Then she slapped her forehead. "Oh, yeah, I'm the one who's supposed to help you heal."

Rather than wait for him to respond, she spun around and marched off down the sidewalk. When she'd gone a short distance, she stopped to look back. "Well, are you coming or not?"

Leif was already back at his truck and climbing in. She guessed she had her answer. Well, crap, that was a rotten end to what had been a pleasant evening. There was nothing to be done about it now, though, so she started walking again and counted the minutes until she would reach the sanctuary of her apartment and that bottle of wine in the fridge.

*   *   *

About three blocks later, a familiar red pickup cruised past her. It slowed at the next corner, where it hung a U-turn and headed back in her direction. He stopped a short distance ahead of her, where she'd have to go right past him. What did Leif want now?

In no mood for more theatrics, she wanted to keep walking and ignore the idiot. Obviously, however, Leif couldn't take a hint, leaving her no choice but to deal with him now. Putting off the confrontation wouldn't make it any easier. She kept walking at a steady pace despite being painfully aware of those dark eyes watching her every move. She slowed to a stop when she reached the side of the truck.

The passenger-side window slid down, and Leif leaned over from the driver's side to look down at her. Zoe took the initiative and spoke first.

"What is it now, Leif?" Crossing her arms over her chest, she added, "And make it quick. It's getting late and I have to work tomorrow."

"Can I give you a ride the rest of the way to your place?" He added "please" almost as an afterthought.

In no mood to make it easy for him, she shook her head. "I can get there on my own."

"I know you can, and if you'd rather I get out of the truck to do my groveling, I will."

As if to prove he meant it, he straightened up and opened his door. She took pity on him. "Fine, I'll get in."

Even after she was inside the cab, he sat staring out the front window. Finally, he sighed and turned to face her. She hated the defeat she saw etched in his handsome face.

Angling herself in the seat to see him better, she offered him a chance to explain. "No groveling required. Just lay it all out there and tell me how I can help."

He leaned his head back against the headrest and gripped the steering wheel with both hands. "Look, my temper is pretty unpredictable these days, especially when it comes to my leg. I get that people are only trying to help, but all that attention gets old pretty damn quick. I'm not helpless."

Leif shot a quick glance in her direction but then looked away again. "Hell, somehow even my hard-ass sergeant has turned into an effing nursemaid. I swear Nick constantly frets about what I eat, how much I sleep, if I've taken my pills or if I take too many. He wants to do my laundry for me and hates me doing anything more strenuous than washing the dishes."

He paused to pound his fist softly on the steering wheel. "Earlier tonight, when I was leaving, the big jerk chased me all the way to my truck, wanting to come with me. It was like he thought I couldn't even find my way into town and back, much less eat a meal on my own."

All of that came out on one breath as if he'd been piling up all those words and all that frustration until the dam finally broke. It was probably a relief to get it all out. She chose her next words carefully.

"I know it's hard, Leif, and you've got a lot going on right now. Have you told Nick how you feel about all the fussing?"

Leif drew in a deep breath and let it out slowly. "Not in so many words, because I know a large part of it is due to the fact that he holds himself responsible for what happened to me and our friend Spence. That's bullshit, but there's no convincing him any different. Nick was in charge that day, and Spence died on his watch. There's no changing that, but it doesn't mean Nick was at fault. That honor belongs to the bastards who planted the IED and then lobbed in a couple of mortars just for grins."

Then he patted his injured leg. "It doesn't help that every time he sees me limping or downing a pill, it all comes rushing back. I don't have the heart to tear him a new one for trying to make it up to me. Then there's the fact that if he had helped Spence first, I would've been the one to die. We're both sort of feeling our way through all of this."

Zoe couldn't resist the need to connect with him in some small way. She put her hand on his arm and said, "Yeah, I get that, Leif. In some ways it's harder on our loved ones when they see us hurting and can't wave a magic wand to make the pain go away. Even so, bottling it all up inside and not telling him how you feel isn't helping either one of you."

"Yeah, I know. On the other hand, he'll be leaving in a few days, so it won't be a problem, at least not until he gets back. By then, I'll be back to walking normally again."

Well, the jury was still out on that last part, but she wasn't about to point it out right now. When she'd first touched his arm, the muscles had been rock hard. Some of the tension had eased now.

"If you find yourself needing to talk about this stuff, I'm always available, Leif. There's also a support group of veterans that meets at the church. They're a great bunch of guys and always welcome new members. Several of my other patients have found it helpful to talk to them."

Leif nodded, but it was impossible to tell if he was open to the suggestion. She understood that. She had no interest in joining the group herself, despite Jack Haliday's best efforts to coax her into giving it a try. Finally, Leif turned the key in the ignition. "Thanks for listening, and I am sorry that I took my frustrations out on you."

Zoe let her hand drop back down to her side. "That's why they pay me the big bucks, Corporal."

Although it wasn't her job credentials that had her wanting to wrap this man in her arms and hold the rest of the world at bay. Calling him by his rank helped put some of that professional distance back in place. Barely.

He put the truck in gear and pulled away from the curb. "Which way?"

Clearly he was done talking, so she gave him directions and waited in silence until they reached her apartment.

Damn, he wished Zoe's place was a lot farther away than six measly blocks. Going to the bar by himself no longer held much appeal, but he wasn't ready to go back to Spence's house either.

He studied the cedar-sided building. "Looks like a nice place. Which one is yours?"

Zoe had been about to open her door, but she stopped when he spoke. "I'm on the second floor. It's nothing fancy, but there aren't a lot of rentals here in town. Eventually, I'll get around to buying a house of my own. I wanted to make sure I liked living back here in Snowberry Creek before making a commitment of that magnitude."

Leif knew all about the reluctance to set down roots too quickly or too deeply. It was easier to move on to the next duty station if he wasn't leaving anything special behind. He thought about all the people he'd met and grown fond of here in Snowberry Creek: Zoe, Isaac, Gage Logan and his daughter, Bridey, and Clarence Reed. Clearly he'd already made connections that would make it harder to leave when the time came.

"Yeah, I get that. That's why I'm staying at Spence

Lang's place with Nick. It's only temporary, until my leg gets back to full strength. Then it's up to the army where I'll be living."

He paused to stare up at the night sky. "It will sure be weird to be deployed again without Spence or Nick. Not sure if I like that idea at all."

"Yeah, leaving friends behind is definitely the downside of military life."

Something in her voice made him think that whoever it was she'd left behind had been more important to her than just a friend. But when she didn't offer up any more details, he didn't ask. Zoe was entitled to her privacy, and sharing hamburgers and banana cream pie in a small-town diner didn't entitle him to her life story.

She was reaching for the door handle again. Letting her go would be the smart thing, but he wasn't feeling all that bright. He opened his door and climbed out too quickly for her to try to stop him.

"There's no need to see me to the door, Leif."

Okay, so that eliminated any chance of being invited in for a drink. He wouldn't push it, but neither was he ready to give up completely.

"My mother taught me to always see a lady to her door."

He almost pulled it off with a straight face, but Zoe wasn't buying what he was selling. "Oh, brother. Tell me, does that line usually work for you?"

He gave up and laughed. "Considering that's the first time I've used it, I'd have to say no."

That didn't keep him from following her to the bottom of the stairs that led up to the second floor. Damn it, no elevator. Well, there was no way he was going to attempt that many steps after the day he'd had.

Zoe knew it too, so there was no use in pretending

anything different. He managed a small smile. "I guess Mom will have to be satisfied with me escorting you this far."

Zoe followed his lead and kept it light. "If you need a note for her, let me know."

"Will do."

He seemed to have run out of steam, caught between saying good night and wanting to stretch out the evening for a few minutes more. At least Zoe seemed to be stuck in the same spot with him.

Feeling a little daring, he tucked a tendril of her dark hair back behind her ear. "Thanks again for letting me join you for dinner. I enjoyed myself."

"So did I."

"Well, except maybe for when I was being a jerk."

Her full lips quirked up in a teasing smile. "Yeah, except for that."

He couldn't seem to tear his eyes away from her mouth. Was it as soft and kissable as he imagined? Was she swaying toward him or was that his wayward mind seeing what it wanted to see? Only one way to find out.

"I probably shouldn't do this."

"Do what?"

Her words sounded breathy, and he was pretty sure that her pulse was racing as fast as his was. Being a man of action, he answered her not with words but with the softest of kisses. A mere brushing of his lips across hers. Friendly, nothing over the top. When she didn't immediately pull back, he did it again, ramping up the intensity enough to satisfy a little of his curiosity without scaring her off.

Damn, he wanted more, but this wasn't the time or the place. And he knew it. He backed off slowly, trying to make sure she felt his regret.

"Good night, Zoe. And thanks again."

She retreated to the safety of the steps. "You're welcome. Maybe I'll see you at the clinic next week when you come in for therapy."

Even if he understood why, he hated that she was already morphing back into his nurse practitioner. "I'll be there."

When she started up the stairs, he walked back to his truck, doing his best not to limp in case she was watching. When he finally looked, she had already disappeared inside. He drove back to the main drag through town and sat at the stop sign to consider his options.

Did he still want to check out BEER and see if anyone wanted to play pool? Somehow the whole idea had lost its appeal. Maybe he should have asked Zoe if she'd like to go with him, but he hadn't wanted to risk putting her in the awkward position of having to turn him down.

Okay, decision made. He headed back toward Spence's house. He'd take a shower and a pill, and then crawl into bed.

Alone. Damn.

Chapter 9

Leif could barely watch this. It hurt like hell seeing the Sarge back in uniform and packing up to leave at this ungodly hour of the morning. Nick had gotten a clean bill of health from the medics on the shrapnel damage to his upper arm, so there was nothing to prevent him from returning to active duty.

Leif would give anything to be going with or, better yet, instead of Nick. After all, the sergeant had already made up his mind that his military service would end with this current enlistment a few weeks from now. He'd already started building a post-army life with Callie right here in Snowberry Creek.

Nick tucked the last of his kit in his duffel bag and zipped it shut. "Well, that's everything, I guess."

"Not quite."

Leif tossed a small package to Nick, who caught it with his usual quick reflexes. He gave the gaudily wrapped package a suspicious look.

"Aw, Leif, I'm pretty sure you shouldn't have."

Leif figured Nick might just be right about that. There was no way to know for sure until his friend opened the box. "It's nothing big, Sarge. Just something I thought you might like."

"No, I meant exactly what I said, Leif. You shouldn't have." Nick pulled the pink bow off the package and tossed it straight back at Leif. "I don't do pink."

Leif shoved the bow in his pocket just in case he got the chance to slip it back in Nick's luggage. "I could claim it was the only color I could find, but that would be a lie."

His friend gave him one more narrow-eyed look before tearing into the wrapping paper. When he finally opened the box, all traces of trepidation disappeared. He unfolded the trifold picture frame and stared down at the photos it contained. His mouth quirked up in a sad smile as he ran his fingers across the glass in the frame.

When he looked up, his eyes had a suspiciously bright sheen to them, not that Leif would point that out. He'd felt the same way as he'd slipped the photos into place. The picture in the middle was one Leif had taken last week when he'd caught Nick and Callie holding hands out by the gazebo. The one on the left was Mooch sitting on the front porch steps with Callie.

He'd known without a doubt that Nick would appreciate having those two pictures to take with him. It was the third one he wasn't so sure about, but finally he'd gone with his gut reaction and included it. A friend had snapped it back in Afghanistan right after their squad had won a basketball game against a bunch of marines.

Spence had made the winning free throw and the three of them were high-fiving in celebration. There'd been few really happy moments during that deployment, but that had been one of the best.

Nick jerked his head in a quick nod as he carefully folded the picture frame and stowed it safely back in its box. He unzipped the duffel and wrapped one of his shirts around the small package to give it some extra protection. Why wasn't he saying anything? Had Leif guessed wrong about the whole picture thing?

But as soon as Nick finished zipping the duffel closed again, he headed straight for Leif and gave him an awkward man hug. It was the kind of emotional moment neither of them was ever really comfortable with, but Leif figured they both needed once in a while. Leif hugged him in return and then stepped back.

Nick finally spoke as he snagged his duffel and headed for the door. "I've got to tell you, I hate like hell to be leaving right now."

Leif let his friend lead the way down the steps. "We'll be here when you get back."

Mooch joined the party, acting pretty subdued, as if he sensed what was happening and wasn't sure what to do about it. "Mooch and I will watch over the house and Callie for you."

Nick stopped to look around the house. "As soon as I get back, we'll really get to work on this place."

"That's the plan."

Leif wasn't sure about how helpful he'd be for all the remodeling Callie and Nick had in mind, but he'd give it his best shot for as long as he was still in town.

Nick was still talking. "And I also appreciate that you're going to Austin Locke's hearing with Callie. I wouldn't want her to have to face him and his father by herself."

"That's for damn sure."

Spence's younger cousin, Austin, had broken into the house that Spence had bequeathed to Callie several times in order to steal valuables he could sell for cash. The punk and his old man thought Spence should have left his home to them despite how Vince had treated Spence when he was a kid. They didn't see what Austin had done as robbery, but as reclaiming back a little of their own. Unfortunately, only Austin would be getting some jail time. As far as Leif and Nick were both concerned, Spence's uncle, Vince Locke, should be going with him.

It was time to go. Leif followed Nick out onto the porch, where Callie was waiting. Leif limped down the steps to her. "Are you sure you don't want me to ride along with you?"

She immediately wrapped her arms around him and gave him a quick squeeze. What was up with all this hugging today? He wouldn't complain, though. It was going to be hard on both of them while Nick was away.

"I'll be fine. Besides, you've got your therapy appointment this morning."

True, he did. This was a long one, too. He was scheduled to start off the morning with Isaac before meeting with Zoe. It would be the first time they would be alone since their chance meeting at the Creek Café almost two weeks ago. He'd seen her from a distance a couple of times, but that was all.

Not all of the knots in his gut this morning were because of Nick leaving. Was Zoe actively avoiding him or was she just really busy? He wished he knew. He guessed he'd know more by how she acted when he saw her.

"I could still blow off the appointment if you needed me, Callie."

She rose up on her toes to kiss his cheek. "I know, but

there's no point in you missing your therapy. Nick's already made me promise to just drop him off out front at the airport. It's not like I can hang out at the gate with him until he has to board, anyway."

Nick had been busy saying good-bye to Mooch. He wiped his face on his sleeve. "Damn, dog, now I'm covered in slobber."

Callie chided him. "Doggie kisses are not the same as slobber."

He snorted. "Feels the same to me. Guess we should hit the road."

When Mooch tried to jump into the cab of Nick's truck, Leif caught him by the collar and pulled him back toward the porch. The dog sounded pitiful as he whined and tried to break free of Leif's grasp. How did he know that Nick was going farther than just to town and back? Did he realize what was up because of Nick's duffel? Maybe he was sensing everyone's ramped-up emotions.

"Settle down, Mooch. I don't like watching him leave either, but soldiers like us can handle anything."

Evidently his words got through to the dog, because Mooch immediately relaxed and leaned against Leif. He sat and scratched the dog's head for several minutes. Although he'd never admit it in a million years, he needed the comfort as much as Mooch did.

But enough was enough. He pushed himself back up to his feet. "Come on, Mooch. Let's have some breakfast. I'm going to need all my strength to get through the day."

As usual, his four-footed companion brightened up at the mention of any word that referred to food. Considering that the dog had spent most of his life half-starved and living on the streets, Leif didn't blame him.

As he opened the screen door, Leif gave Mooch a hard look. "Stay out from under my feet while I'm cooking, dog, and I might even share my bacon with you."

Mooch yipped his acceptance of the terms and bolted straight for the kitchen.

Chapter 10

Zoe picked up her keys and headed outside for some fresh air. It was well past her usual bedtime, but despite being tired to the bone, she was far too restless to settle in for the night. It had been a long day at work, and she'd been unable to shed the stress since walking out of her office. Looking back over the day, she realized that all but one of her appointments had been routine, not a bad average.

But that one had been a doozy. Isaac had shot her an e-mail with a copy of his report on Leif's progress attached only minutes before the corporal had limped his way down the hall to her office. She'd barely had time to assimilate the content before having to explain it all to Leif.

The good news was that he was making progress. The bad news was he was hoping for a miracle cure, and there wasn't one. Not for the kind of damage his leg had sustained. She knew better than to remind him he was lucky to have a leg at all. He wouldn't see the bright side of anything unless it was a full recovery with no residual damage.

In the end, she'd laid it all out for him. Progress of any kind was a good thing. Patience was as much a part of his recovery as was diligence in doing his therapy. No one, especially not her, could give him a hard date where he would be able to walk out her door and not look back.

The more she'd talked, the quieter he'd gotten. She would've been more comfortable with a show of temper than she was with the unnatural calm that had masked his real reaction. She had been tempted to whack him on the head with her rubber hammer to try to break through the stone wall he had erected between them.

It was hard to believe the chilly stranger sitting across from her was the same man who had been so charming the night they'd had dinner at the café and at the potluck before that. As the two of them sat in her office, the distance between them had grown far greater than the width of her desk. She couldn't imagine ever having kissed the guy, much less wanting to do so again.

Didn't the idiot realize how fragile the human body was? Doctors sometimes worked miracles, but they could do only so much with what they had to work with. The reports on Leif's leg and ankle had made it clear that the surgeons had been working on a jigsaw puzzle where not all the pieces were made to fit back together.

In the end, he'd thanked Zoe for her time and quietly promised to continue his exercises and appointments with Isaac. He'd said all the right things, but she couldn't quite believe he had meant any of it. She'd cursed and thrown his chart against the wall as soon as he walked out the door.

But that was then. Right now, she needed to get past the frustration so she could sleep. At least tomorrow was her day off. Outside on the sidewalk, she debated which way to go. She ignored the late-night siren call of the Creek Café and a piece of Frannie's pie. A long walk would be a far better use of her time. The exercise would burn off the tension and give her a good workout at the same time.

She set off at a brisk pace, following a familiar route that would take her down to the park by the creek. Experience had taught her that a few minutes listening to the soothing sound of the water rippling over the rocks would help her relax enough to sleep.

Her steps slowed when she reached the edge of the park and realized she wasn't the only one out for a stroll. A man stood by the creek, his attention riveted on something down at the edge of the water—a dog.

Well, there was no need to disturb the pair. She could cut across to the path a little farther up the creek and walk upstream from there. Still, something about the guy seemed awfully familiar, maybe in the way he stood leaning a bit to one side. She slowed her steps as she studied him from a distance.

It finally hit her that the guy was leaning on a cane. Could it be? He was the right height and build. He stood with his back to her at the edge of some dark shadows, so it was impossible to tell for sure. Come to think of it, the dog looked familiar, too.

Deciding it was worth the risk, she changed directions again. After making her way to the edge of the water a short distance from where he stood staring out into the night, she called his name.

"Leif?"

No response. Okay, so maybe it wasn't him. She edged a little farther away and prepared to retreat to the street behind her. Before she'd gone two steps, he finally realized he was no longer alone.

"I'm sorry, ma'am, but did you . . . Zoe, is that you?"

The familiar voice had her spinning back around again. "Leif, I'm sorry. I didn't mean to intrude, but I was pretty sure that was you."

The nurse in her noticed he was leaning pretty heavily on the cane as he stepped onto the lighted pathway. However, it was the woman in her who took note of the broad shoulders, the ruggedly handsome face, and the engaging smile that he aimed in her direction.

"I see I'm not the only one who needed a breath of fresh air before turning in for the night."

She nodded. "Sometimes the day closes in on me, and I need to get out for a while."

The dog had been sniffing along the edge of some bushes. As soon as he realized she was talking to his human, he came trotting over to check her out.

"Who's your handsome friend, Leif? We were never formally introduced at the potluck."

"That's Mooch. My unit adopted him after he saved us on a night patrol in Afghanistan."

She knelt down to pet the dog. "Seriously? He did? That's great you guys could bring him back to the States with you." Leif shifted restlessly as if the subject made him uncomfortable. "I'm sorry. I didn't mean to pry."

"No, it's all right. We'd been clearing streets for hours and were dragging our exhausted asses back to camp. From out of nowhere, this half-starved mutt started following us. Mooch would've sold his soul for a piece of beef jerky and was smart enough to peg Spence Lang as the soft touch in our squad."

He paused for breath. "Anyway, a few minutes later Mooch started pitching a fit and barking at something in an alley we were about to pass. Turns out one of the locals had a little surprise planned for us. The bastard shot Mooch to shut him up."

"Oh, no!"

The dog whined softly and licked her hand as if to remind her that he'd clearly survived the incident.

"Yeah, our boy there definitely took one for the team. You can still feel the scar underneath the fur on his shoulder."

Leif leaned down to give his buddy a good scratching. "When we got back to camp, Spence got the dog patched up, figuring he deserved that much. Our deployment was winding down, and Spence couldn't stand the thought of tossing Mooch back out on the streets when we left. Actually, none of us could."

Leif sounded embarrassed to admit that about himself, but she thought it was sweet. "I can understand why. He's a handsome fellow."

"Not so sure about that," Leif said with a soft laugh. "Anyway, Spence did all the grunt work on the arrangements to have Mooch shipped home. It was Nick who made sure it happened when Spence couldn't, figuring he would've wanted it that way."

Aware that he wouldn't want her sympathy about what had happened to him and his friends, she settled for giving his furry companion a quick hug before straightening up. "Were you two heading back home?"

"No, we just got here. Mooch likes to explore off his leash, so I was letting him wander a bit. I thought I'd walk along the creek for a while before we go back to the house."

"Mind if I walk with you?"

"Not at all as long as I don't slow you down too

much." He patted his leg again. "As long as I don't push it, it feels good to be out moving around."

"I'm glad to hear that, Leif."

A few steps later, he said, "I was a jerk again today in your office. It was a lot to process."

On impulse, she looped her arm through his in the hopes he would understand that the gesture meant his quasi apology was accepted. "I know it was, Leif, but let's agree that what happens in the office stays in the office. Out here, we're simply two people and one heroic dog out to enjoy the evening air. Fair enough?"

His smile was more genuine now. "Fair enough. Come on, Mooch, keep up."

The silence that settled between them was comfortable and relaxed. Once again, she'd given in to the temptation to enjoy this man's company. It wasn't smart, but she couldn't seem to help herself. He was hurting; they both were. Yeah, she was skirting the edge of impropriety with a patient, but right now he needed her more than she needed to follow the rules.

That was her excuse and she was sticking to it.

Early the next morning, Leif was wide awake and feeling pretty perky, especially considering how late he'd gotten to bed. After he and Zoe had walked along the creek, he'd coaxed her into splitting a piece of Frannie's pie. Since Mooch was with them, they'd wound up outside on the wooden bench where some of the town's old codgers sat during the day.

Afterward, Zoe had insisted that they walk to her place so she could drive Mooch and him back home. Since he'd gotten to bed well after midnight, he shouldn't be feeling perky at all. Leif frowned. Okay, maybe "perky" wasn't a manly enough word to describe his mood. It was more like something Spence would've said to get a rise out of his friends.

Leif stared up at the ceiling, determined to linger in bed a little longer. "Spence, you always were a pain in the ass, but I miss you, buddy. It seems strange to hang around here in Snowberry Creek with people who knew you, too."

Rather than the usual sharp pain of grief, he found himself grinning. "You must have been a holy terror when you were a teenager, Wheels. Frannie at the diner has promised to share some hair-raising tales about your high school exploits next time I'm there. Wish I had known you back then. We'd have kept the cops around here on their toes—that's for sure."

The patter of claws on the hardwood floors served as warning that Leif's horizontal time was at an end. Rather than wait for Mooch to pounce on the bed, Leif rolled upright and sat on the edge of the mattress.

Disappointed that his favorite morning game had been canceled, Mooch parked his backside on the rug by the bed and waited impatiently for Leif to get moving. The dog's tail did a slow sweep across the floor when his human managed to stand up.

"Come on, dog," Leif grumbled as he shuffled out of the den and headed toward the kitchen. "I'll let you out while I start breakfast."

Mooch barked his approval and headed over to wait by the door. Leif left it propped open so the dog could come back in when his business was done. Mooch's morning routine was pretty involved. He would start by marking his territory and then do a full perimeter search of not only this yard but also the one next door. After all, who knew how many squirrels had invaded his territory during the night?

Lucky bastard. Leif envied the dog's easy acceptance of his new purpose in life. Mooch had it good: a permanent home here in Snowberry Creek with two people who would make damn sure he lived out his days in peace.

Leif should have it so good. When he tried to picture himself settling down here in Snowberry Creek, the picture wouldn't quite come into focus. It came close, though, especially since he knew his friends would be living there.

Tired of his own pity party, he slammed a skillet down on the stove and got out the bacon and eggs. When Mooch started barking like crazy, Leif glanced outside. Callie was headed his way but was having trouble walking with Mooch bouncing all around her like a damn yo-yo.

Leif stood in the doorway and yelled, "Dog, if you want any of this bacon I'm cooking, you'll stop that before you trip her."

Mooch immediately settled down to trot by Callie's side. Leif returned to the counter and set out another coffee cup. "I'm just starting the bacon, Callie, but the coffee's about ready. Help yourself."

She poured each of them a cup, automatically loading his up with sugar and cream.

"Want some eggs, too?"

"I wouldn't turn down a couple of pieces of real bacon. Mom is watching Dad's cholesterol like a hawk, which is a good thing, so I'll have to depend on you to keep me supplied with the good stuff."

Leif dutifully added another couple of strips to the

skillet while Callie set the table for two and put bread in the toaster. He waited until she sat down at the table to speak.

"So, what brings you out so early this morning?"

Callie bent down to rub Mooch's belly before answering. "Gage Logan stopped by yesterday evening to talk to me. He'd hoped to talk to Nick, too, but hadn't realized he was already gone. He wanted to update us on Austin's hearing that's scheduled for next week. Thursday at ten o'clock."

"I know. I wrote it down."

He pointed toward the calendar on the side of the refrigerator with the tongs he was using to turn the bacon. Deciding it was done, he set the strips on a paper towel to soak up the excess grease and dumped the eggs into the skillet.

"He didn't need to drive out here to remind us of the court time. What else did he have to say?"

Callie took a sip of coffee before answering. "It seems the public defender staged a preemptive strike and asked the court to consider giving Austin probation and maybe community service instead of more jail time. Since it's his first offense, the judge is actually considering it."

There had to be more to this than just the lawyer's request.

Callie was frowning big-time now. "It seems Austin's boss and several of his coworkers have come forward on their own as character witnesses to testify he's been a good employee, reliable and all of that. The attorney is claiming the break-ins were out of character for Austin, and that he was only driven to take such desperate action because he was working for minimum wage and needed to help support his ailing father."

What a load of crap. "So what does all of this have to do with you and me?"

Because Callie wouldn't be avoiding looking him in the eye if it was only about her and maybe Nick.

"According to Gage, it would really help Austin's case if I were to support the idea. The only real question is about Austin's attack on you. He admits he broke the window, but he denies ever hitting you. He claims he heard you hit the floor and ran in to check on you."

"Bullshit! I was knocked out cold that night. I even have the scar to prove it."

Callie held up her hands as if to surrender. "I know, I know, Leif. But here's the thing: When I was dusting that room the next day, I found blood on the corner of the end table next to the hide-a-bed. What if you did fall getting out of bed when you heard the glass break and hit your head there?"

He found himself rubbing his temple, trying to remember the details of that evening. The trouble was he'd been on some pretty heavy pain meds and had no memory of how he came to be passed out on the floor. Translation: The kid's explanation was possible.

"He also said he put a pillow under your head before he took off. I don't know how else the pillow would've gotten there. In fact, Nick apologized to me later for ruining the pillowcase when he used it to wipe the blood off your face."

Again, the explanation was plausible—not that it excused Austin for breaking into the house in the first place. However, Callie's words were tentative, as if she was actually considering offering that punk a lifeline.

Like hell! This wasn't some teenager. He had to be in

his early twenties. At Austin's age, Leif had already done his first tour in Iraq and was on the verge of beginning another deployment.

No matter what, though, Callie didn't deserve the sharp side of Leif's temper. With considerable effort, he reined it in and bought himself some time by buttering the toast. The eggs were done, too, so he scooped them into a bowl. After putting the food on the table, he sat down across from Callie.

After they'd each filled a plate, he made himself ask, "Are you actually buying that line of crap?"

She'd been about to take a bite of her bacon, but she set it back down on her plate. "Not exactly. We both know that if Austin does do hard time in prison, he'll come out worse than he went in. That is, if he survives at all. So, yes, I'd rather give him a chance to make restitution and turn his life around. If he screws up again, at least I will have tried. It's not like I have any big emotional attachment to any of the stuff he took. It all belonged to his family anyway."

Leif knew right where this was headed. "And despite knowing that Spence wanted you to have all of his stuff, you feel guilty about ending up with everything."

Her shoulders sagged. "Yeah, I do. Maybe that's stupid, but I can't help feeling that way."

They both lapsed into silence as they ate. Who was he to blame her for feeling guilty about the situation they all found themselves in? After all, if Nick had made a different choice that day, it would've been Leif who died in the street. Nick felt guilty because he'd been the one in charge, and Spence had died on his watch. Callie felt guilty because she'd profited from a friend's death. There was plenty of guilt to go around.

Aw, heck, what the hell?

"If you want to give the punk a break, I'll back your play." He pointed his fork at her. "But if Nick explodes over this, I won't take the heat alone. In fact, I'll tell him you waited until I was in a pain-pill stupor and browbeat me into accepting the idea."

She laughed, just as he'd hoped. "It's a deal. If he asks, it's all on me."

"Is there anything we need to do other than show up at the hearing?"

"I'll call Gage and found out. And, Leif?"

"Yeah?"

She got up and came around to his side of the table to give him a quick hug. "Thanks for being so understanding, even if you really do hate the whole idea."

"You're welcome. But I repeat, if Nick comes unglued, I'm throwing you to the wolves."

"Fair enough."

She sat back down, her mood obviously improved. "I saw you and Mooch leave for a walk last night. How did that go?"

"Fine. We only went as far as the park. I mostly let him run around for a while."

"And you didn't see anybody else?"

Her question sounded a little too coy for it to be totally innocent. What did she know? Enough, it would seem, considering the smug smile she was shooting in his direction.

He might as well fess up and get it over with. "I might have run into Zoe Phillips at the park."

Her eyebrows shot up. "Might have? You don't know for sure?"

Busted. "Okay, I did run into her at the park. She was out for a walk, too. We talked for a little while, had a piece of pie at the diner. Afterward, she drove Mooch and me back here. Then I went to bed. Alone, in case you're wondering."

"I've always liked Zoe." Callie poured herself another cup of coffee. "And before you ask, I wasn't spying on you. Bridey happened to be driving by when you two were leaving the park. She mentioned it when I stopped by her shop for a latte on the way back from my run this morning."

Okay, that did it. He set his mug down with a little extra force. "You went to Bridey's and didn't bring me back a muffin?"

Callie looked guilty. "Actually, I did. But while I waited for you to show some sign of life over here, I lost control and ate it. Next time I'll know to buy two."

"Better make it three, since you already owe me one. The second one is the penalty you pay for eating mine in the first place. The third one is for insurance to make sure mine arrives here intact."

Callie laughed and started to clear the table. "It's a deal. I've got to go in a minute. I promised my mother I'd help her out in the yard this morning."

Before she was out the door, he called after her, "Callie, it's a nice thing you're doing for Spence's cousin. Let's just hope he's smart enough to realize it."

But Leif wouldn't be putting any money on the chance that he would.

Chapter 11

꧁ ꧂

The rest of the weekend sped by in a blur. Leif spent most of it sitting on his ass or doing his stretches. On Sunday evening, he'd taken Mooch for another walk at the park, but they hadn't run into Zoe again.

He'd been tempted to call her to see if she'd like to go somewhere for dinner, but he wasn't sure how she would react to that. There were times he was convinced her interest in him went beyond her concern over his recovery, but not always. Not wanting to push things, he'd also resisted the urge to kiss her again the other night when she'd dropped him off at Spence's place.

Had she taken that for a lack of interest on his part? He wasn't scheduled to see her at the clinic today, but maybe he'd run into her anyway. If so, he might take a shot at setting up something with her later in the week. Feeling better than he had in a while, he locked Mooch in the house and headed into town for his physical therapy appointment.

As soon as he walked in, Isaac closed the chart he'd

been reading and headed straight for Leif. "How did your appointment with Zoe go on Friday?"

The question came off as more curious than accusatory, but the concern on the other man's face made it clear something was up. "Fine, I guess. She went over the numbers with me and talked about the importance of keeping up with my treatment."

Not that he gave a rat's ass about the measurements. He didn't need a bunch of facts and figures to tell him that his leg was a long way from normal.

"Why? What's going on?"

His answer didn't seem to satisfy Isaac. "Because she wants to see you again today. Zoe said it wouldn't take long and to let Brandi know when you were done in here. She didn't say what it was about, and I wanted to make sure there wasn't a problem of some kind."

It was a puzzle to Leif, too, even if he and Zoe hadn't parted on the best terms after his appointment on Friday. They'd certainly gotten along fine on their impromptu walk that evening.

"There's no problem that I'm aware of, so maybe it's some paperwork snafu. You know how easy it is to get all tangled up in red tape."

Isaac looked relieved. "So true. I spend half my time dealing with all that crap. Either way, keep me in the loop."

"Will do."

Rather than worry about what might have gone wrong in the interim, Leif plunged into his exercise program, keeping up a running conversation with Mitch about the upcoming baseball play-offs as they did their reps.

The hour passed quickly. Isaac made a few more notes on Leif's chart before letting him leave.

Leif picked up his pack and headed out the door that

led into the main clinic. When he didn't immediately see either Brandi or Zoe, he stopped at the front desk.

"I'm Leif Brevik. Zoe left a message with Isaac that she wanted to see me for a minute."

The receptionist smiled and reached for the phone. "Have a seat, and I'll let her know you're here. It may be a few minutes if Zoe is with a patient."

"That's okay."

It's not like he had anywhere he had to be. He settled into a chair and picked up one of the year-old magazines from the pile on a nearby table. He skimmed an article on the war, probably not the smartest thing he could have done. It didn't matter that it was months out of date. For the boots on the ground, the war was pretty much the same now as it had been then. And wasn't that just a damn shame?

"Mr. Brevik, Zoe can see you now."

He closed the magazine and tossed it aside. Pasting a smile on his face, he followed the receptionist down the hall past the same office where he'd met with Zoe the first time. They kept going until they reached a door he hadn't noticed before.

"She's waiting for you at the picnic table in back."

He thanked the receptionist and stepped outside to look around. Okay, this was getting stranger and stranger. Granted, it was a nice day, and it was a relief to breathe air that was fresh and free of the medicinal smell of the clinic. But why would Zoe prefer to speak to him out here?

There was only one way to find out. He walked around the corner of the building. His leg was tired from his therapy, which meant his limp was more pronounced. It wasn't as if Zoe hadn't seen him hobble before, but that didn't mean he liked it.

He finally spotted her sitting on the top of an old wooden picnic table with her back to him. Her dark hair was pulled back and braided. Damn, he'd love to set it free, especially if he could then see it spread out on his pillow. Yeah, like that was going to happen—but a man could dream.

She waited to face him until he was just a few feet away. Her expression definitely wasn't a happy one, making him wonder what the hell had happened since they'd parted company on Friday night. All the pieces fell together. If this had been about his leg or his physical therapy, they wouldn't be meeting out here next to the parking lot.

"What's up, Zoe? What do you have to say that couldn't have been said inside instead of out here?"

"I wanted to talk to you about Friday night. You know, about us."

"I didn't even realize there was an 'us,' Zoe. What's happened to make a simple walk in the park a problem for you?"

He perched on the tabletop right next to her. She scooted a few inches farther away, clearly not liking that he was crowding her.

"We were seen together."

"Yeah, I heard that Bridey saw us leaving the park Friday night. I didn't think it was any big deal."

Although it was obvious it was a big deal for her. "She saw us, too?"

"Yeah, she mentioned it to Callie earlier this morning. Who else saw us?"

Zoe swallowed hard. "Brandi. I swore her to secrecy, but that's not fair to her. She's not the one with something to hide."

Okay, that was a bit over the top. "What are you

talking about? We're both adults. We went for a walk and had pie. Neither of those are crimes as far as I know."

"No, they're not, but I'm definitely bending the rules here. Ours has to be a professional relationship, not personal. I can't afford to have it get out that I'm hanging out with a patient."

He was trying to remain calm, but it was getting harder with each passing second. "I'm guessing from your reaction that could be a bad thing."

"Yeah, it could be, Leif. Even though I'm a nurse practitioner, I'm still bound by the same rules that set the boundaries between a patient and a doctor."

"And those rules say two adults can't share a piece of pie or a walk along the river?"

He didn't bother to wait for her response. "So you're saying that as long as you're overseeing my care, none of that can happen again."

Leif hadn't phrased it as a question, but she answered him anyway, her blue eyes looking so sad. "I'm sorry, but yes. I don't like it either. Leif, I didn't make the rules, but I do have to live by them. It's for your own protection."

Just that quickly his temper snapped. He could protect himself. He'd been doing it for years. "That's bullshit, Zoe, and you know it. I can take care of myself, but that's not what's in play here. No, you're protecting your own ass. Fine, I get that, but don't tell me that it's better for me in the long run."

Not when the evenings he'd shared with her had been the biggest dose of normal that he'd had in a long time. For those few precious hours he'd been able to put the war and all its pain behind him.

"But, Leif—"

He cut her off. "You've made your point, Ms. Phillips. I'll be going now."

His leg cramped up as soon as he put his weight on it, causing him to stumble a bit. Zoe was off the table and grabbing his arm in an instant. He tried without success to break free of her grasp.

She held on with the tenacity of a terrier. "Damn it, Leif, don't be an idiot! Let me help you."

He froze long enough to regain his balance. "You can let go now."

When her hands fell away, he missed their warmth against his skin, not that he would admit it to her now. "Thank you for your concern, Ms. Phillips, but I can make it to my truck on my own."

Stubborn woman that she was, Zoe shadowed his footsteps. Finally, he'd had enough of her hovering. His anger faded, and all he could feel was tired.

"Go back inside, Zoe. You wouldn't want anyone to see you walking me to my truck. I'm pretty sure that goes beyond your customary service to your patients. God knows we wouldn't want people to talk."

Okay, that was a cheap shot. He stopped walking. "Look, I get what you're saying—no more late-night walks, no more pie. I'll see you around—or not."

She let him walk away this time. And yet he really wished she hadn't.

Mitch made it to his car by sheer willpower alone. If he didn't know better, he might have suspected that Isaac had added on that extra round of reps just to see how much Mitch could take without pleading for mercy. His gut told him that his old friend had set out to challenge, not torture, him.

Besides, he knew from his past rounds of postsurgery rehab that it was up to him to pound the mat when it got to be too much for him. It was his body, making it his call when to back off a bit.

He'd pay for his stubborn pride later, but that didn't stop him from being pleased about how much more he'd been able to do today. As he unlocked his car, he caught sight of Leif coming around the end of the building. Where had he been all this time? He'd left the therapy room half an hour ago. Whatever Leif had been doing had left him huffing and puffing like he'd been running a marathon.

Under other circumstances, Mitch would've met the man halfway in case Leif needed some extra support, but right now he wasn't in any shape to help anyone. He leaned against the front fender and watched to make sure Leif made it to his truck safely.

When the other man noticed Mitch was staring at him, his eyes narrowed in suspicion. "What the hell are you looking at?"

Mitch considered a few answers but went with his first thought. "I'm looking at a man who looks as bad as I feel. You know, like he could use a beer." He let himself smile. "Or maybe even a six-pack. God knows, after what Isaac put me through this morning, I'm all about heading to the closest bar."

Leif hobbled closer, his face flushed from the exertion it cost him to get that far. "My buddy told me there's one around here with some decent pool tables. He said the building wasn't much to look at, more like a bunker than anything, and the only sign on it just says BEER."

Mitch laughed. "Yeah, I know the place. It sits right at the edge of the city limits. It used to be called Parton's Bar, but I heard someone else took it over recently. Want to follow me there?"

Leif looked back toward the clinic with the oddest expression on his face. Whatever was on his mind at the moment couldn't be good. "Oh, yeah. Lead the way. I'll even buy the first round." He headed for his truck. "Get me there fast enough, and I might even spring for the first two. On the way, though, I have to stop and pick up a friend."

Suddenly Mitch had a new surge of energy. "Sounds like a plan."

Thirty minutes later Mitch was halfway through his first beer. He took another sip and looked around the room while he waited for his turn at the pool table. It wasn't the kind of place he was used to hanging out in anymore, but today the dingy interior and twangy music certainly suited his mood. Leif's, too, considering he was already on his second longneck and had a third lined up next to it as backup.

"Move, Mooch."

Leif stepped around the dog to line up his next shot. He'd insisted on stopping to pick up Mooch on the way to the bar. Something about soldiers never abandoning a buddy when on a mission. The bartender had protested when the three of them had walked into the place, but Leif flashed his dog tags and then Mooch's.

A pair of bikers over in the corner had immediately sided with Leif once they heard the dog's name. It seems Leif's buddy Nick had told them all about the dog's heroics back in Afghanistan. At first the bartender thought it was a line of bull that Leif and the other two were using to convince him to let the dog stay.

But when Leif had shown the man the scar on the dog's shoulder, he'd backed off and even cooked a burger for the mutt. Amazing. Mitch hadn't wanted to doubt Leif's story, but he didn't believe it himself until he surreptitiously ran his fingers along the dog's shoulder himself. Damned if there weren't a long scar buried under all that white fur.

He didn't know a damn thing about bullet wounds, but he was willing to give Leif and the dog the benefit of the doubt.

"It's your shot, Mitch."

He took another sip of his beer and set it aside while he walked around the table eyeing his options. "You could have left me something to hit."

Leif leaned against the wall with a big smirk on his face. "And here I thought a hotshot quarterback like you would be able to hit anything he aimed at."

Mitch shot Leif a dark look. "That would be true if I were throwing a football. Pool takes a whole different skill set. I used to be pretty good at it, but I honestly can't remember the last time I played."

It felt like forever. He'd been too caught up in life in the fast lane to leave much time for hanging out in the kind of place that boasted well-worn pool tables and a postage stamp–sized dance floor. He could just hear what his teammates would say about this place.

Make that his *former* teammates.

He shut the door on that line of thought. Instead, he concentrated on the sweet glide of the cue stick through his fingers. Time to start calling the shots, and not just in this game of pool.

"Green in the corner pocket."

He gave the cue ball a solid tap, which sent it rolling in a straight line toward the far end of the table. When the white ball hit its intended target with a soft thunk, the green one went tumbling in the corner pocket.

Mitch smiled and moved on to the next shot. As he

studied the table, he realized that for the first time since his knee had been ripped apart, he was enjoying himself.

When the next ball tipped into the side pocket, he reached for his drink, held it out to clink bottles with Leif. "Here's to BEER, my friend, and to shooting pool. The next round is on me."

"I'll drink to that," Leif said, grinning widely. "Bartender, two more and a bottled water for my furry friend here."

He reached down to pat his buddy Mooch on the head. The dog wagged his tail and licked Leif's hand before settling back down in the corner he'd staked out as his own.

While they waited for their drinks to arrive, Mitch ran the rest of the table.

"Rack 'em up again, Corporal. I'm on a roll."

Leif made a quick trip to the men's room. When he stepped back out into the bar, he frowned and sniffed the air. Something smelled good enough to have his stomach rumbling. Had he eaten anything since breakfast other than stale peanuts? Not that he could remember. Rather than heading straight back to the pool table where Mitch was practicing some trick shots, he stopped by the bar.

"Can we get six burgers, two plain and the rest with the works? A couple of orders of fries and onion rings, too."

He pulled out his wallet and handed over a couple of twenties. "Keep the change on that and give us a yell when it's ready."

When he strolled back over to the pool table, he whistled for Mooch. The dog had been remarkably patient and seemingly content to doze in the corner while Leif and Mitch played pool and tried out a few trick shots.

"Come on, boy. You're due for a trip outside."

The dog sprang up, tail wagging a mile a minute. Before they left, Leif figured he should let Mitch know where he'd be. He waited until the quarterback made his shot.

"Mooch and I are going to take a lap around the parking lot. I ordered some food for the three of us. It's all paid for, so keep an eye on the bartender. He's going to give us the high sign when it's ready."

"Will do."

Leif headed for the door and let Mooch out. He immediately reached down to catch him by the collar to keep him from charging out in front of an enormous pickup pulling into the lot in a spray of gravel and dirt. Assholes.

"This way, dog. We need to stick to the woods so you don't end up as some idiot's hood ornament."

Mooch dutifully followed the line of sorry-looking shrubs along the side of the building to the tree line. He took care of business and then wandered around for a few minutes, nose to the ground and tail in constant motion.

After he'd done a thorough job of inspecting the area, Leif called him to heel. "Come on, buddy. I suspect lunch is ready."

Then he really looked around. When had it gotten dark? "Make that dinner. Damn, no wonder my stomach is growling. Let's get back inside before Mitch eats all the fries."

Mooch ranged out ahead of Leif as if taking point. When he was within a few feet of the door, he slowed down. His tail quit moving and his head came up. The dog glanced back at Leif and growled softly. What the hell had set off that reaction?

As a precaution, Leif changed his grip on his cane so that he was holding it about halfway down its length. As much as he hated the damn thing, at least it could prove useful as a weapon. He opened the door, glad for once that the interior was almost as dim as the light out in the parking lot so that his eyes needed no time to adjust.

Mooch continued to growl. He looked up at Leif, probably wanting to take his cue from him. Yeah, trouble was brewing. Three guys that Leif hadn't seen before had Mitch cornered. So far, only words were being exchanged, but Leif had witnessed enough bar brawls to know when fists were about to fly. He, Nick, and Spence had waded into more than a few themselves.

He hadn't known Mitch long, but damned if he was going to stand there and watch the man get beaten to a pulp. Flexing his fingers on the cane, he and Mooch sidled around to the left, trying to reach Mitch's side before all hell broke loose. As they made their move, he listened in on the conversation between Mitch and the newcomers.

On the surface, the quarterback sounded all reasonable, but there was a thread of tension in his voice warning he could switch gears any second. "Well, boys, I understand that you usually use this table, but my friend and I are playing here today. I'll be glad to let you know when we're done with it."

The biggest of his three opponents was shaking his head. "Listen, prick, I said that was our table. If you walk away now, we might just let you leave peacefully."

Mitch stood leaning against the pool table looking relaxed as he smiled at the three men. Leif might have even bought the charade if Mitch hadn't had the cue ball in his throwing hand and his left hand resting oh so casually on a cue stick. He was willing to bet that the first man that made a wrong move would get hit with the ball and the second would see the business end of that stick swinging straight at him.

Mitch shook his head sadly. "I'm pretty sure it's first come, first served around here. My friend just ordered another round of beers and some burgers, so we're here for the long haul. Leave now, and we might just wave bye-bye when you walk out."

Oh, yeah, things were about to get interesting. Leif risked a quick glance toward the bartender. Was he the kind of guy who broke up fights with a ball bat or called nine-one-one and let the police bat in the cleanup position? Good—he was already dialing the phone.

Meanwhile, most of the rest of the customers were heading for the back exit. The only ones hanging back were the two who'd met Nick and knew about Mooch. He didn't expect them to wade in on the fight, but at the very least they might prevent anyone else from doing so. There was no telling how many friends the trio had in the bar.

Meanwhile, the big guy was back to shooting off his mouth. "You talk pretty big, mister, for a man with no backup. Where's this friend of yours? 'Cause he'll need to scrape up your bloody carcass and haul it out of our way so we can play pool without stepping over it all night. Wouldn't want to get blood all over my work boots."

"Good one, Butch!"

The other two yucked it up, clearly thinking their friend was quite the comedian. Leif gave up all pretense of stealth and positioned himself near Mitch, but not so close that they would get in each other's way.

"I'm right here, asshole."

Mooch stood between Mitch and Leif with his hackles standing straight up and a deep growl rumbling in his chest. The canny dog stared at the spokesman for the trio, clearly taking his measure and snarling his opinion.

The guy might not be afraid of Mitch, but he took a step back after getting a good look at Mooch's teeth. "Hey, who the fuck said you could bring a dumb animal in here?"

Leif laughed. "I guess they figured letting you hang out in here all the time set the precedent."

It took Butch a couple of seconds to recognize the insult and react. "You son of a bitch!"

His fist delivered a glancing blow to Leif's jaw about the same time Mitch took out Butch's wingman with the cue ball. Mooch retaliated by grabbing the guy on the left by the leg of his jeans, which threw the man off balance until one swing of Mitch's cue stick took him out of the fight completely.

The police were already filing in the front door by the time Leif and Mitch piled on Butch and dragged the big man to the floor. Unfortunately, they still had to cross the length of the bar to get to them. Leif's head was ringing and his jaw hurt bad enough to prevent any clear thought except the need to fight back. He aimed for the ribs and kept swinging hard and fast until someone grabbed him by the collar and yanked him off the pile.

Leif came up sputtering and ready to wade right back in and engage the new enemy. Someone hollered his name and shoved him against the closest wall hard enough to break through the red glaze of pure fury that had him by the balls.

"Stand down, Corporal! Right now!"

Breathing hard and hurting, Leif fought to fill his

lungs with air. Finally, he raised his head and squinted in the dim light of the bar to reassess the situation. When he recognized Gage Logan standing in front of him, it finally sank in that the battle was over, and he held up his hands in surrender.

Chapter 12

Leif figured he should be worried about spending the night in a jail cell, but he wasn't. In truth, he was far more concerned about what would happen to Mooch if that happened. The dog didn't deserve to spend hours locked up in an animal control cage because of him.

"You doing okay?"

The question was accompanied by a moan, meaning Mitch sounded as bad as Leif felt right now. He popped one eye open long enough to study his condition. Yep, just as he expected—the football player had one helluva shiner blossoming around his right eye, and his knuckles were bruised and bloody. How had the other three idiots fared? Not that he cared; not much anyway.

He finally answered the man's question. "I'll survive. Probably. Not sure I want to, though."

As soon as he opened his mouth, a shaft of pain reminded him to duck the next time somebody's fist came flying straight toward his face. He rubbed his jaw. Nothing was broken, but it could be a couple of days before he'd be up to chewing anything more solid than scrambled eggs.

"Any idea how much trouble we're in? Does Chief Logan have a reputation for being hard-nosed when it comes to bar brawls?"

Mitch gave him an incredulous look. "How the hell am I supposed to know something like that? It's not like I've had much experience in getting arrested, especially back here in Snowberry Creek."

Then he grinned and added, "Lately, anyway."

In truth, neither did Leif. There'd been a time or two that he and Spence had come close, but Nick had managed to rescue their sorry asses, or at least facilitate a last-minute escape.

Right now all Leif wanted was a handful of aspirin and his bed. He'd never gotten to eat even a single bite of the burgers he'd bought and paid for, which meant all that beer on an empty stomach had left him hungover and queasy. Whenever he opened his eyes, the room spun like a fucking top, but he wasn't sure if that was because of the punch he took or because of the alcohol.

Most likely it was an unfortunate combination of both.

The ominous sound of footsteps heading their way had both men sitting up straighter. Even at the cost of a fresh wave of nausea, Leif wouldn't face his fate cowering in a corner.

Gage Logan stepped into the room and glared first at Leif and then Mitch. The man looked just as pissed now as he had when he and his deputy had grimly set about separating the five men. At the time, Leif had been busy throwing punches as part of the brawling mob rolling around on the floor back at the bar. Oh, shit, had any of those flying fists connected with one of the policemen instead of its intended target? If so, there'd be hell to pay.

Gage definitely didn't like it when Mitch started laughing for no apparent reason. "You find this funny, Calder? If so, you might want to share the joke."

Leif expected the man to have the good sense to shut up, but for some reason Mitch clearly found Gage's question hilarious. He finally regained enough control to speak two words that he directed toward Leif.

"Principal's office."

Okay, now Leif had to swallow hard to keep from joining in the merriment. Mitch was right, though. The two of them had already been called on the carpet in Isaac's office for bad behavior. This was just more of the same, even though a helluva lot more serious.

If he hadn't happened to glance at the police chief at the right moment, he would've missed seeing that Gage was fighting to hide his own smile. Maybe the man had his own experience in that vein even if that small bit of good humor disappeared as quickly as it had come.

"What the hell were you thinking?" He definitely had his chief of police hat on now. "Because I'm telling you right now that you've managed to rack up quite a list of charges."

He held up his hand and ticked them off on his fingers. "Drunk and disorderly, assault, resisting arrest, property damage, cruelty to an animal. Need I go on?"

That last one sobered Leif up faster than a pot of strong coffee would have. "Where's Mooch? Is he okay?"

"The dog is fine, which is more than I can say for you two idiots."

Gage pulled over a chair and swung it around and straddled the seat, resting his arms on the back. "Here's how this is going to play out. You will write the bar owner a check for the damages. Lucky for you, Grainger is only asking for the price of one cue stick and an hour's salary at time and a half for the mess his bartender had to clean up."

Gage paused, maybe to give their beer-soaked brains time to catch up. "If his bill is paid by noon tomorrow, he won't press charges. To be clear, that's noon on Wednesday. Since it's already after midnight, it's now Tuesday morning. I'm guessing neither of you will be in any shape to do much of anything until you get some sleep."

"What about the other three guys? They started it."

As soon as Leif asked the question, he wished he hadn't. Gage clearly didn't appreciate it, either.

"They started it? Seriously, is that all you have to say for yourself? Tell me, Corporal, are you stuck back in grade school?" Gage pinned Leif with a hard look. "But to answer your question, those three are a constant thorn in my side. Again, luckily for you, the bartender and a couple of the other patrons backed up your version of the story. I've already read them the riot act and sent their worthless asses back home in a squad car."

"Sorry, sir. No disrespect meant." Something about Gage's demeanor left Leif fighting the urge to salute. He doubted the police chief would appreciate the gesture, though. "I'll make sure he gets the money."

Mitch spoke up again. "No, I'll take care of it. I was the one who egged them on in the first place. Besides, you paid for the burgers and fries."

What did that have to do with anything? Either way, he wasn't going to fight over their financial issues in front of Gage. "We'll get it handled, Gage."

"Damn straight you will. And even though Grainger isn't pressing charges, I'm not going to let you off that easily. We have a volunteer community service program run out of the mayor's office that helps elderly citizens with their yard work. Here's the contact information. I expect you both to put in a few hours."

He held out a business card to each of them. "Now, Mitch, get your ass out of here. My deputy will drive you home. You can pick up your car at the bar tomorrow."

Mitch looked confused. "But what about Leif? I already admitted that I started the fight."

That wasn't exactly true. Even if Leif appreciated Mitch's effort to shoulder the blame, he couldn't let him. "Yeah, but when they complained about a dog being in the bar, I'm the one who told them that the bartender had to let Mooch in because Butch's presence had established a clear precedent that the place catered to dumb animals."

This time Gage didn't bother hiding his grin. "Seriously, that's what you said?"

Leif gave a careful nod, not sure he should risk acting proud of his actions. "Yeah, I did. That's when Butch punched me in the jaw."

Mitch took over. "I hit the second guy with the cue ball and his buddy with the pool cue. It took both of us to take Butch to the ground. I know it was two against one, but in our defense, we were both hampered by our injured legs."

He gave in and grinned again. "Well, that and the copious amounts of beer we'd consumed by that point."

Gage held up his hand. "That's enough, both of you. Don't tell me any more. Mitch, go now or I will lock you up."

The quarterback still hesitated. Leif waved him on. "Go while the getting is good. I'll be fine."

He hoped so, anyway. Finally, Mitch limped toward the door. "Leif, if you need anything, call me. Otherwise,

I'll see you at physical therapy. Afterward, we can go pay our bill at the bar."

"Sounds good, man. And despite it all, I had a good time tonight. We'll have to do it again."

He shot Gage a sheepish look. "At least parts of it."

Mitch was chuckling again as he disappeared down the hall. By the time he was out of hearing, Gage was back to giving Leif the evil eye.

"Okay, Leif, do you have any idea how worried Callie was about you? She actually tried to report you as missing when you didn't come home by late in the evening. She said you left for a therapy appointment yesterday morning, but then both you and Mooch disappeared with no explanation. I can tell you right now that I don't ever want to see her that scared again, not because of something stupid you've done."

Leif folded his arms across his chest and leaned back in his chair, trying to look far more relaxed than he was. "Why would she panic like that?"

"Because she cares about you. With Nick gone, she doesn't need this kind of crap from you."

Now the sick feeling in Leif's gut had nothing to do with beer or a bar brawl. "I'm sorry she worried, but I'm fine."

"Yeah, right. Sure you are."

Gage continued to stare at Leif, but now there was a bit more intensity in his gaze. "She's waiting out in the lobby for you. Personally, I would've left you to rot in a cell. Maybe that would help you get your head screwed on straight."

The lawman stood up and shoved the chair back into the corner. "Listen, Leif, I know you've been dealt a tough hand lately, what with your leg and Spence and everything. For that reason, I'm willing to cut you some slack, but just this once." He took off his hat and studied it for a few seconds. "Hell, I was an Army Ranger myself, and I know it's a bitch to be stateside where it's safe while your friends are still in the line of fire."

God, the last thing Leif needed right now was to be lectured. Even if Gage did have firsthand knowledge of what it was like for him right now, he wanted to shout, "Enough already!"

Instead, he gave a nondescript grunt in response and hoped that would end the matter. It didn't.

Gage pulled a business card out of his pocket. "This is the number for Reverend Jack Haliday over at the Community Church."

Okay, that was too much. Leif's hold on his temper was slipping badly. He clenched his teeth and fought for control. "I don't need to listen to a bunch of sermons."

The lawman didn't give an inch. "I never said you did, Leif, but you sure as hell need help of some kind. If you don't believe me, think back to when I pulled you off Butch tonight. It may have started off as your basic bar fight, but it went way past that point with you. When I dragged you off him, you were doing your best to do some serious damage. I shudder to think how badly you would've hurt the stupid bastard if we hadn't gotten there when we did. You damn well weren't showing any sign of stopping on your own."

There was nothing Leif could say to that, not when the man was right on target.

Gage kept talking. "Reverend Haliday is a veteran with multiple deployments under his belt. And before you ask, that was before Jack became a minister. Before that, he was infantry, so he's been right where you are now.

That's why he started the veterans' support group in the first place."

Gage held out the card. "Bottom line, the price for getting to skate on this fight is that you attend at least one meeting. Fail to show up, and I'll haul your ass right back here. Got that?"

Leif stared at the lettering on the small piece of paper. "Seriously, I don't need this, Gage. I'm doing fine on my own."

A snort was the lawman's only response.

Okay, that pissed Leif off, but he was careful not to show it. "How about you, Gage? If I were to hit one of the meetings, would I find you there?"

The police chief's expression changed and his eyes lost their focus. What kind of hell was he revisiting in his mind? Leif didn't bother to ask; he could guess.

Gage blinked twice and was back with Leif, no longer lost in his memories. "If you want me to go with you the first time to introduce you around, give me a call."

Leif tucked the card in his pocket. Maybe he would go and maybe he wouldn't. Right now he felt like hell and his temper was too close to the surface to discuss it anymore. It was time to collect his dog and get the hell out of here.

He made himself act grateful. "Thanks for everything, Gage."

As he stood up, his much abused leg demonstrated its unhappiness by refusing to support his weight. Gage lunged across the room to catch Leif before he hit the floor. *Son of a bitch, could this night get any worse?*

"Let me get your cane, Leif."

Gage was out the door before Leif could stop him. To prove he could make it on his own, he took a step by himself. From the amount of pain ripping up through his leg, tonight's activities might have set his recovery back a bit. Okay, a whole lot. And wasn't that going to make his next appointment with Isaac really pleasant?

He bit his lip and shuffled sideways so he could keep his hand on the wall as he walked. Better. At least he'd made it all the way to the door before Gage got back. The man didn't have to know that Leif had taken the long way around to get there.

"Here."

Leif accepted the proffered cane. He needed it, even though it burned him to have to admit it. "Thanks."

Gage stood back out of the way until Leif had navigated his way out of the room and into the hall. They did a slow march down the hall to the small lobby of the police department. Sure enough, Callie was there, pacing the floor while Mooch watched her every move.

The dog spotted Leif first and came bounding across the room. Leif grimaced and braced himself for the impending impact. Getting knocked on his ass would be the perfect ending for a night that was already the purest definition of FUBAR.

Callie yelled, "Mooch, no!"

She made a passing grab for the dog, but he dodged to the side, so she missed him entirely.

Gage's deeper voice rang out next. "Dog, heel!"

Evidently the police chief's message got through; Mooch immediately put the skids on and slid to a halt just short of his intended target. Leif and everyone else breathed a sigh of relief. He stooped to reassure the dog he was all right and happy to see him, too.

When he straightened up, Callie asked, "Are you ready to go home?"

God, could this get any more embarrassing? Probably,

so he kept his response to a nod and a simple "Yeah, let's get out of here before Gage changes his mind."

"I'll go pull the car up out front. Mooch, you come with me."

She took off, with the dog following right on her heels. When they were gone, Leif crossed his fingers and took a step forward, hoping his leg would hold up long enough to get him home. One step. Two. Three. Great, he was on a roll. Gage kept pace with him all the way outside, where Leif coasted to a stop. Damn, steps. There were only four of them, but right now there might as well have been a million.

"To your right, soldier."

Leif looked around and spotted a gently sloping ramp. He felt as if he'd aged a hundred years as he made his way down to the sidewalk. At least Gage allowed him the dignity of letting him walk it by himself.

When he reached the bottom, he made himself turn back to face the police chief. "Thanks again, Gage. I swear I'm usually not this much of a fuckup."

The older man waved him off. "I know, Leif. However, you might want to remember I only give one get-out-of-jail-free card to each customer."

All things considered, that was probably one more than Leif deserved. "I won't forget."

Which meant he'd have to check out the veterans' group. Great. When Callie pulled up to the curb, Leif eased himself into the front seat and pulled the door closed. They rode in a chilly silence until they reached Spence's house. Leif started to let himself out of the car but stopped. He had one more apology to deliver.

"I am sorry you had to come get me, Callie. Gage shouldn't have called you."

She angled herself in the seat to look directly at him. "He shouldn't have had to, Leif. You should have. I'm not your babysitter, but I had no idea you'd made friends with Mitch Calder. It never occurred to me that you might be off having a good time with him."

He hated the catch in her words as if she were fighting the urge to cry. Now he really felt like a bastard. "I really am sorry, Callie. I didn't mean to worry you. If you want to kick me down the road, I'll go peacefully."

Callie shook her head as she reached out to touch his arm. "I don't want you to leave, Leif, and I'm guessing I've overreacted. I've already lost Spence, and now Nick is gone, too. Even though I know he'll be back, I can't help but worry. It didn't take much to send me right over the top."

She leaned over and kissed Leif on the cheek. "Now, go get some sleep. You look like hell."

He laughed, which set off the throbbing in his jaw. "Yeah, I suppose I do. After Mooch has a quick run, we'll both turn in for the night. I don't have to be anywhere until my appointment Wednesday morning, so I'll check in with you later in the afternoon. Go get some sleep yourself, lady."

"Will do."

Leif waited until she was gone before attempting the steps. By the time he made it to the top, Mooch was back from his nightly patrol and ready to go inside.

"Come on, dog. Let's go lie down before we fall down."

Because he'd already done enough of that for one day. Inside, he gave Mooch fresh water and filled his food bowl. The dog gulped down the kibble as if he hadn't eaten all day. One burger at the bar wouldn't have held Mooch until breakfast, and Leif hadn't even had that much. He settled for a bowl of cold cereal and a banana. Definitely feeling less shaky, he took a quick shower to wash away the stench of spilt beer and sweat.

After toweling off, he swallowed two pain pills with a swig of milk right out of the carton. Bed beckoned, but he still needed to do a little first aid. He dumped a tray of ice into a plastic bag and wrapped it in a dish towel before putting it on his jaw.

His small burst of energy was disappearing quickly. He crawled into bed while he had the strength to get that far. Damn, it felt good to get horizontal. The ice helped numb his aching face, and elevating his leg on a pillow slowed down the throbbing there a bit. As soon as he had himself situated, he patted the mattress.

"Come on, dog. Lights-out."

He winced when Mooch jarred the bed jumping up, but the dog quickly settled in. The mutt had had a long day, too. A few minutes later, Leif slid into sleep with the comforting warmth of Mooch stretched out along his side.

Chapter 13

❧❧

"Hey, Zoe, have you got a minute?"

Isaac stood in her doorway, his eyebrows drawn down low and his mouth set in a tight line. She immediately closed the file she'd been working on and prepared to listen.

"What's up?"

"Have you seen our boy this morning?"

Although she suspected exactly who he was talking about, she made herself ask, "Which one?"

Isaac didn't dignify the question with an answer. "Seems he and our local star athlete decided to get in a damn bar fight Monday evening. That pair of chuckleheads were lucky they didn't set their recovery back by weeks."

The staccato beat of her pulse thrummed in Zoe's ears. "Do you need me to check them over?"

"It probably wouldn't have hurt, but they're gone now. Something about needing to pay off their tab at the bar before Gage Logan hunted them down with guns blazing."

She pressed her fingertips to her forehead and rested

her elbows on the desktop to support her suddenly aching head. "So the police were involved?"

Isaac came the rest of the way into her office and perched on her low filing cabinet like he always did. "Yeah, Leif mentioned playing a get-out-of-jail-free card. Not sure what that was all about."

The therapist frowned. "Leif's temper has been running on a razor edge lately, but I thought he was doing better. I wonder what happened to set him off."

Okay, maybe there is an easy answer to that question.

An image of the hurt and fury reflected in Leif's dark eyes when they'd parted on Monday morning flashed through her mind. She'd known he was upset, but she never imagined for an instant that their conversation might set off a drunken binge. Surely not. The real question was what, if anything, she should do about it.

"How badly were they hurt?"

Not that Mitch Calder was her patient. Technically, he was still under the care of the team doctors, but he'd made arrangements for Dr. Tenberg to handle anything that came up locally.

"Mitch has one of the prettiest shiners I've seen in a long, long time. His knee didn't seem much worse for the wear, which was my main concern. Leif's jaw is sporting a dandy, fist-sized bruise, but he claims it's fine. His knuckles were busted up some, too, but that's to be expected. "

Zoe should have been relieved that the damage was no worse than it was, but she was far more worried about what had triggered the whole episode.

"Thanks for telling me, Isaac. It sounds as if you've got a handle on the situation, but let me know if you need my help. Otherwise, I'll wait until Leif's next visit to talk to him about it."

Brandi appeared in the doorway. "Your next patient is ready, Zoe."

She was instantly up and moving. "On my way."

Isaac headed back toward his office while she picked up the chart for her next patient. She had a full schedule of appointments to get through before her day would end. Her patients all deserved her undivided attention, so she shoved her worry about Leif to the back burner for now.

Later, after she got off work, she'd figure out if there was anything she could do to keep the man from going completely off the rails.

After a quick knock on the examination room door, she pasted a friendly smile on her face and walked inside. Time to get back to work. "Hi, Mrs. Brooks. Tell me you brought pictures of that new grandbaby. I've been looking forward all day to seeing them."

Six hours later, Zoe slowed her car as she approached the driveway that led to Spence Lang's old place. Once she knew Leif was all right and not about to self-destruct, she could go home, heat up a frozen dinner, and rest her tired feet.

Not exactly an exciting game plan, but there it was. Steeling herself for an unfriendly welcome, she flipped the turn signal on and slowly steered her car into the driveway.

It took all of her concentration to maneuver her small SUV around the worst of the ruts in the gravel. At least it gave her something to think about other than the man who had just stepped out onto the porch. Leif's expression was reserved. Mooch, on the other hand, immediately came bounding down the steps to greet her as soon as she got out of her vehicle.

Darn it, she'd thought she'd long ago outgrown the ability to feel shy. If she couldn't bring herself to greet the man she'd come to see, maybe she could ease into the situation by talking to his dog.

"Hi, Mooch. How are you doing, fella?"

The dog barked and then raced around the yard, doing two quick laps before once again coming to a stop at her side with his tongue hanging out in a doggy grin. She picked up a handy stick and threw it as far as she could, which sent the dog off in a frenzied chase.

After a couple of more tosses, she finally worked up the courage to face Leif. He stared down at her in silence, letting her look her fill. He hadn't shaved today, which emphasized his rugged good looks. But despite the dark shadow of his whiskers, she could see the faint outline of the bruise along his jawline.

"Does it hurt?"

At least he didn't pretend to not understand. "Isaac has a big mouth."

She defended her friend. "He was worried about you."

"That doesn't explain why you're here. I wasn't aware that you made house calls."

Clearly he was still angry over her efforts to keep their relationship strictly professional. Her mere presence here meant she was once again sending him conflicting signals. How could she hope that he would understand their relationship when she didn't get it herself?

It was time to go. "Forget I stopped by."

For a man who often had trouble getting around, he made a surprisingly fast move to prevent her from making her escape. Zoe was no stranger to tough situations, but right now she didn't want to face the waves of anger radiating from Leif. This had been a monumentally stupid decision.

When she didn't immediately look up at Leif, he crooked his finger and used it to lift her chin until their eyes met. But instead of lashing out at her, Leif's expression now looked more curious than angry.

"So why did you stop by, Zoe? Isaac knew full well that I was only bruised up and sore. I'm also betting you didn't stop by to check on Mitch Calder."

"He's not my patient." Before he could respond, she kept right on talking. "Look, I know you are fully capable of taking care of yourself. I also know if you'd been really hurt, Isaac would've hog-tied you before letting you walk out of the clinic without being seen."

She stepped back, and this time he let her. "I was concerned that our discussion the other day might have set this all off. I wanted to apologize again for handling the situation so clumsily."

When Leif didn't say anything, she resorted to babbling to fill the void. "As I said, I'm sorry, and I'm glad you weren't seriously hurt. I'll be going now."

Once again Leif blocked her way. He stared at her for several seconds as he ran his fingers through his hair in obvious frustration. "I haven't eaten yet."

All right, that one sure came flying out of left field. What did that have to do with anything? "Then I should get out of your way."

"No, wait. Zoe, what I was trying to say is that I haven't had dinner yet, and if you haven't either, maybe you'd like to join me. It won't be anything fancy. Burgers and a salad pretty much exhaust my culinary talents, but you're welcome to stay."

She shouldn't. That much was obvious, but the last thing she wanted to do right now was get back in the car. Damn, this shouldn't be so hard. "Are you sure, Leif?"

*   *   *

Leif thought about it hard before finally nodding. As he waited for Zoe to make up her mind, he picked up the stick that she'd been throwing for Mooch and gave it another toss. The dog chased it down and returned to drop it at Zoe's feet.

"Mooch would definitely be happy if you joined us. He'd love the company. I suspect he's tired of mine."

He could tell she was torn, which pleased him. He'd hate to think he was the only one whose gut was tied up in a big knot at the moment. When Mooch backed away and barked, begging Zoe to come play with him, she finally caved.

"All right, if it means that much to you, Mooch, I'll stay."

It meant that much to Leif, too, but for once he managed to keep his mouth shut on the subject. "I'll meet you around back. I've already got the grill heating, so dinner will be over before you know it."

He started to walk away and thought better of it. "That came out wrong, Zoe. What I meant was I know you've already put in a full day and coming out here to check on me has only added to it. You're welcome to stay as long as you'd like. Head on around back and make yourself comfortable, and I'll bring you something cold to drink."

She tossed the stick for Mooch. "Make mine nonalcoholic. Even ice water would be fine."

"After the other night, I've been sticking to root beer myself. I'll bring out a couple."

He knew he'd sounded gruff, but Zoe didn't seem to notice. When she disappeared around the end of the house, Leif dragged himself up the steps to the porch. Suddenly, the boring evening that had been stretching out in front of him had possibilities.

He made quick work of setting the table after putting

away the paper plate he'd planned to use for himself. Zoe deserved better. He grabbed the drinks along with the platter of burgers for the grill and headed back outside. At first he didn't see Zoe and feared she'd changed her mind about staying.

Then he spotted her standing out in the gazebo that he and Nick had built right after they'd arrived in Snowberry Creek. She was studying the back wall, where they'd painted their names when they dedicated the gazebo to the memory of their friend, Spencer "Wheelman" Lang.

He set down his load and joined her. Zoe traced the letters with her fingers and read the words aloud. Sighing, she turned toward Leif, her eyes looking a bit shiny. "I noticed this when I was here the other night. It's a really special memorial, Leif. One of the best I've seen for one of our fallen."

As nice as the gazebo was, it also served as a constant reminder that Spence was dead. Leif didn't regret helping to build it, but neither was he comfortable with seeing it every day.

"It was Nick's idea. He thought Callie would enjoy it. When she turns the place into a bed-and-breakfast, we figure her guests will like it as well."

They started back toward the patio, where Leif got busy arranging the food on the hot grill. "In truth, building that thing really gave Sarge an excuse to stick around long enough to convince Callie she wanted him to hang around permanently."

Zoe laughed. "Gotta love a soldier with ingenuity. You guys sure did a beautiful job. I can imagine curling up out here with a book on a rainy day."

"That's the whole idea." He held out her root beer. "Nick's next project is considerably bigger, since he plans to do most of the work on Spence's house himself. I'm supposed to help."

He frowned as he studied the big Victorian house. "I suppose one of these days we'll have to start referring to the place as Callie's, but even she still thinks of it as Spence's."

"Give the woman some time, Leif. She grew up with Spence, and it was his home for twenty-plus years. It's only been hers for a few months."

There wasn't anything Leif could say to that. He couldn't imagine the hole that Spence's death had left in their lives would disappear anytime soon, if ever.

While keeping one eye on the food sizzling on the grill, Leif watched as Zoe wandered along the perimeter of the yard, stopping periodically to smell one of the roses. She took such obvious pleasure in the yard that it surprised him that she lived in an apartment. It was too bad, really, because if she had a yard, he could have ordered the materials to build a gazebo for her. The strength of that desire surprised him.

Maybe it was some kind of weird mating ritual here in Snowberry Creek.

"Is something funny?"

"Uh, no."

At least nothing he was about to share with her right now. She was skittish enough. He changed the subject as he turned the meat on the grill. "How do you like your burgers?"

"Medium rare."

"Then we're almost ready to eat. I set the table inside, but we can eat out here if you'd rather."

"Inside is fine."

He transferred everything to the serving platter he'd brought out while she picked up their drinks. At least she made no effort to take the tray from him, evidently trusting that he'd ask for help if he needed it.

Mooch charged past them into the house and stood by his empty bowl. He stared up at the pile of burgers with a hopeful look and a slowly wagging tail.

"Damn it, dog! I keep telling you burgers are people food. Contrary to what you think, that group doesn't include you."

But even as he groused about it, he filled Mooch's bowl with kibble and then broke apart one of the burgers and piled it on top. The dog attacked his dinner with the gusto of a soldier who'd been living on MREs too long.

Zoe clearly found the dog's antics amusing. "From the way Mooch devoured that burger, I have to think you must be one heck of a chef, Leif."

He disagreed. "That mutt grew up on the streets of Afghanistan. Considering he'll eat anything you put in front of him, up to and including old combat boots, his approval isn't much of an endorsement. Besides, it's pretty hard to screw up something as simple as hamburgers."

Zoe took a seat at the table and began piling condiments on her bun. "That might be true, Corporal, but a burger sure beats the frozen dinner I was going to eat tonight. As a matter of fact, I'm pretty sure the name on tonight's entrée was Combat Boot with Alfredo Sauce."

He grimaced at the image that created. "Okay, then feel free to be dazzled by my cooking."

Their conversation over dinner stayed light and easy. Zoe still didn't seem comfortable with spending time with him outside of the office, even though she was the one who'd sought him out. There wasn't much he could do except to steer clear of topics that might send her running for the door.

"I've got ice cream for dessert if you'd like some. It's chocolate, if that makes a difference."

She finished drying the last of the dishes. "Chocolate always makes a difference. That's what makes it impossible to resist."

Zoe ran her hands down her hips as if unhappy with her curves. Leif respectfully disagreed to himself, but then, he liked a woman with a little meat on her bones. She had a great ass, the perfect size to grip in both hands while he went down ... *Whoa, don't go there, soldier. It's not happening. Maybe not ever, and wouldn't that be a damn shame?*

Meanwhile, Zoe was still speaking. "I really shouldn't, but I'd love some. Just a little, though. One scoop will be plenty."

Still lost in his imagination, it took him a minute to make sense of what she was saying. One scoop of what?

Oh yeah, right. Ice cream. That's what they'd been talking about. A nice safe topic. "Why don't we eat it out on the front porch so Mooch can patrol? If he doesn't make his rounds on a regular basis, those sneaky little squirrel bastards come creeping right back into his territory."

Zoe hung up the dish towel. "Well, we can't have that, can we? Come on, Mooch, let's go make sure we haven't been invaded."

The dog yipped and charged for the front door as if he'd understood her call to arms. Later, Leif would slip the mutt another burger for providing such a great buffer between the two humans. Sometimes it was hard not to be jealous of the dog's easy transition to life in the States.

That didn't mean Leif didn't have his own special arsenal of weapons. As he gathered up the ingredients, he murmured, "Yeah, the fur ball might have all the charm, but I've got the chocolate and all the toppings."

Leif served up two heaping bowlfuls, added a sprinkling of walnuts and a sliced banana, and topped it all off with a generous squirt of chocolate sauce. He stuck a spoon in each bowl and carried them out to the front porch. Zoe's eyes widened in surprised horror when he held out her bowl.

"What happened to just a little?"

He gave her a smug smile. "It's not my fault you didn't specify the size of the scoop."

She wasn't buying it. "Well, I didn't think you'd use a shovel."

Leif took the rocker next to hers. "You don't have to eat all of it. It's your choice."

He paused to take a bite of his own ice cream. "But I'm pretty sure there are laws in this country against wasting chocolate in any form. I'd hate to have to report you to Gage Logan, since I wouldn't be able to bail you out. I already used the get-out-of-jail-free card he gave me. He told me it was a one-time deal."

Zoe stared at her bowl before picking up the spoon. "Fine, Leif. But if I can't get into my pants in the morning, don't think I won't be right back out here."

Leif came awful close to spewing out the bite he'd just taken at the thought of Zoe showing up on his front porch half-dressed. To avoid the risk of revealing the direction his thoughts had taken, Leif kept his eyes firmly on the woods across the yard.

Maybe she figured it out on her own, though. "Okay,

that sounded a whole lot different in my head. Let's just say that I'll need to walk off a lot of calories if I eat this whole thing, or even half."

Hmm. Perhaps she'd presented him with an opportunity to extend their time together this evening. "I had planned to take Mooch for another walk to the park along the creek tonight. You'd be welcome to join us."

Zoe pursed her lips as if she were about to refuse. He should've guessed she wouldn't risk being seen in public with him again. It was amazing how much that pissed him off. "Never mind, Zoe. Forget I said anything."

Her hand bridged the distance between them to rest on his forearm. "I was only thinking about the time, Leif. I have to work tomorrow, so I can't be out real late."

He relaxed slightly. "Sorry. I don't mean to be so testy."

She set her half-eaten ice cream aside. "Tell you what. I'll go if you don't mind me driving us back to the park instead of walking from here. That way I don't have to come all the way back here for my car."

"It's a deal. Let me lock up and grab Mooch's leash."

He took their bowls back into the house. What had started off as another in a long line of boring evenings had definitely taken a turn for the better. And if he hoped that they might just end up somewhere a lot more private than the trail along the creek, well, he'd keep that thought strictly to himself.

Chapter 14

❦ ❦

This was a stupid idea, not to mention dangerous and flat-out crazy. Yet Zoe couldn't seem to help herself. Just like that heaping bowl of chocolaty goodness that Leif had given her, the man himself was a temptation she couldn't seem to resist. Sure, she could pretend this stroll along the creek was just two friends enjoying the night air. No different than if she'd met Brandi for a brisk walk to get some exercise.

Only Brandi wouldn't have ended up slinging her arm around Zoe's shoulders as they walked. And Brandi also wouldn't have been wearing a soft flannel shirt that had Zoe wanting to snuggle in close.

"You're thinking way too hard."

He held her close enough that she felt the rumble of his deep voice as he spoke. As much as she hated to spoil the moment, she felt compelled to point out that they were once again treading too close to that line she'd drawn between them. Heck, they weren't merely treading too close. They were jumping up and down on it.

"We're playing with fire, Leif. This has got to be the last time we do this."

She half expected him to jerk his arm free of her shoulders and go stomping off with Mooch in tow, leaving her alone in the gathering darkness. Instead, he kept walking forward, still keeping her tucked in close to his side. Not that he was calm. Oh, no, there was a definite new strain of tension thrumming between the two of them. She braced herself for the imminent explosion.

As they passed a gap in the trees, Leif veered off the path, dragging Zoe along with him. When they'd gone about ten feet, he came to an abrupt halt.

There was still enough light for her to see his face clearly. What she saw there sent her pulse into overdrive. The man's temper was definitely running hot, and he had her in his sights.

"Leif, what are you doing?"

He trailed his fingertips down her cheek to follow her jawline until his hand wrapped around the back of her neck. Although he was still at arm's length from her, she felt cornered and panicky.

But that heat glittering in his dark eyes sent shivers dancing across her skin. Her voice cracked when she repeated the question he'd yet to answer. "What are you doing?"

His answering smile was predatory. "I'm going to show you what it really means to play with fire, Zoe."

He eased closer, still giving her room to escape, not that she could find the strength to move. When she didn't give in to panic, he narrowed the gap between them even more.

"You see, fire has nothing to do with rules and regulations."

She swallowed hard. "It doesn't?"

"No, actually, it doesn't. It has everything to do with a man and a woman who crave each other's touch. They can't imagine waiting another minute to explore . . . the possibilities."

Oh, God, each word he spoke licked at her senses with hot little flames and warmed her in places that had been cold for far too long. The cool chill of the evening air wasn't the reason her nipples pebbled up and her breasts ached to be touched, kissed, massaged, or all of the above.

No, that was all because of Leif. In that moment her entire body craved his touch. The intensity of that desire had her turning away from him, no longer able to face—or deny—the truth of what he was telling her.

Something hit the ground, making her jump. She realized he'd dropped his cane to free up both hands as he moved up behind her. Leif didn't hesitate as he slid his arms around her waist, tugging her back against the hard planes of his big body. The thick ridge straining beneath the zipper of his jeans made it clear that she wasn't the only one profoundly affected by this encounter.

He pressed a series of nibbling kisses along the side of her neck. Her knees nearly buckled when his hands settled on her waist, only to slowly ease upward. They stopped short of where she wanted them to be. Needed them to be.

And Leif knew it, too.

"What do you want, Zoe?" He whispered the word right next to her ear, his warm breath sending yet another burst of heat pulsing up and down her spine.

Stupid man; stupid question. She wanted him. Right here. Right now. That much should be obvious. Rather than point that out to him with words, she took action and tugged his hands up until they settled over her breasts. He smiled against her skin as he gave them a gentle squeeze.

Zoe reached her arms up and back to encircle his neck, which served the dual purpose of pressing her back more solidly against his chest while thrusting her breasts more firmly against the palms of his hands. Leif rubbed them gently, only gradually increasing the pressure enough to satisfy her hunger for more.

When Leif released his hold on her, she protested until she realized he wasn't stealing his warmth and abandoning her to the chill of the night air. Instead, he gently turned her around to face him, then once again wrapped her in his arms. His mouth claimed hers with an all-out assault on her senses. The heady flavor of his kiss had chocolate ice cream beat all to heck.

She was about to share that little tidbit with him when the situation spun completely out of control. Someone or something started crashing through the underbrush, headed straight for them. Before she could make sense of what was happening, Leif exploded into action.

"Fuck, no!" His whisper was harsh as he issued orders. "Hit the dirt!"

His eyes were wild as he stood ready to defend them both against the perceived attack. When she didn't immediately comply with his demand, Leif shoved her toward the nearest trees, sending her stumbling backward.

"Damn it, woman, take cover and stay down."

She bounced off the trunk of a nearby Douglas fir with a bone-jarring jolt. At least it kept her from hitting the ground. She came right back at Leif, even though he was now holding his cane like a club.

His head was pivoting back and forth as if he was trying desperately to make sense of their surroundings. His fears fed into hers, dredging up the nightmares she'd lived with for years. It took every ounce of willpower she had to shove them back down where they belonged. One of them had to stay calm and rooted in the present. Holding up her hands as she approached, she kept her voice pitched low and soft.

"Leif, please, we're safe. We're in the woods by the creek, not Afghanistan."

He shook his head in denial. "No, they're coming. I heard them."

That much was true. Some guy was talking to Mooch, and the two of them couldn't be more than a few feet away from where she and Leif were standing. She listened to hear what was being said. "Hey, dog, are you out here all by yourself?"

The words carried clearly on the night air. "See, he's just worried about Mooch. Put down the cane, Leif. We need to reclaim your pal."

Something of what she was saying must have gotten through, because Leif looked calmer, but not by much. She inched close enough to put her hand on the cane and gently pushed it down.

"Yes, Leif, you're right. Someone is close by, but he's not the enemy. He's worried about Mooch running loose. We need to go get your buddy."

The stark fear in Leif's expression drained away. "Son of a bitch, Zoe, I'm sorry. Wait here. I'll go straighten things out."

He shifted his hold on the cane to use it for support as he hobbled back toward the trail. At least his flashback hadn't lasted long. He'd been gone for only a minute or two, but she had to wonder how often he got lost in the past. With his hold on reality so shaky, now was not the time to ask.

She started to follow him, but thought better of it as her own reality came crashing down. What had she been thinking? All that crazy talk about playing with fire and what followed afterward served as absolute proof that Leif Brevik was pure temptation. That was bad enough, but it terrified her that his flashback had almost triggered hers.

She cocked her head to see what he was saying. He sounded calm as he explained that the dog had gotten off his leash and that Leif hadn't been able to catch him. All lies, but at least they were believable ones.

Leif's voice still sounded a bit rough to her, but he apparently had the situation under control. "Thanks again for your help in catching my dog."

"No problem, man."

She bet Leif hated the small note of pity in the other voice. He also sounded young, which reduced the likelihood that he would've recognized Zoe if he'd actually blundered into the small clearing instead of sticking to the path.

Thank goodness the situation hadn't spiraled completely out of control, but it had been close. She had to do something to prevent the same thing from happening again. That left her two choices: stop seeing Leif outside of the office or hand off his care to someone else.

Leif walked back into the clearing with Mooch at his side. Despite the close call, Zoe started right for him. It was a bit dicey having to maneuver around his cane on one side and the dog on the other, but she still managed to find herself back in Leif's arms for a quick hug.

He was trembling from the aftereffects, which nearly broke her heart. She knew all too well what it was like to get blasted by the memories, the fear, all of it so damn real that you could taste the dust and grit that got into everything downrange.

She stepped back, still fighting the whisperings from her own past. "We need to go."

"Yeah, I know."

Leif didn't sound happy about it, but then neither was she. Here, within this small circle of trees, she'd been able to shut out the worries and rules of the world outside. For a sweet few moments, the whole universe had consisted of only two people. The scary part was that if they hadn't been interrupted God knows how far they would've gone.

Even now, Zoe hungered for more of what they'd shared, but she wanted to experience it someplace more private. Somewhere they could get skin to skin as they explored the growing attraction between them. Having to stop before they got that far was pure frustration, even if it was a smart decision.

From what had just happened, it was obvious that Leif had a lot going on in his life and in his head. Dealing with his leg was bad enough, but the nightmares were no doubt worse. He might not believe her, but he didn't need the complication of a relationship on top of everything else he was dealing with right now.

They walked in silence back to her car. Despite all of her misgivings, she actually considered inviting Leif to come home with her. What was she thinking? When they reached her car, he took the decision out of her hands.

"Zoe, things got out of hand back there on two fronts. Not that I'm complaining about what was happening between us before . . . well, you know."

He drew a ragged breath. "However, if we're ever going to take that step together, I don't want it to cause you problems in your job."

Leif gently pushed a strand of her hair back away from her face. There was too much regret in his voice for the touch to be comforting. "There's also the fact that I'm pretty screwed up right now. Most of the time I can hide it, but every so often it blindsides me. Until I know how things are going to play out for me with my leg and everything, I've got no business getting involved with a woman like you."

Everything he was saying made sense. It also made her mad, which was just plain crazy. "What's wrong with a woman like me?"

The nitwit actually grinned, which only made her madder. "Not a damn thing, Zoe. In fact, it's the opposite. There's too much right about you. That should have been obvious from the way we went from zero to sixty in five seconds back there."

He checked their surroundings before pressing a quick kiss on her lips. "But you deserve better than a busted-up soldier with his entire future on hold. Right now I don't have much of anything to offer to you. Until I do, we need to back away from the precipice."

The noble idiot was right. That didn't mean she had to like it. "Fine, Leif. If that ever changes, let me know."

He retreated again, this time putting more than simply physical distance between them. "Believe me, Zoe, you'll be the first person to know."

After climbing into her car, she rolled her window down. "Maybe I'll see you at the clinic on Friday."

He didn't answer but simply walked away, his limp more pronounced than before. Even with Mooch by his side, Leif looked so damn alone. Her heart ached for him. She knew just how he felt. Putting the car in gear, she drove away, watching him in the rearview mirror until he disappeared from sight.

Earlier, before breakfast, Leif had cut himself shaving. Then his toast popped up burned to a crisp. As he and

Callie headed into city hall for Austin's hearing, he hoped those two events weren't some kind of omen about how things were going to turn out.

Gage was waiting for them in the lobby. "Let's head on downstairs. The bailiff said the judge will join us in about ten minutes."

He led them around behind the staircase to the elevator tucked in a back corner. It rattled as it descended at a snail's pace and finally hit bottom with a heavy thunk. Leif doubted Gage made a habit of using it; he expected he had done so this time only because of Leif's bad leg. It was thoughtful of him, but Leif hated the weakness it implied.

As they walked into the small courtroom, Gage gestured toward a row of seats right behind a low railing that separated the business end of the courtroom from the rest. As they sat down, a door on the far side of the room opened, and a pair of deputies escorted the prisoner over to a nearby table. So that was Austin Locke. Leif sat up taller to get a better look at him. From what Callie had said about him, the guy had just turned twenty-two. Right now, Austin looked a helluva lot younger and a whole lot scared.

Callie gasped softly, clearly having the same reaction to Austin's appearance. Leif reached over to squeeze her hand to let her know he was there for her. What would it do to Callie if they sent Austin to jail? No matter who it had been, the whole situation would've been hard on her, but this was Spence's cousin, and someone she knew. Yeah, Austin had been dealt a bad hand in life, but he'd also made poor choices, ones that had led him straight to this courtroom.

Several other people had straggled into the room. Most looked around with some degree of curiosity, but there was one who strutted in as if carrying a big chip on his shoulder.

The man paid no attention when Austin lifted a hand in greeting. Instead, he dropped into a seat in the back row and looked around the room, clearly disgusted by the whole situation. The second he spotted Callie, he snarled as he came up off the chair and started toward her. "You greedy bitch! This is your doing!"

Gage recognized the threat at the same time Leif did and moved to intercept the guy. He caught him by the arm and spun him around.

"Sit down now, Vince." He pushed the older man back down in his chair and wasn't all that gentle about it. "And just so you know, there's nothing I'd like better than to throw your worthless ass in the cell right next to your son's. One more word out of you, that's exactly what I'll do."

To underscore that he meant business, Gage waved one of his deputies over to sit a few seats away from the angry man.

Leif watched the confrontation, holding his cane in a white-knuckled grip. "I assume that's Austin's old man."

Callie looked a bit pale as she nodded. "Yes, that's him."

Gage seemed to have the situation under control for now, but Leif wasn't going to take any chances. Right now, Callie had the aisle seat. "Switch places with me."

It spoke to how rattled she was that she immediately did as he asked. The woman wasn't much for taking orders. More than once she and Nick had tangled over her stubborn insistence that she could take care of herself.

Finally the bailiff announced the arrival of the judge. Good. The sooner this circus was over, the better. Once again Leif squeezed Callie's hand as they settled back to watch how the whole mess played out.

Chapter 15

Three hours later Leif found himself back at the courthouse for the second time in one day. Callie asked so little of him; it was the least he could do for her. Besides, the last thing he wanted was for her to be the one to meet with Gage and Austin Locke, and not just because Nick would kick his ass for letting that happen. There was no telling what that punk would do once he walked out of his holding cell. Besides, the time Leif spent with Austin would let him get a read on the kid.

If Austin was gaming them, he'd be more likely to let his mask slip around Leif than in front of Callie, especially if Leif pushed a few buttons. After reading Austin the riot act this morning, the judge had warned him that one screwup was all it would take to land him right back in that courtroom. And the judge had made it very clear that if that were to happen, Austin would be handed a one-way ticket to hard time in prison.

For now, Austin would be given supervised probation

as long as some very specific criteria were met. Gage had asked that either Callie or Leif be present when he explained everything to Austin one more time before releasing him from custody. It would be interesting to see how the meeting played out.

On paper, Austin wasn't that much younger than Leif himself, but they were worlds apart in experience. The army had given Leif a sense of self-worth and a purpose in life. Austin was still caught in that no-man's-land between punk kid and adulthood.

So while Leif had Austin to himself, they were going to have a little come-to-Jesus talk to make sure they started off on the right foot. Meanwhile, he stretched his leg out in front of him and tried not to flash back to a few nights ago when he'd been sitting in this very same room with Mitch Calder and wondering if they were going to be overnight guests at the Snowberry Creek jail.

He shifted his weight, trying without success to find a more comfortable position. When the doorknob turned, Leif rose to his feet. Austin walked in with Gage right behind him. The kid acted just as freaked out by everything as he had been earlier in the courtroom. His eyes flitted around the room as if he couldn't quite believe what was going on.

Gage performed the introductions. "Austin, in case you don't remember, this is Corporal Leif Brevik. He's a friend of Callie's and served in Afghanistan with your cousin Spence."

When Leif held out his hand, Austin reacted as if it were a snake about to bite him. After a quick glance toward Gage, who nodded, he finally stuck out his own to grip Leif's. His palms were clammy and cold. Yeah, the kid had a bad case of the screaming heebie-jeebies. No surprise there.

"Leif's here to talk to you about the job Callie offered you."

It would've been hard to miss the flash of furious resentment in Austin's eyes. Earlier in court, his employer had stepped forward as a character witness on Austin's behalf, but he'd also regretfully delivered the message that the company had rules against employing convicted felons. The judge had tried to convince him differently, saying that Austin's record could be expunged if he made restitution and went a year with no further infractions.

The man had made it clear that the corporate office had left him no wiggle room on the matter. On his way out, at least he'd stopped long enough to apologize to Austin before leaving the courtroom. It had clearly been a hard blow.

Austin shoved his hands in his jeans pockets. "I can find my own fucking job."

Leif jumped right on that. "Well, maybe you could, but the judge said the only way he was going to let you out of jail was if you already had one. I'm guessing it's hard to look for work from behind bars. If you'd rather serve time instead of accepting Callie's offer, fine with me. I'll let her know."

As Leif feigned heading for the door, Gage joined in. "Don't be stupid about this, Austin. A lot of people worked hard to make this chance possible for you. It sucks about losing your job, but at least give your boss credit for showing up today. He didn't have to do that. He also told me off the record that the second your record is expunged, you'll be welcomed back."

None of that seemed to make much of an impression. "Yeah, right. He'll just find another excuse when the time comes."

Austin stared right back at both Leif and Gage, which

Leif sort of admired. It couldn't be easy dealing with all of this even if he had brought it on himself. "Gage here thinks you're smart enough to take advantage of this chance you're getting to turn things around. Me, I'm not so sure, but I'm willing to be proven wrong."

Gage backed his play. "So what's it going to be, Austin? Will you accept the job offer and walk out of here a free man or are we headed back down those steps to arrange your transfer to the state pen?"

Austin's wide-eyed gaze ping-ponged back and forth between them. He obviously felt cornered, but finally he nodded. "I'll take the damn job."

Gage's big hand came down hard on Austin's shoulder. "Smart decision. Is your father picking you up or do you need me to have one of my deputies give you a ride home?"

Austin shook his head. "He couldn't hang around all day, waiting for you to let me out. I'll walk."

Leif surprised them all by saying, "It was pouring rain outside when I came in, so why don't I give him a ride? It will give me a chance to talk to him more about the job."

Gage didn't even give Austin a chance to turn down the offer. "That's a good idea. Now, both of you get on out of here. I've got work to do."

Leif was glad he hadn't been standing between Austin and the door because he suspected he would've been mowed down. Before the kid made it out of the room, Gage had a couple more things to say.

"Leif, I haven't forgotten about that meeting I mentioned to you. I'd better hear from you soon."

"I haven't forgotten either."

In fact, as much as Leif wanted to deny it, Gage had been right about him not being able to handle everything that was going on all on his own. "I've been meaning to call."

"Meaning to doesn't cut it with me, soldier."

Without waiting for Leif to respond, Gage turned his attention back to the kid. "Austin, one more thing. Remember this: You get this one chance. Blow it, and I promise you'll regret that decision the rest of your life. Got that?"

The kid jerked his head in a quick nod. "Yeah, I got it."

The short trip to Austin's apartment was spent in total silence. Leif turned on the radio in the hope that music would dispel the heavy cloud of tension between them. No such luck. His companion stared at the lit dial in horror.

Leif had to laugh. "So I take it you don't much like country music."

When Austin didn't respond, Leif tried again. "Well, it can be an acquired taste."

The kid sneered. "I don't see that happening anytime soon."

Okay, at least he was talking. Progress was being made. "Fine. Since you're obviously a music critic, I'm open to suggestions. You pick the station."

At first he didn't think Austin would take him up on the offer. When he did switch to another station, his choice surprised Leif. Maybe there was hope for the kid after all. The sound of a guitar riff filled the cab of the truck. Leif listened for several minutes before speaking again.

"I didn't know they had a dedicated blues station around here." Leif tapped the steering wheel in time to the music. "That's one of my favorite songs. Do you like acoustic or electric blues guitar better?"

"Both are good. Depends on the performer." Austin

pointed straight ahead. "That's my apartment building at the end of the block on the left."

As they turned into the narrow parking lot, Leif was about to ask more about Austin's taste in blues players, but the kid started cursing at the top of his lungs. He pounded his fists on the dashboard a couple of times.

Leif reached over to stop him from hurting himself or the truck. "Hey, stop that. What's gotten into you?"

Instead of answering, Austin ripped off his seat belt and bolted out of the truck while it was still moving. Leif slammed on the brakes and clambered out after him, landing hard on his left leg. He ignored the shooting pain as he limped over to catch up with Austin. The kid stood at the side of a big Dumpster, staring down at a bunch of clothing and other crap scattered on the ground.

Austin started kicking the piles. When he began hitting the Dumpster with his fist, Leif caught his arm to prevent him from doing some serious damage to himself.

"Damn it, what's wrong, Austin?"

The younger man's eyes were bleak when he finally looked up. "This stuff is mine. The manager must have tossed it all out here."

Now Leif wanted to punch something. If this mud-soaked pile represented the sum total of everything Austin owned, no wonder he'd turned to theft to make ends meet. But, by God, even if the entire mess wasn't worth a damn dime, he deserved better than to come home to this.

"Does the manager live on-site?"

Austin nodded. "Yeah, he has an apartment on the first floor. It's the last one on the far end."

"Good. Let's go have a little talk with him."

Before going two steps, Leif pivoted back to face Austin. "On second thought, I don't want you involved."

He looked around and spotted the perfect place to tuck Austin out of sight. Pulling out his wallet, he handed the kid a couple of bills. "This shouldn't take long. Wait for me over there at that coffee shop. Order whatever you want to drink and get me a tall drip with cream and three sugars. There should be enough there to buy yourself something to eat, too."

"I don't need your money."

Leif wasn't going to risk blowing Austin's parole. "Take it. You can buy next time."

"Okay, but what are you going to talk to Mr. Roche about?"

Leif was supposed to set a good example for Austin, which meant he had to control his temper no matter how much he'd like to kick the apartment manager's ass right now. "I'm going to find out why he did this. While I'm talking to him, is this everything? Are you missing any furniture or anything?"

"The apartment was furnished, but I had dishes and—"

Stopping in midsentence, Austin muttered another string of curses as he flung back the lid of the Dumpster. His tirade only increased in intensity as he started yanking another bunch of clothing and other stuff out of it.

He tossed it all to the pavement with careless disregard as he continued to hunt for something. After a couple of minutes, he stopped and let the lid drop back down with a heavy clunk.

"They're not here."

"What's not here?"

"My acoustic guitar, my iPod, and my CD collection." Then he looked around the parking lot, his eyes wide and worried. "My truck's gone, too. Chief Logan said he had it towed back here after the cops arrested me."

"Go get coffee. I'll be along in a few."

Austin started to protest, but Leif cut him off. "No, let me handle it. You can't afford to get involved in a shouting match with the guy. If he were to call the police, your one chance to stay out of jail would be shot all to hell and back. I'll either get your stuff from him or find out where it is."

He waited to make sure Austin was going to listen to reason before heading toward the front of the building to find the manager's apartment. Luck was with him. Just as he rounded the corner, the man stepped out of his door. He appeared to be in his late sixties and was as run-down as the building he managed.

"Mr. Roche?"

"Who the hell wants to know?"

"I'm a friend of Austin Locke's."

Okay, that was a stretch, but this guy didn't have to know that. "He asked me to stop by and check on his apartment."

Roche spit on the ground. "He don't have one anymore. Emptied it out yesterday."

Leif took two steps forward, deliberately crowding the guy a bit. The manager wasn't much shorter than Leif, but he was skinny to the point of being skeletal.

On impulse, Leif took a shot in the dark. "Austin told me he'd paid through the end of the month, plus you'd collected a deposit when he moved in. One way or the other, you owe him a refund."

Roche resorted to bluster. "Then he's a damn liar. The law says I can deduct cleaning costs from his deposit and storage fees for his crap."

Leif was now within arm's length of the man. "Considering you tossed his clothes and things out in the trash, I can't imagine there are any storage fees. And where's the rest of his stuff?"

From the way the man's eyes were darting around and looking for a means of escape, Leif already knew he wasn't going to like Roche's response. He pulled out his cell phone. "Answer me or the next call I make is to the police."

Roche swallowed hard. "I sold it all to the pawnshop down the street just this morning. Figured the kid wouldn't be back for any of it, seeing as how the paper said he's in jail and on his way to prison."

"Bad news for you. He's not going anywhere." Damn, he wanted to hurt this asshole. "His truck also seems to be missing."

When Roche hesitated again, Leif started punching numbers into his phone. "Okay, okay, I had it towed. Told them it was an abandoned vehicle."

What were the chances he could stick the bastard with the impoundment fees? Zero to none. Probably the same thing on the money he'd gotten for selling Austin's stuff.

"Give me the pawn slip and the number for the towing company."

"I'll need to go inside to get the information."

Leif stepped back far enough to let him pass. As soon as Roche lunged through the door to his apartment, he tried to slam it shut in Leif's face. How predictable. Leif had expected him to try to pull some kind of stunt, and so he shoved his size twelve boot in the way.

"Really, Roche, don't be stupid about this."

Still grumbling, the man rooted through several piles of paper before coming up with the receipt for both the truck and Austin's other things.

"And I'll need your number, too."

While he waited, Leif tucked the receipts in his pocket. He tore the scrap of paper from Roche in half and scribbled the address of Spence's house on it before handing it back.

"Mail the refund on Austin's deposit to him at that address. If it doesn't arrive by Monday, I'll be back to collect it in person."

He put enough growl in his voice to make sure the man took him seriously. Then he walked away.

Twenty minutes later, he and Austin were back in the truck after stopping at the pawnshop to retrieve the kid's guitar and CDs. They'd gotten there too late to get the iPod back, but the guitar was the important thing. Even so, the kid was looking pretty defeated.

"You know I can't pay you back for buying my stuff for me."

After a quick stop to pick up some trash bags at the corner store, Leif turned into the parking lot behind Austin's former apartment. "I don't recall asking for any money."

"Yeah, well, I don't take charity."

Considering Austin's upbringing, it was no surprise that he didn't know how to deal with someone doing him a favor without expecting anything in return. "Don't sweat it. We'll add it to your tab."

"Fine."

Austin looked only marginally happier about the situation. Leif parked the truck by the Dumpster, not caring if he was blocking the parking lot. If anybody wanted to get by, they could fucking well wait.

"Toss whatever you want to keep in the back end. I've got a call to make."

While Austin sorted through the sodden mess of his life, Leif made two quick calls. The first was to the towing company to make arrangements to bail out Austin's truck first thing in the morning. The second was to Gage to fill him in on what had happened.

Just as Leif expected, the officer didn't take it well when he heard how that mangy landlord had ripped Austin off. Old Man Roche didn't know it, but his life was about take a turn for the worse, especially if he didn't come through with a check for Austin's deposit. Then there was the money he'd gotten from pawning the kid's belongings.

Austin was back. "I guess I can crash with my dad for now. He lives in the next town over."

He made the announcement with all of the enthusiasm of someone who had just learned he needed two root canals and the dentist was fresh out of novocaine. Leif didn't blame him. He knew from what both Callie and Spence had told him that Vince Locke was an abusive, vicious drunk. The thought of sending Austin back to live with a man like that made Leif sick.

He couldn't believe what he was about to do, but he pulled out of the parking lot and headed directly back to Spence's house.

Austin sat up straighter and looked around. "Hey, my dad's place is the other way."

If Austin didn't know how to handle Leif buying back his gear, he sure wasn't going to like being told where he would be staying tonight. Leif kept on driving and lied through his teeth.

"Somebody is supposed to be keeping an eye on you. I can't do that if you're staying with your father."

"So where are you taking me?"

Austin looked a bit green when he realized they were nearing the turnoff to the jail. "Chief Logan didn't say anything about me having to sleep at the jail nights."

Leif gunned the truck to get past the building a little faster. "We're going to Spence's house. You'll be bunking upstairs in one of the spare rooms. Since your job will be helping Nick and me remodel the place, that will make it more convenient for all concerned."

The kid's temper was fueling up for a major explosion. "I already said I don't want your damn charity. I can find someplace else to stay."

Crossing his fingers that Callie would back his lie, Leif faked a look of total disgust. "Shove the charity crap, kid. Part of the deal Callie offered you included free rent. And before you say another word, it's the same deal she offered me and Nick."

Austin stared at him for a long time before finally relaxing enough so that Leif knew the battle was over for now. He pulled into the driveway and parked in front of the steps.

"Haul your stuff inside and take it straight to the utility room. God knows what kind of cooties your clothes picked up in that Dumpster. While you get started on your laundry, I'll make us something to eat. Afterward, you can finish settling in. You probably know where everything is around here."

Austin dropped one of the trash bags full of his crap on the porch. The bag sloshed as it landed. Austin didn't seem to notice; he was too busy glaring at Leif.

"Why? Because you know I got caught snooping around the house?"

Leif gave him the hairy eyeball. "No, although you did exactly that. I was referring to the fact that you used to live here when your old man was Spence's guardian."

He shoved the key in the lock. "Now do me a favor and hold off on the attitude for a while. I'm long overdue for a nap, and I'm in no mood for any more crap out of you or anyone else, for that matter. Any other questions?"

Austin started back down the steps for another load. "Any preference which room I take?"

"The big room on the second floor is Nick's. I'm still bunking in the den because it's easier on my leg if I avoid the stairs as much as possible. Otherwise, take your pick."

"Okay." Austin stopped halfway down the steps to look back at Leif. "One more thing you should know. I wasn't lying in court this morning."

Leif frowned. "About what?"

Austin's chin came up as he spoke, and his eyes remained firmly locked on Leif's. "When I said I didn't punch you that night. I heard you hit the floor after I broke in. I was going to call an ambulance when I heard your buddy Nick coming back."

Leif weighed the kid's words and decided they rang true. Austin had admitted to everything else he'd done, so there was no real good reason for him to lie about this.

Leif stared out toward the trees. "My leg was hurting pretty bad back then. I was also on some heavy-duty pain pills, so I don't remember much of that night. Having said that, I'm choosing to believe you, Austin. Now, let's get inside. Mooch has been locked in most of the day, and I need to let him out for a run."

As Austin rejoined him on the porch, they could both hear Mooch pitching a fit through the door. Austin grimaced. "I suspect that dog hates me."

Leif laughed as he finished unlocking the door. "Don't sweat it. Mooch isn't the type to hold a grudge."

The dog bolted right past them, for the moment too intent on chasing off a couple of birds to pay any attention to the two men. "But just in case, before you go back out for another load, I'll show you where we keep his favorite treats. Slip him a couple of those, and he'll be your best friend forever."

Leaving Austin and Mooch to make peace with each other, Leif threw together a pile of sandwiches, opened a bag of chips, and called it good. If his new roommate expected gourmet meals, he'd have to cook them himself.

Leif knew that after they ate and Austin went upstairs, he should give Callie a call and tell her what had happened and make sure she felt okay with it. Luckily, she'd had to drive up to Seattle for the afternoon and wouldn't be back until late. He hoped she'd be happier about the situation than he was. All in all, he'd made the only decision he could live with by dragging Austin back to the house with him. He was pretty sure Callie would understand. Nick, on the other hand, was bound to be pissed about it.

But then Nick wasn't the one here dealing with the situation, was he? Gritting his teeth against the pain in his much-abused leg, Leif eased down onto one of the kitchen chairs and let out a long sigh of relief. That nap was sounding better and better by the minute.

Maybe he'd even take a couple of pain pills. All things considered, he deserved a little oblivion right now. On second thought, until he got a better feel for how far he could trust Austin, he'd make do with ibuprofen. He reached for a sandwich and bellowed out an invitation to his new roommate.

"Hey, kid! Come eat or I'll feed your half to Mooch."

Chapter 16

✥ ✥

Zoe deliberately wandered by the PT room, pausing long enough to peek through the window in the door. Leif was over on the far side, working on a set of exercises designed to improve balance. Judging from the grim set to his face and the sweat stains on his shirt, it was pretty tough going for him right now.

Before she could head back to her office, Leif froze and slowly pivoted to stare right at her. He'd had his back to her, but somehow he'd sensed her presence. What had given her away? Not that it mattered. She managed a small smile and a wave. Leif barely nodded in response before turning away.

Nothing like being caught again, but she couldn't help being curious about his progress. After they had parted company Tuesday night, she'd made a deliberate choice to avoid checking on him during his Wednesday-morning appointment. Nearly two more days had passed, and she needed to know he was all right.

It had been difficult to stay away even that long, which

made it all the more important that she not linger now. Just as she took a step back from the window, she heard a shout, followed by a loud thump. Spinning back toward the window, she watched in horror as Leif windmilled his arms, fighting to regain his balance, only to stumble backward into Mitch Calder. The two men went down hard in a tangle of legs and curse words.

Isaac gave first Mitch and then Leif a hand up off the floor. The football player laughed and went right back to his plyometrics. From the ease with which he handled jumping up and down the steps, he was no worse for the experience.

Leif's elbow was dripping blood, but he didn't seem to notice. Instead, clearly frustrated and embarrassed, he picked up a small free weight and moved as if to throw it against the wall. Isaac caught his arm before he could let it fly, but clearly it was taking all of his strength to stop him. Whatever Isaac said to him had Leif shaking his head, but she couldn't hear what it was through the thick glass.

The blood continued to run down Leif's arm to land on the floor. Drip, drip, drip. God, would it ever stop?

Zoe had started for the door, intending to join the effort to talk Leif down off the ledge. But that wasn't going to happen, not when her eyes saw nothing but swirls of black peppered with small bits of light.

"Oh, hell, not now!"

Grabbing the edge of the windowsill for support, Zoe fought to keep her balance. She struggled to remain vertical while she felt as if she were being buffeted by gale-strength winds.

It had been so long since she'd had a full-blown flashback that dumped her right back into the hell that had been her time in Iraq. All she could hear was the swishing rush of blood pounding in her ears as snapshots of the horror filled her head. Mangled bodies carried in on an endless line of stretchers. More wounded men and women dragged in by their friends. Bloody boot tracks across the floor. Too many injured. Too much pain. Too many lost.

She fought through the maelstrom, forcing the simple words of her mantra out through clenched teeth. "Breathe in. Breathe out."

The saying had become her strongest defense against getting lost in the past. Controlling her breathing was a solid step toward controlling her thoughts and fears. Gradually, her vision cleared and her pulse slowed. Prying one hand free from the sill, she straightened up and stood taller. When the world remained steady around her, she let go completely.

Next stop would be the sanctuary of her office, but not until she made sure Leif was all right. Sure enough, he was back at his workout, sporting a new bandage on his arm and acting as if nothing had happened. He was even laughing at something Mitch said. Good.

Feeling steadier, she walked away from the window. Thank God no one had noticed her momentary lapse. She stopped in the restroom to splash some cold water on her face. Patting her skin dry with a paper towel, she studied her image in the mirror.

God, she looked haggard. She could only pray that the lapse was a onetime thing brought on by her concern for a patient. After all, she'd gone months this time without it happening, at least not this severely. There was no reason to think the memories wouldn't fade back into the shadows of her mind.

She hoped so. The last thing she needed was to live and breathe that pain and fear again. Back then, the smell of blood had hung so heavily in the air that the scent of it still haunted her all these years later. The past came whirling back, as her fingers burned from the phantom touch of a wounded marine's hand clasped in hers. His dying whispers . . .

A knock at the door jerked her out of the downward spiral. "Zoe, are you in there? Your next appointment canceled, so Dr. Tenberg asked if you could squeeze in a couple of kids with ear infections from the walk-in clinic."

Grateful for something to distract her, she called out, "On my way, Brandi. Tell the doctor I'll be glad to take them."

She wadded up the paper towel with shaky hands and tossed it in the trash on her way out. With luck, there'd be a steady stream of patients to keep her mind occupied for the rest of the day. Staying too busy to think about anything else beyond the next appointment and then the one after that was the best way she knew of shoving the past back where it belonged.

"You up for beer and pool tonight?"

Leif tossed his pack in the cab of his truck and considered Mitch's offer. The last time the two of them had indulged in a few beers and pool all hell had broken loose. Good times. Maybe it would improve his current bad mood.

He stared at the football player. "Yeah, as long as we take a solemn vow that the evening won't end up with another visit from the local police. I can't handle that kind of grief right now."

Mitch raised his hand and solemnly said, "I so swear. No fights. No cops."

Leif gave him a hard look. "No cheating?"

That brought a grin to Mitch's face. "Well, I wouldn't go that far. I do try not to lie to my friends."

Leif allowed himself to smile a little. "Fair enough. Why don't I meet you at the bar around seven?"

"Sounds good."

Then Leif remembered he had Austin to deal with. "I might have to bring another guy with me. Hope that's okay."

"The more the merrier. See you then."

On the way back to Spence's house, Leif finally gave in to the irritation that he'd been struggling with ever since he'd hit the floor of the therapy room, all while Zoe watched. His ankle had locked up. A skinned elbow. Not all that much pain. No big deal. He'd clearly overreacted, but he couldn't seem to help himself. The real blow was to his dignity. He could only be relieved that neither he nor Mitch had been hurt. Isaac had helped each of them up off the floor and calmly dealt with Leif's little temper tantrum.

It was bad enough to be fussed over and to have taken Mitch down with him. The worst part was knowing Zoe had seen him at his weakest again. Feeling that way was stupid, but that didn't make it any less true.

He'd maintained a feigned disinterest until he'd moved on to the cool-down portion of his therapy. As he waited for the ice to dull the throbbing pain in his leg, he'd replayed the whole scene like a movie in his head. It had all happened so fast that some of the images remained blurry.

Even so, he was convinced there had been something odd about Zoe's reaction. When he'd been sitting on the table while Isaac gave him a quick going-over, Leif had looked to see if Zoe was still watching from the other side of the window.

She'd been there, all right. But even though she was looking in his general direction, he was convinced she wasn't actually seeing him at all. When he'd tried to make eye contact with her, she'd stared into the distance, her eyes wide and unblinking. Whatever she'd been focusing on had left her pale and maybe even a little scared.

What was up with that?

Maybe he was imagining things, but he didn't think so. Right now there wasn't anything he could do about it. Maybe he'd check in on her later. Sure, they'd promised to keep some distance between them except on his scheduled appointments, but she'd already broken that agreement.

Granted, it was a pretty weak excuse to do something he wanted to do anyway. Yeah, maybe later he'd go for a long walk that just happened to take him right by her place. If he was careful, his leg was strong enough now to handle the steps to her second-floor apartment. He would climb them, knock on the door, and tell her ... What?

That he'd made it four days without speaking to her but that was his limit. Or how about that he thought maybe she'd been scared earlier and he wanted to make sure she was all right?

He could only imagine her reaction to either of those scenarios. She'd probably kick his ass right back down the steps to the parking lot. That image should have worried him, but instead it only made him grin. If he gave in to the temptation, it would be interesting to see how it all played out.

When he pulled up in front of Spence's house, Austin was out in the yard playing catch with Mooch. He climbed out of the truck as the kid tossed the ball one more time. All signs of good humor disappeared from his face as he turned to face Leif. Yeah, he got that Austin resented every minute he was forced to spend in Leif's company. It probably didn't help that with his truck still impounded he was trapped at the house.

Too fucking bad. He'd brought all this on himself.

"Sorry I'm later than expected. My therapy ran long."

Leif started up the steps to the porch as Austin and Mooch trailed after him. "Let's grab a quick sandwich, and then we can go bail out your truck."

"Okay."

Inside, Austin pitched in and helped. Maybe he figured that hurrying the process along would get his wheels back all that much faster. Fair enough.

Just as they were sitting down, Leif's leg locked up again and caused him to list heavily to the side. Austin lunged toward him, catching him before it gave out completely. Damn, could this day get any fucking worse?

He jerked his arm free from Austin's hands and lowered himself into the closest chair. With his voice little better than a growl, he snapped, "Back off. I'm okay."

Austin held up his hands and stepped away, looking disgusted. "Fine. Next time I'll let you fall on your ass."

"Oh, hell." Leif sighed and said, "Sorry, kid. I don't mean to be a complete jerk. It's been one of those days."

Austin didn't respond, but at least he didn't go storming off. The two of them shoveled their mouths full of food, probably because that meant they didn't have to talk. As a result, they made quick work of their meal.

"Like I said, we can go get your truck out of hock now if you want."

"I want."

Austin cleared the table, dumping the dishes in the sink. "About the money I owe you. I plan to pay you back as soon as I can."

Right now Leif wasn't worried about a couple of hundred bucks, but it was clearly important to Austin. Maybe that was a good sign that the kid was taking his situation seriously.

"Not a problem. We can set up a spreadsheet on my laptop for the restitution you owe and tack on the rest."

The kid looked up from putting a plate into the dishwasher.

"Here's the thing." The younger man flushed red and shifted from one foot to the other. "I don't know a lot about computers, much less how to create a spreadsheet."

Seriously? In this day and age? What the hell kind of school had the kid gone to that hadn't at least taught him the basics?

He hadn't realized he'd said that last part out loud until he saw the expression on Austin's face. "We moved around so much that I missed a lot of class. I got sick of playing catch-up all the time, so I dropped out the day I turned sixteen."

Austin shoved his hands in his pants pockets and stared at the floor. "I've done okay without a diploma."

Yeah, if you considered a dead-end job flipping burgers doing okay. The kid sounded defensive, but who could blame him? Leif mentally added that to the list of reasons Vince Locke deserved to have his ass kicked.

"When we've got time, we'll sit down and set up the spreadsheet together, and I'll show you how to update the data as you go along."

The knot in his thigh muscle finally gave it up and relaxed. Leif allowed himself to enjoy a few seconds without pain before trying to stand up again. He tossed Austin the keys to his truck. "Let's get going. You drive. We can start on the program after we get back."

Austin snagged the keys out of the air. "Fine."

Despite the one-word answer, Austin looked pleased by the offer. Maybe it was a good time to bring up Leif's plans for tonight.

"By the way, I'm supposed to meet Mitch Calder to play a few games of pool tonight after dinner. If you want to tag along, you'd be welcome. You don't have to decide now. Just let me know."

Austin's eyes flared wide in surprise. "Mitch Calder, as in the big-time professional quarterback who grew up here in Snowberry Creek? You're really friends with a guy like him?"

Sometimes Leif had a hard time believing that himself. "Yeah, we share the same physical therapist."

"Cool. Yeah, I'll go."

"Fair enough." Leif led the way to the front door. "Come on, Mooch. You can ride along this time."

Outside, Austin opened the driver's-side door and stood back to let the dog jump in first. Leif rode shotgun as Mooch settled into the narrow backseat. After Austin started the truck, Leif held out a piece of paper. "Here's a map and the address for the tow yard." Austin studied it briefly. "It's not far from where I used to work."

Leif stretched out his legs and closed his eyes as they left the driveway behind. "Good. Wake me when we get there."

Chapter 17

"One more mile, and then I'll be able to sleep."
    Hoping that last part was true, Zoe kept trudging on down the street. Shoving her hands in her jacket pockets, she ignored the chill of the air, in fact preferring it to the dry stuffiness of her apartment. Maybe that was all in her head, but all she knew was that she could breathe more easily once she headed out into the night.

At the next corner, she hung a right and kept walking. Unfortunately, no matter how far or how fast she walked, the memories kept pace with her. After making it through the rest of the day at work, she had hoped the flashback was a solo performance.

No such luck. As soon as she didn't have the constant hubbub at work to keep her mind occupied, the stark faces from her past came flooding back. She'd always tried to concentrate on the successes, especially the patients she'd helped along their way back to normal.

But God knows, there'd been so many others whose lives had been changed forever. They had all been so brave, each and every one of them. Too many to remember by name. That didn't mean she'd ever been able to forget any of their faces, nor did she try. They deserved that much from her.

Technically, the park along Strawberry Creek was closed this late at night. But she needed the soothing sound of the water far more than she needed to follow the rules right now. Cutting across the grass, she headed for the picnic table that sat between the path and the edge of the creek.

Before she reached her goal, the sound of squealing tires had her spinning around to look back the way she'd come. Damn, had one of the deputies noticed her?

Luck was with her. Or maybe not. It was a pickup truck, not one of the local police cars, backing up to the park entrance. From this distance it was hard to pick out much detail, but it looked all too familiar. Her suspicions were confirmed as soon as the passenger door opened and the interior light came on.

Leif.

It was too much to hope that he hadn't seen her, not when he was already headed straight for her. Rather than wait for him, she deliberately turned away and continued on her original trajectory until she reached the picnic table.

She perched on the top of it with her feet on the bench and stared out across the creek. The silver light from the moon overhead painted the water with its cool shine, causing it to sparkle as it tumbled over the rocks. The soft babble did nothing to muffle the sound of Leif's uneven tread as he approached.

Without bothering to look at him, she said, "We seem to always end up here, don't we?"

"Yeah, we do."

He joined her on the table, a heavy sigh the only hint about how his leg was doing. She didn't ask, and he didn't tell. Leif propped his cane on the seat and scooted closer. She managed to resist leaning into his warm strength.

"Wasn't that your truck?"

He nodded. "I'd had a couple of beers with Mitch while we played pool, so my new roommate was behind the wheel. When I spotted you, I had him drop me off and told him I'd walk back home."

She was surprised that he would trust anyone with his new truck. When she said so, Leif's smile gleamed in the darkness. "It was all part of my crafty plan to make sure Austin stuck to soft drinks tonight while the two of us played pool with Mitch. The kid has had a major run-in with the law lately, and I didn't want him to risk any more trouble with Gage Logan. That would be last thing he needs right now."

How noble of him. "But, Leif, as I recall, you and Mitch have had your own issues with Gage and his men. Didn't that involve beer and pool, too?"

He laughed. "Yeah, well, Austin doesn't have to know about that. Besides, the pool and beer weren't the real problem that night. Gage was more concerned about the fight that came afterward."

"Oh, well, that's different."

Leif leaned in closer, giving her a soft nudge with his shoulder. "Besides, Mitch and I took a solemn vow beforehand that there would be no fights or cops tonight. Cheating, on the other hand, was still on the table. We didn't want anyone to get the idea that we're a pair of Goody Two-shoes."

Zoe followed his lead and kept things light. "I can only imagine how careful you have to be not to damage the manly reputations of both the U.S. Army and the

NFL. Please tell me you both remembered to curse and swagger on your way into the bar."

"Oh, hell yeah, you bet we did. I even spit a couple of times for good measure."

"Your mom would be so proud."

"Poor lady, she tried her best to civilize me. Some of it stuck, but not everything. Of course, I wouldn't have expected her to know much about barroom etiquette."

Somehow his hand had become entangled with hers as they'd talked. She didn't mind, but what had happened to that line they'd drawn? Hadn't they agreed that neither of them was in a position to pursue any kind of relationship outside of the clinic?

So much for their resolve.

Leif gave her hand a gentle squeeze. "I was surprised to see you here this late at night, especially after working all day."

"Sometimes I need to unwind before I can sleep. Sitting here by the creek is especially soothing."

"It is a beautiful night, I'll grant you that much." He released her hand and leaned back on his elbows to stare up at the sky. "So many nights here are cloudy even when it doesn't rain. It's nice to have a clear view of the stars."

"True."

His voice grew rougher in the darkness, although his expression remained serene. "It's also nice to be able to enjoy a moonlit night without worrying about who else might be out and about."

She shuddered. He was right about that, too. She risked sharing a little more. "I had a lot of friends in the military who truly hated night patrols."

"With good reason." He sat back up. "Sorry. I didn't mean to spoil the mood. After three deployments, worrying about snipers and IEDs pretty much becomes second nature. I guess I'll eventually get over it."

That would be nice. If Leif could somehow put his past to rest, maybe there was hope for her to do the same. Just that quickly she needed to be up and moving again.

"I'd better be heading home."

Leif reached for his cane. "I'll walk with you."

She shouldn't let him, but she couldn't find it in her to miss a chance to spend more time in his company. His quiet strength made her feel safe. With Leif setting the pace, they made their way back toward Main Street. Once they were on more level ground, Leif wrapped his arm around her shoulders. She didn't protest that either.

It was tempting to stretch out their time together over a cup of coffee and some of Frannie's pie, but Leif didn't even glance at the diner as they walked past. Yet he seemed relaxed and in no hurry to get shed of her company as they reached the final stretch to her apartment.

If only she felt as calm, but right now her pulse was picking up speed at an alarming rate. Did she have the resolve or even the desire to say good-bye to him in the parking lot? That would be the smart thing to do because each step he took closer to her front door only increased the likelihood that she would invite him inside. From there, it was only a short trip down the hall to her freshly made bed.

Was that what she wanted? The truth? Yes, she did. The real question was why? Granted, she found Leif attractive, and had from the first moment they'd met. But why was she so willing to cross that all-important line tonight? If it was solely because she was too afraid of her own dark memories to face the night alone, that wasn't fair to Leif.

She assessed her companion as they walked across the parking lot. He was handsome, strong, a hero. Everything she liked and desired in a man. Was that reason enough to want to lose herself in his arms?

"You're thinking way too hard, Zoe. Say the word, and I'll wait until you're safely inside and walk back home."

She didn't bother to deny her concerns. "We both know a lot of reasons why I should do exactly that. It would be the smart thing to do, Leif. Not just for me, but for both of us."

He turned to face her. His big hand cupped the side of her face, its heat soothing her soul. "And if I'm not feeling all that smart?"

Neither was she. If he walked away right now, it might just shatter her. On the other hand, his touch, his kiss, and the promise of his passion might actually save her. Her decision made, she smiled up at him. "Leif Brevik, would you like to come upstairs with me?"

"To be clear, are you offering me coffee or something else, Zoe?"

She owed them both honesty. "I want you in my bed, Leif. Coffee afterward is optional."

His eyes glittered with a hot promise of passion. "Then I'd love to come upstairs with you."

Under any other circumstances Leif would've cursed the slow pace Zoe set walking up the steps to her apartment. He normally hated giving in to the need to favor his bad ankle. At least right now, the longer they took to reach her door, and from there her bed, the more time they would have to savor the anticipation.

She was right about the reasons they shouldn't be doing this, but it would've taken a lot stronger man than he to walk away. How many nights had he stared up at the ceiling in the den at Spence's place and imagined what it would be like to have Zoe curled up at his side, her dark hair spilling across his pillow, a satisfied smile on her pretty face?

It took Zoe two tries to get the key in the lock, but then the door swung open. She stepped inside to turn on the lights, giving him his first glimpse of her home. The living room walls were a soft cream, but the furnishings were done in a riot of strong colors ranging from a dark green to a deep red. Comfortable and welcoming. He liked it. Liked her.

"Aren't you coming in?"

He realized that he was still hovering right at the threshold. "Do you still want me to?"

If there'd been any hesitation in her response, he would've found the strength to walk away. But no, she simply nodded and held out her hand. After closing the door, he turned the lock to shut out the rest of the world along with all its doubts and its stringent rules about what the two of them should and shouldn't be doing.

After tossing his cane aside, Leif crossed to where Zoe stood. She didn't exactly look reluctant; "skittish" was a better way to put it. He needed to move slowly, to coax and not demand.

He placed his hands on her shoulders and then slid them up and down her arms several times in hopes that a gentle touch would coax those first flickers of heat he saw in her eyes into flames. When Zoe responded in kind and the palms of her hands settled on his chest, he gathered her into his arms, trapping her against the length of his body. He smiled and pressed a soft kiss on the top of her head as she melted against him.

For the moment, it was enough to hold and be held, taking comfort in the simple healing of human touch. If that was all Zoe needed from him tonight, it would be enough. Solace had its own value.

But he craved her passion. With that in mind, he whispered, "Zoe, look at me."

She slowly tipped her head back enough to meet his gaze. Her blue eyes darkened as her mouth softened in invitation. Leif smiled and brushed his lips across hers. Softly. Slowly. Teasing and tasting until she grew restive in his arms.

"Leif, kiss me."

He nibbled her lower lip. "I am."

"No, you're not. You're only playing. Kiss me like you mean it, Corporal."

The tart note in her voice had him grinning.

She didn't like it. "Are you laughing at me?"

"No, ma'am, not at all. I was just thinking that was the first order an officer—even a former officer—has given me that I couldn't wait to carry out."

"Let's see a little more action and a lot less talking, soldier."

All right, then. Leif had his marching orders, a mission to carry out. This wasn't a raid where speed and a quick retreat were in order. No, making love to Zoe, with Zoe, meant taking his time, scouting out the territory.

He kissed her again, slowly savoring the give-and-take as first one and then the other took the lead. They still hadn't made it any farther than the center of the living room. It was time to push on. After tugging her jacket off her shoulders, he let it drop to the floor and did a little scouting.

He began by slipping his hand under the hem of her T-shirt and then splaying his fingers across her lower back. Her skin was like living satin: soft, smooth, and so warm. Trailing his fingers downward, he eased them inside the waistband of her jeans, but was careful to leave the thin barrier of her panties between his touch and her skin. She shivered in response.

At the same time, Zoe did a little exploring of her own. She cupped his ass and squeezed. Hot damn, he liked a woman who was willing to make a few demands of her own. He was so hard for her, he hurt. If his bad leg would've supported them, he would've ripped her jeans down and taken her right up against the nearest wall.

He eyed her oversized sofa, which was within easy striking range, but rejected it. He wanted more room to maneuver when they finally got down to it.

Zoe broke off kissing him long enough to tug at his shirt. He surrendered it without protest. When she tossed her own on the floor, he smiled. Oh, yeah, this was going to be good. As he moved to stand behind her, he settled his hands at her waist and enjoyed exploring the curve of her waist, her hips, and then back up, stopping just below her breasts.

"Tease," she complained as she attempted to tug his hands higher to where she wanted them to be.

"Yeah, but you like it."

He held his position and tried out some different tactics. First, he leaned down to trace the shell of her ear with the tip of his tongue. When she cocked her head to the side with a soft sigh, he rewarded her by giving her breasts a gentle squeeze. She leaned forward into his palms, which had the added effect of pressing her backside right against his erection.

She shot him a smug smile back over her shoulder when he groaned. Okay, time for some payback. He flicked the front fastener on her bra open and pushed it aside. Rolling her nipple between his finger and thumb with one hand, Leif reached for the snap on her jeans with the other. He made quick work of it, but took his time lowering her zipper.

Zoe tried to spin around to face him, but he held her

trapped against his chest with one arm. Then slowly, so slowly, he eased his fingertips beneath the elastic of her panties. Her breath caught in her throat as he tested her readiness for him with soft strokes.

He didn't know how Zoe was faring, but he was driving himself crazy. "I think it's time we get horizontal."

Zoe immediately took his hand and led the way down the hall to her bedroom. "Wait here for a second."

She left him standing at the door while she crossed the room to turn on a small lamp on her dresser. It was just bright enough to bathe her skin in a soft glow. He approved. After she pulled back the covers on her king-sized bed, she reached into a drawer and set a box of condoms on the top of the bedside table. Finally, she returned to stand in front of him.

"Now, where were we? Oh, yes, I was about to do this."

She reached for the snap on his jeans, obviously aiming for a little payback herself as she took her own sweet time lowering the zipper. After tugging his pants down far enough to free his cock, she took him in hand and showed him the real meaning of teasing. He had to brace himself against the doorframe with both hands as he fought for control.

God, he loved that she gave as good as she got. He wasn't sure how much longer he could take this. "About that bed."

Then it was the race to strip off the last vestiges of their clothing and inhibitions.

When they finally tumbled onto her mattress, Zoe did her best to drag Leif on top of her.

Frustrating man that he was, he resisted her demands. "We'll get there, honey, but not quite yet."

In an obvious attempt to distract her, he kissed her hard and deep before moving down over her body, exploring and tasting each inch along the way. The wet heat of his mouth on her breast was amazing; it was as if she could feel each tug and lick everywhere at once. Her legs thrashed restlessly, needing his weight to help ground her in the moment.

He stopped long enough to put one of the condoms to use. But when he finally spread her thighs wide, he made no move to take her. Instead, he scooted farther down the mattress. What was he doing? Did he mean to . . . ? Yes, he did.

When he tasted her, she saw fireworks. She couldn't take much more. She really couldn't. But Leif didn't seem to care. He held her in place as he slowly, deliberately pushed her higher and higher until she was panting his name and begging for release.

Then he stopped. Just like that. With her balancing on the sharp precipice between completion and insanity.

"Leif, please."

"I will, but look at me. I want you right here with me."

She forced her eyes to open, to see his handsome face. He was breathing hard, his skin covered in a slick sheen of sweat. Good. She didn't want to be the only one who felt this desperation. "I'm right here with you, Leif."

He nodded as he rose over her again, this time poised at the entrance of her body. Then, with his dark eyes staring into hers, he flexed his hips hard and fast to bury himself deep within her. It had been a long time since she'd been with a lover, and the sudden invasion burned. She didn't care but couldn't help but wince.

He froze. "Did I hurt you?"

She didn't bother to deny it. "It's been a while."

"Do you need me to stop?"

Was he crazy? "No way. Not now."

He must have believed her, because he made no attempt to withdraw. When he did move again, he took such care, going slowly, giving her every chance to adjust. Zoe let out a breath she hadn't realized she was holding and relaxed. After raising her knees up higher on his hips, she dug her fingertips into his backside and held on.

"Now, Leif, please!"

He obliged her, driving deep and fast. She loved the flex and play of his muscles under her hands. He had the perfect warrior's body, all lean power and strength. His life as a soldier had left its mark on him, but it only made him stronger in her eyes.

Once again he was pushing her toward the edge, her entire body tensing as he raised up to support himself at arm's length, allowing his hips to swing freely. Again and again and again, he drove forward. She bowed beneath him, meeting his thrusts with her own.

"That's it, Zoe—let go and fly."

She did as he ordered, her entire body burning hot as she screamed out her release. Caught up in the grip of her own climax, she felt him plunge over the cliff with her. His powerful body shuddered in release deep within hers in a final burst of hard thrusts.

Gradually, reality returned. When the last of their desperation drained away, Leif gave her a crooked grin and kissed her on the nose.

"Corporal Brevik reporting in, ma'am. Mission accomplished."

She lost it and gave in to a fit of the giggles as he rolled over and tucked her in at his side. Feeling better than she had in . . . well, in forever, she snuggled close and held on to the amazing man next to her.

Mission accomplished, indeed.

Chapter 18

Leif stared up at the ceiling, unable to sleep and torn about what he should do next. He had no real desire to leave Zoe's bed. For one thing, he truly savored the skin-to-skin contact with the woman curled up next to him. Then there was the hope that they might stage a repeat performance of the mind-blowing sex that they'd shared earlier.

The trouble was that he'd told Austin he would be back home tonight. He figured he owed it to Callie to keep an eye on the kid now that he had free run of Spence's house. After all, it was Leif who had told Austin he could stay there. The bottom line was that he couldn't linger in Zoe's bed until dawn.

With that in mind, he shifted to roll onto his side. Gently brushing Zoe's hair back from her face, he studied her quiet beauty. There was such strength in her—which normally showed in her animated expression. But here in the dim moonlight seeping in past the blinds on the window, there was no missing the faint dark circles under her eyes, and her lips still looked a bit swollen from their kisses. He'd definitely left his mark on her body in other ways as well, starting with the love bite right at the juncture of her shoulder and the delicate skin of her neck. That was only fair because she'd left her mark on him as well, even if it didn't show on the outside.

When Zoe finally stirred, she turned away from him, but kept her body pressed back against his. In the process, the covers slipped down to her waist, leaving her upper body exposed for his perusal. She made no move to cover herself; perhaps the combined warmth of their two bodies was enough to keep her comfortable. Regardless of the reason, he could only be grateful.

True, a better man might have tugged the blanket back up to afford her some modesty. He didn't know what it said about him, but he couldn't find the strength to deny himself a clear view of all those delicious parts of her that he'd already tasted and touched. He couldn't wait to do it again.

No time like the present.

He palmed her breast and slowly kneaded it until her nipples came to attention, a clear sign that she was aware of him on some level. Next, when he traced small circles on her belly, she twitched a bit as if his touch tickled her skin. From there, he turned his attention to the curve of her fabulous ass, sliding his hand down and down to seek out the feminine secrets that were his ultimate goal.

Zoe moaned and stretched, keeping her back toward him but shifting enough to encourage him to continue his explorations. She reached back to grasp his erection and gave it a gentle squeeze.

"Better suit up, big guy, before we go any further with this."

He hated to stop even for such a vital reason, but he

did. While he sat up, Zoe remained right where she was, offering him an unobstructed view of the elegant lines of her back that practically had him drooling.

Hot damn, he wanted some of that. In fact, all of that. He rolled back onto the bed next to her. "I wanted to take it nice and slow this time, but I'm pretty sure that's not going to happen. Consider that your fault."

She offered him a siren's smile. "How do you figure? As I recall, I was sound asleep when you started all this ruckus. That makes me the innocent one."

"True enough. But, even asleep, there's nothing innocent about the effect you have on me, lady."

"And what would that effect be exactly?"

Although she knew. There was a wealth of feminine awareness in the heated look she gave him, and the teasing wiggle she gave her hips was definitely intended to incite trouble. Fine. If she didn't want to own up to her wicked, wicked wiles, he'd have to let her feel the fire she'd unleashed.

"Brace yourself, honey. This is going to be a hard ride."

Zoe went willingly when he gently tugged her hips into the perfect position for him to take her from behind. As he slowly pressed forward, she dropped her head down to rest on her arms and moaned in approval. When he stopped to savor the moment, she looked back over her shoulder.

"Bring it on, soldier. Give it your best shot."

He had every intention of doing just that, but he'd forgotten to take one thing into consideration: his injured leg. For one delicious moment, they proceeded as planned with nothing but pure pleasure pounding through his body, and his entire focus was on satisfying the amazing woman in front of him. Damned if she wasn't the most unselfish lover he'd ever had.

Then without warning something snapped, crackled, and popped in his left calf. Leif's lungs forgot how to work, as agonizing pain sliced through his leg. He tasted blood as he bit down on his lip to keep from screaming, collapsed to the side, and begged the universe for mercy.

The fact she was naked didn't matter. Zoe's training automatically kicked in to assess the situation. It didn't take a genius to identify Leif's injured leg as the source of his agony. Figuring out how to treat it was a whole different issue. Before she could do anything constructive, she needed to know exactly what had happened. Right now Leif was too caught up in the pain to focus on anything else. They needed to get past that if she was going to be of any help to him.

More light would be a good start. She clambered off the bed long enough to turn on the ceiling light. On the way back, she tried calling his name in a soft voice in hopes that the soothing sound would help draw him out of his daze.

No luck. Leif remained curled up in the fetal position, his hands holding on to his left leg so tightly that his knuckles were bone white. Trying not to jar him unnecessarily, she knelt beside him on the bed and captured his face with her hands.

"Corporal, look at me."

His eyes fluttered as if he were trying to open them. She kept talking. "That's it, breathe through it, Leif. Tell me what's wrong. Do I need to call an ambulance?"

"NO!"

After another ragged breath, he managed to shake his head as he growled through gritted teeth, "Cramping. Burns like hell. Should pass."

He said it, but he didn't believe it. She'd bet her last

nickel on it. Maybe she could help that along. Grabbing a bottle of lotion off the bedside table, she positioned herself by his leg. If he was right about the problem, massage would help ease the pain. If he wasn't, she still needed to get her hands on his leg to make the right diagnosis.

"Leif, let go of your leg so I can look at it."

His pain-racked eyes locked onto hers. He gave a sharp nod and then jerked his hands back out of her way and laced his fingers behind his head. His big body thrummed with tension as she poked and prodded his calf muscle. He cursed a blue streak under his breath as she felt her way from his ankle all the way up to his thigh and back down.

"I think you're right that it's a cramp, but I can't be sure. The prudent thing would be for me to take you to the hospital and have an orthopedics doc take a look at it."

Leif was already shaking his head. No surprise there. "Had enough of them."

"Okay, then let's see if we can't get it to ease up for you. If this doesn't work, though . . ."

She left the rest unsaid. After pouring some of the lotion in her hand, she smeared it on his leg and then started the slow process of working out the knots. Judging by the grim expression on Leif's face, it had to hurt like hell, but he didn't utter a single complaint.

Her hands were aching and tired by the time the last of the tension faded away and his muscles smoothed out. Leif offered her a small smile and slowly stretched his leg out completely. They both held their breath until it was clear that the crisis had passed, at least for the moment.

Leif took her hand in his and tugged her down beside him. He kissed her palm. "Zoe, you definitely have magic hands. Thank you."

She wanted to rail at him. He needed to be more careful with his leg unless he wanted to risk further damage or at the very least a major setback in his recovery. But considering that she'd been actively encouraging him, she couldn't assign all the blame to him. They'd both been too caught up in the moment.

Leif stroked her back as he kept talking. The rough note in his voice sounded different now, as if it had been stripped of the pain, leaving only the intensity behind. "So, Zoe, where did we leave off?"

She couldn't believe her ears. "Are you crazy? I don't want to hurt you."

His eyes flashed hot with temper. "Screw that, Zoe. Let me worry about me. I'm fine and have every intention of finishing what we started. Unless you've changed your mind."

He guided her hand down his body to give testament to the power of his determination. One touch and a slow burn started deep inside her. How was she supposed to set him straight on the subject when her own body betrayed her? She also recognized muleheaded stubbornness when she saw it.

No way was she going to let him abuse his leg again. Not on her watch. Not in her bed. In a quick move, she straddled his hips and leaned down to kiss his mouth, starting off soft and gentle.

Growing bolder, she planted one hand on his chest while she grasped his erection with the other. Rising up, she guided him to the entrance of her body, and sank back down, taking him deep and taking her time to enjoy the ride. Leif's head kicked back on the pillow, his dark eyes mere slits as he watched her slowly roll her hips.

For his part, Leif palmed her breasts, squeezing them

to just the right side of pain. She smiled in approval. "Oh, yeah, just like that."

She wanted more. Faster. Harder. As if sensing her growing frustration, Leif grasped her hips with his big hands and guided them both into a virtual frenzy. He drove his hips up to meet hers on the downward stroke. Someone yelled. It might have been her. She wasn't sure and didn't care. All that mattered was that they kept going, kept driving hard, kept this amazing connection running hot between them.

His mouth curved in a wicked smile as he touched her in just the right place with just the right force. That was all it took. She broke apart in a million pieces, completely shattered and then remade whole again. He followed right after her, shuddering in release as he held her firmly in place and thrust upward.

When he collapsed on the mattress, she joined him in a boneless heap, remaining on top of him with her head tucked up by his chin. As much as she was enjoying the moment, the nurse in her still had concerns.

"How is your leg?"

The warmth in his dark eyes disappeared, the flame extinguished by the blunt question. She couldn't help but worry, but no doubt her timing could have been better.

"I told you once already. It's fine."

Maybe it was, but she suspected he would've given her the same answer even if it was a flat-out lie. She had no choice but to take him at his word for now. At least he kept his arms wrapped around her and made no move to put any physical distance between them. Emotional distance might be a different matter, but all she could do was play the cards she'd been dealt.

*   *   *

A few minutes later, Leif sighed and rested his forearm over his eyes, never a good sign. She braced herself for whatever he had to say. "Leif, just tell me."

"I should leave." He traced her lower lip with his thumb. "I don't want to."

At least the regret sounded honest, so she tried her best to ignore the stab of pain his words caused her. "Why do you need to go?"

Although, in all honesty, his leaving would save them both that awkward morning-after stress. It had been years since she'd had the kind of relationship that included sharing breakfast with a lover.

Leif's arm tightened around her as if he was worried that she was about to bolt from her own bed. His voice was a deep rumble when he finally answered.

"You already know that I'm living at Spence's old place. What you might not know is that we had a break-in at the house a short time ago. The perp turned out to be Spence's cousin, Austin. Since it was his first arrest, the judge offered the kid a second chance if he promised to make restitution. As it turns out, one of the requirements the judge mandated was that Austin had to have a job waiting for him. Unfortunately, he lost his old one because of his arrest."

Leif sat up far enough to rest on his elbows as he kept talking. "Callie offered to hire him to work on the house with me and Nick, and I ended up giving him a ride when he got released from jail. When I took him back to his apartment, we found out the landlord had thrown all of Austin's stuff out in the trash, figuring he wouldn't be back. The bastard hocked anything worth having.

"Long story short, I sort of invited Austin to move into the house with Nick and me, telling him room and board were part of the bennies that came with the job.

Now Austin is out at the house all alone and up to who knows what. It's too soon to think we can trust him. The thing is, I also need him to trust me. I told him I'd be back tonight, so I think I should be there."

What a relief that his reasons for leaving had nothing to do with her and what had happened with his leg. No, they had everything to do with the kind of man he was. The kind who took things like duty and honor seriously, putting them ahead of his own needs. Feeling a little happier about the situation, she rose up high enough to smile down at him.

"Leif Brevik, you're a nice man."

He snickered. "Not always."

"No one is, but this Austin kid is lucky to have someone like you take an interest in him. I hope he's smart enough to realize it."

She showed her approval of his actions with a kiss. "Give me a minute to get dressed, and I'll drive you home. And before you protest, I don't want you to have to walk that far."

He didn't look happy as he stared down at his leg, maybe judging how well it would support him. "It's not that far, Zoe. I can walk."

As he spoke, he turned his back toward her and pushed himself up off the bed. Damn stubborn men! She got up and started pulling on her own clothes.

"I wouldn't offer if I didn't mean it, Leif. Besides, I won't be able to sleep until I know you made it safely. I would do the same for any friend."

He pulled up his jeans before responding. Although clearly not happy, he gave in. "Thanks. I appreciate it."

They both gathered up the rest of the scattered bits of their clothing and dressed in near total silence. She wished there was a way to bridge the sudden bit of strained tension between them. Maybe if she understood its source she could say the right thing.

"Are you ready?"

Leif nodded and followed her out into the night. When he remained quiet for the entire drive, she realized that she felt as alone with Leif in the car as she would have if he hadn't been there at all.

Chapter 19

The short trip back to Spence's place took forever. Zoe didn't seem inclined to talk, and Leif's own thoughts had him too twisted up right now to carry on any kind of conversation. He was being an idiot, shutting Zoe out like this, but he couldn't seem to help himself. He didn't want to hurt her, but what the hell could he say, anyway?

The chance meeting in the park had been a happy accident. The walk back to Zoe's had gone off without a hitch, and the first round of sex had topped his own personal all-time greatest hits list.

Then his damn leg had to seize up and throw a damper on everything that followed. Certainly his body had enjoyed every second of round two, but he hadn't been able to shut out the churning thoughts in his head. Did she think he wouldn't figure out why she'd chosen that particular position? She'd been afraid of what would've happened to his leg if he'd picked up where they'd left off.

Normally, he had no problem with a woman wanting to take charge in bed, but this time the experience had made him feel weak. If he admitted that to Zoe, he'd only come off as some macho jerk. Not to mention that his leg still hurt, and no way in hell did he want Zoe to find out. She'd be all over him to go to the ER or some other fool thing. Yeah, he got that she was a nurse; it was her job to take care of her patients.

But when he got naked with the woman, he wasn't her patient. Plain and simple. Except that it wasn't, was it? Hadn't Zoe warned him repeatedly about the dangers of letting that line become blurred? No doubt she was already making plans to ship his case off to someone else. Her professional ethics would demand that much of her.

One thing he did know was that he wouldn't trust his care to anyone else. As she pulled up into the driveway, he blurted it out. "Don't transfer my case to anyone else."

She waited until she had stopped in front of the house to respond. "I have to, Leif. I can't be involved with you and be your health care provider at the same time. It wouldn't be right for a lot of reasons, some of them legal issues. I'm mostly worried that my feelings for you could cloud my professional judgment."

Which meant it all came down to which was the more important role right now. Leif hadn't been wrong when he'd told her the other night that he was in no position to get involved with anyone.

"If that's the way it has to be, fine. Right now I need to be your patient."

She slowly shook her head. "That doesn't change what we did tonight, Leif. If someone were to find out . . ."

Did she think he liked this any better than she did? He twisted in the seat to face her. "So who's going to tell? I don't shoot my mouth off about who I sleep with and neither do you. This was between us. Period."

He reined in his temper. "It's only until my leg's back to normal. After that, we'll be free to figure out where we go from there without all these complications."

Flexing her hands on the steering wheel, Zoe didn't mince words. "Yeah, right, Leif. We both know that if your leg gets back to normal, you'll be gone. The army is your life, and I get that. I'm only just now realizing there won't be any 'us' if that happens."

She slumped back in the seat and sighed. "It's no reflection on you at all, Leif. But I made the decision to leave the military behind for a lot of reasons, and none of those have changed. I won't be part of that lifestyle again. I can't risk it. The price is just too high."

Where had that last part come from? Her words pummeled his already hurting head. "You've always known I was a soldier. You also knew I want to go back."

Zoe's face looked washed out and pale by the light of the dashboard. "You're right. I did, and I'm sorry for letting things get this far. I have so much respect for you and the sacrifices you make for our country, Leif. I also understand why you want your old life back. Regardless, all any of us can do is make the decisions we can live with. As I said, the reasons I left the military are my own, but I didn't make the decision lightly. I can't let myself get tangled up in all of that again. I guess that means tonight should be a one-time thing."

She finally looked at him. "But it was a good thing, wasn't it?"

He owed her honesty at the very least. "Way better than just good, Zoe. It was the best, and I'm not saying that lightly. It's the truth."

He wanted to kiss her and needed to hold her, but her rejection of everything that he was, respect or no respect, left him twisting in the wind. Once again the gap between the two of them was so much wider than the few inches of space in her car. "I'd better go in. Guess I'll see you at my next appointment."

Climbing out of her car hurt like hell, but it had nothing at all to do with his leg. Before making his way up the steps, Leif waited to wave one last time as Zoe drove away. He had no idea if she noticed or even cared if she had. What a screwed-up ending to the night.

On his way into the house, he finally realized that Austin had left the porch light on for him, and the kid's truck was still parked next to Leif's. Good. He'd stuck around. That was something. Leif tried the door and found it locked. At least the kid cared something about keeping the house secure.

Leif unlocked the door and stood back, knowing that Mooch would come charging out. Sure enough, a white blur whizzed by to disappear into the trees on the far side of the yard. Leif debated whether to go on in or to wait. It was hard to tell how long Mooch would be. Besides, once he had a chance to take the weight off his leg, he might not be willing or even able to get back up.

Leaning against the doorframe, Leif waited a couple of minutes and then put two fingers in his mouth and let loose with a shrill whistle. His four-legged buddy eventually reappeared at the edge of the woods but made no move to return to the house. There was no way Leif could leave Mooch out all night. There were coyotes and God knows what else in the woods that would happily chow down on a Mooch-meal.

"Come on, dog, make it short."

Mooch yipped and came trotting back, making a couple of stops to lift his leg on the way across the yard. Leif followed Mooch inside just as a light came on in the hall upstairs. Austin appeared at the top of the steps dressed in boxers and an undershirt.

He rubbed his eyes and blinked down at Leif. "Everything okay?"

"Yeah," Leif lied. "I was waiting for Mooch to haul his ass back inside. Do you need anything before I crash for the night?"

Or what little was left of it.

"No, but you'll want to call Callie in the morning. She was kind of surprised to find out I was living here now."

Leif winced. "My bad, kid. I meant to call her. How pissed off was she?"

Austin started down the steps. "Actually, she didn't seem mad at all. She said she'd talked to Nick about my job and wanted to check in with you about it."

Leif hobbled into the kitchen and flipped on the light. He poured himself a glass of water to wash down a couple of pain pills while Austin helped himself to some milk and two brownies from a plate on the counter. Leif grabbed a couple for himself and parked his backside at the kitchen table. Austin joined him, but only after he refilled Mooch's water bowl and tossed the dog a couple of treats. The dog gulped them down, then collapsed on the floor next to Leif's feet.

The three males sat in silence, each lost in his thoughts. Leif nibbled the chocolate goodness and mentally thanked Callie for keeping him supplied with high-octane sugary treats. Right now he needed the burst of energy the brownies would provide just to get ready for bed.

Austin finished off the last of his milk. "So what's up for tomorrow?"

Leif hadn't thought that far ahead, other than that he needed to go to that stupid meeting at the church in the afternoon. On the other hand, he supposed if they expected Austin to start earning his keep, someone had to come up with some kind of plan.

"The yard needs mowing, the flower beds need edging, and this house could use some cleaning. If you'll work on the upstairs, I'll do this floor."

Austin looked even less enthusiastic about the proposed plan of action than Leif felt. He managed a sympathetic grin. "Yeah, I know none of that is particularly exciting, but it's a start. Nick will be back soon. That's when things will get interesting around here. He plans to rip this place apart and put it all back together. If you check out the third floor, you'll see where we've already started to make changes."

He pushed himself back up to his feet, wincing as he put his weight on his left leg. "Nick knows a whole shitload about construction and remodeling. Pay attention to what he teaches you, and you'll be able to get a helluva lot better job than flipping burgers."

The kid didn't look all that impressed with the situation, and Leif was too damn tired to put any more effort into convincing him otherwise.

"See you in the morning. Come on, Mooch. Time to hit the rack."

Zoe stared up at the ceiling. "God, what was I thinking?"

It was a stupid question, one with no satisfactory answer. There were good reasons that Zoe had made it a rule to avoid emotional entanglements since she'd left her army career behind to take refuge in the small-town normalcy of Snowberry Creek. Breaking that rule had hurt not only her but Leif as well.

He deserved better, or at least some honesty from her. How likely was it that he'd want to listen to anything she had to say now? Slim to none, and who would blame him?

She looked around the living room. There had to be something left to do, something else that needed to be cleaned, scrubbed, sorted, washed, or folded. Unable to face her empty bed after returning home from dropping Leif off in the middle of the night, she'd first tried watching late-night television. When that failed to provide adequate distraction, she'd folded her laundry. From there, she'd emptied the dishwasher, scrubbed the counters, and kept right on going.

She could always vacuum, but the neighbors downstairs might not appreciate the noise at this hour. She checked the time. The sun would be up soon. Maybe now she could sleep. Once again, she went through her usual nighttime routine, starting with brushing her teeth. After stripping off her sweat-stained clothes, she donned her oldest, rattiest pajamas.

Rather than return to her bed, she waited until the first streaks of sunlight made their appearance before curling up on the couch under an afghan. Crossing her fingers that the daylight would keep her nightmares at bay, she fell asleep to the soft babble of the morning news.

Chapter 20

❧ ❧

"Hey, Leif, are you awake?"

Mooch immediately hit the floor and headed straight for the kitchen while Leif decided how to respond to Austin's question. Ignoring the kid was pretty much at the top of the list; throwing something at him was right up there, too. He burrowed deeper under the blankets and covered his head with his pillow, but that wouldn't hold the day at bay for long.

"Leif? I'm sorry to bother you, but I really need to talk to you."

Okay, give the kid credit for determination. He gave up and answered but stayed right where he was. "Yeah?"

Austin came closer, still moving cautiously. He set a cup of coffee on the table next to the bed and then backed away fast. The rich smell was enough to finally draw Leif out of his burrow. After sitting up, he reached for the cup of life's ambrosia and risked a small sip. It was strong enough to eat through steel. Perfect. Maybe he'd let the kid live after all.

Blinking through bleary eyes, he stared at Austin over the rim of the mug. "So what do you want at this ungodly hour?"

Rather than answer right away, Austin held out Leif's cell phone so he could see the time. Damn, that couldn't be right. If it was, he'd slept through the entire morning. He gulped down another mouthful of the scalding coffee and set the mug aside. Austin patiently waited until Leif was sitting on the edge of the bed.

"Okay, I'm up. What do you need?"

"Callie'll be here in a few minutes. Evidently she's tried calling you several times this morning on your cell. When you didn't answer the last time, she called the landline and got me. She said your phone must be turned off or dead. Something about how you might ignore Nick's calls, but you'd never deliberately be that rude to her."

Leif muttered a curse and reached for his jeans. Could he make it to the shower before Callie got there? Maybe not, but he was going to give it a valiant try. No way he wanted to face her until he cleared out some of the cobwebs.

He stood up and reached for his cane. "I'm going to duck into the shower. Fix Callie a cup of coffee and tell her I'll be out in a few."

"Sure thing."

"And feed Mooch."

"Already did. I also mowed the lawn and edged the front yard. Only reason I heard the phone is that I came back in to get a drink of water. Well, and to make sure you weren't dead."

Leif finally laughed. "It's nice to know you care. Now get the hell out of my way before I show you what this cane is really used for."

Austin held up his hands as if to surrender and retreated toward the kitchen. Leif grabbed his shaving kit, snagged his cleanest clothes, and hustled his ass into the bathroom off the utility room. He made quick work of cleaning up and getting dressed, but didn't bother shaving. It wasn't as if anybody would get close enough to be bothered by the stubble.

"Anybody" being Zoe.

Besides, it went with his shaggy hair. He hadn't had it cut since arriving in Snowberry Creek and probably wouldn't until he had to report back to base. He ran his fingers through it and tried to remember how long it had been since his hair had actually been long enough to part. All in all, he looked strange to himself, as if that guy in the mirror was vaguely familiar but Leif couldn't quite place him.

It was just another part of his life that was out of sync. Maybe talking to Nick would help him get his head straightened out. After he dealt with whatever Callie had on her agenda, he'd check in with the sergeant to see what was up with him. Most likely, Nick felt duty-bound to keep an eye on Leif, even if it was from a distance.

Or he might want to kick Leif's ass for letting Austin anywhere near Callie. That would be fun.

Afterward, he'd try to figure out what to do about last night. Talk about a screwed-up situation. There had been so much right between him and Zoe. How could it have gone so wrong so quickly? Then there was that veterans' meeting at the church to get through.

After he was dressed, he could hear the muffled sound of conversation through the door. Time to face Callie. He left his stuff where it was and walked out into the kitchen. He'd figured she'd been talking to Austin, but instead she was having a heartfelt conversation with Mooch.

"So, boy, wish you could tell me what's up with your buddy Leif. I was afraid he'd been scooped up by the cops again, but Austin assures me that they both behaved last night. A few games of pool, a couple of longnecks, and that's all there was to it. However, Austin also said Leif had ordered him to drop him off at the park when he spotted a lady friend walking toward the creek."

She pitched her voice a tad louder, no doubt aware that Leif was listening. "I have to wonder who this mysterious female is and why he's keeping her identity secret. I'm not entirely sure if I approve of her keeping our Corporal Brevik out to all hours, especially if whatever they were up to results in him sleeping half the day away."

Callie dropped her voice to a whisper. "Mooch, do you think she had her wicked way with him?"

Okay, enough was enough. True, Leif had poked his nose into her business when she and Nick first hooked up, but his situation was different. Besides, it was over between him and Zoe anyway.

He let a little of his irritation show in the look he gave her on his way past her to the coffeepot. "Very funny, Callie. May I remind you I am a grown man and capable of taking care of myself?"

Most of the time anyway.

After pouring himself another cup of caffeine and topping off Callie's, he fixed himself a bowl of cereal before joining her at the table. It was a little late for breakfast, but it would take the edge off his appetite.

"So, what's up, Callie? Austin said you've been trying to call me."

She patted Mooch on the head one last time and then turned in her chair to face Leif. "I wanted to give you a heads-up that Nick is, shall we say, mildly concerned about Austin being here. I tried telling him why I gave him a job and you invited him to move in."

Leif could well imagine how that conversation had actually gone. "Mildly concerned? Am I correct in assuming that translates into him planning on kicking my ass up and down the road a few times for letting you hire Austin in the first place?"

She laughed. "He also mentioned staking you out on a hillside in Afghanistan with a box of MREs and a FREE TO GOOD HOME sign pinned to your chest."

Okay, that sounded like Sarge when he went on a tear. "The good news is that he'll have time to cool off before he gets back here."

"Yeah, he will." Callie's smile faded. "It seems like forever before that happens, though."

"At least you know he's not getting shipped out again." Leif winked at her over the brim of his cup. "Besides, you've got me here."

His cell phone lit up and played Nick's ringtone. Leif braced himself for a tirade. He punched the speakerphone button so Callie could hear both ends of the conversation. With that in mind, he did his best to head Nick off at the pass.

"Hi, Sarge. Sorry I missed your calls this morning. But before you proceed to tear me a new one, you should know that Callie is here and listening."

"What's the matter, Corporal? Too cowardly to talk to me on your own?"

Only someone who knew Nick well would've been able to tell from his ice-cold tone that he wasn't really angry. No, he was green-eyed jealous because Leif was sitting right where Nick would give anything to be.

"Not at all. Callie was missing you, and I was cheering her up by reminding her that I'm much better-looking.

Also, right now I have longer hair, not that crappy buzz cut you're sporting, all of which makes me a lot more manly. I hadn't yet gotten to the part about me not snoring as loudly as you do."

Nick rose to the bait. "Leif, you no good son of a—"

Leif cut him off before he could finish. "Before you start launching grenades in my direction, Sarge, I'll remind you that the woman is so besotted with you that she fails to see my charms. Not sure how you managed to pull that off, but maybe you could give me some pointers. After last night, it seems obvious I could use them."

Well, shit, he hadn't meant to let that slip out. Callie immediately went on point. Now there would be no escaping a full-out inquisition. She'd try to wring every painful detail out of him, and Nick would be right there beside her asking his own tactless questions.

In fact, he launched the opening salvo. "So what woman failed to appreciate your questionable charms this time? Do you need me to call her up and lie about what a great catch you'd be?"

If his friend had sounded smug instead of concerned, Leif would've told Nick exactly what physically painful thing he could do with his offer.

Instead, Leif gave him a limited amount of the truth. "It's not her fault, Sarge. We both know I'm not in a position to get involved until I know how this thing with my leg is going to play out. All I know is being a combat soldier in the army. If I lose that, I lose everything."

Nick wasn't having it. "That's bullshit, Leif, and you know it. There's way more to life than the army."

Yeah, maybe that was true for Nick, especially now that he'd met Callie. He was walking away from his career without a second's hesitation. But then, unlike Leif, Nick had made the decision to leave on his own terms.

Leif might be forced out, and he'd never thought much about what he would do after the army, figuring he had at least another twelve years to decide.

The entire situation left him raw and hurting. "Maybe you're right about that, Nick, but it's all I've ever had."

He lurched to his feet and tossed the phone to Callie. "Here, talk to your woman. She's missing you. I've got work to do. Important stuff like dusting and weeding."

Then he slammed out of the kitchen, not sure where he was headed. All he knew for sure was that he needed to put some space between himself and his friends before all hell broke loose.

His temper ran out of steam about the time he reached the gazebo in the back corner of the yard. He parked his ass and tried to figure out what to do next.

Apologize to Callie? Yeah, that was at the top of the list. Nick? Not so much. The guy code was pretty specific about such things. A punch in the arm when Nick got back to Snowberry Creek and paying for an extra round the next time they hit a bar together should handle it.

The back screen door creaked. Great. Callie was headed his way. It would be both rude and cowardly to make her hunt for him, even if he really didn't want to be found. She was already worried about his mental state. Playing hide-and-seek would only complicate the issue.

He called out, "I'm over here."

Mooch arrived a few steps ahead of Callie. The dog made a complete circuit of the gazebo, nose to the ground, and then ran back out into the yard to check on the squirrel situation. Meanwhile, Callie took a seat on the opposite bench. Smart of her not to crowd him right now. He waved his hand in the air and shook his head.

"It wasn't all that long ago that I couldn't have told

you what a gazebo even was. Now I hang out in one. How weird is that?"

Callie laughed. It sounded a bit forced, but he figured she understood he was trying to lighten the moment. He made himself meet her gaze, hating the concern he saw reflected there. Trouble was, he was worried about himself, too. He cleared his throat and forced the words out.

"Sorry I lost my temper in the house. I'm a jerk sometimes. Lately, more often than not."

Her response was slow in coming. "I don't care about a little show of temper, Leif, but I am worried about you."

God, he hated this shit. Right now all he wanted to think about was rebuilding his leg and his life. He wanted to cut his hair, put on his uniform, and get back to the business of protecting the country. That was the life he'd chosen. It was all he knew. Without it, he would have to start over from scratch and figure out who else he could be.

The thought made his skin hurt.

What he wouldn't give to roll back the clock to that day in Afghanistan when his life went all to hell in the first place. Yeah, first up, he'd make Spence turn right instead of left. Or was it the other way around? He didn't care as long as whichever way they went would take them down a different street, one without an IED and a bunch of crazies trying to kill them.

But there were no effing do-overs in war. Hell, that last part was pretty catchy. Maybe he should have that tattooed on his shoulder, or maybe his ass.

"Leif!"

Had he said that out loud? Judging by the horrified look on Callie's face, that was éxactly what he'd done. Great "Sorry, Callie. Soldier humor can be pretty grim. Didn't mean to shock you. No tats for me. I hate needles too much. Ask Nick if you don't believe me." His cheeks flushed red. "I almost fainted the day I got all my vaccinations. Seriously. Only knowing how much crap Spence would've given me over it kept me upright and moving."

She looked marginally happier. "Yeah, I know how he is." Then she immediately grimaced and pounded her fists on her thighs. "Darn it. I meant to say I know how he *was*. God, Leif, why can't I ever get that straight?"

When her eyes filled with tears, Leif slid around the bench to the other side and put his arm around Callie's shoulders. "It's easy to forget because he was such a big part of our lives, Callie, and he still is. I see something that he'd get a kick out of and expect to hear him laugh or make some wiseass remark. All I get is silence."

His own eyes burned now. "Sometimes I miss him so damn much I want to punch something. But even if remembering what happened to him hurts like a bitch, forgetting him would be so much worse."

The two of them settled into a long silence. Leif cast about for some way to lighten the moment again.

"Let me think of a funny story about Spence. Most of them are R-rated, so it might take me a minute."

She punched his arm. "Hey, I'm a big girl. I can take it."

He shot her a quick grin. "Maybe I'm the one with delicate sensibilities."

Callie rolled her eyes. "Yeah, right."

"Okay, how about this one. We were in a fine drinking establishment a couple of nights before we were due to be deployed. The place catered to the military, so it was a combo crowd of army, navy, and marines."

She winced. "I bet that was a volatile mix."

"Don't you know it, especially with alcohol flowing freely. Anyway, Spence ended up in a game of darts with some hotshot marine. Someone came up with the brilliant idea that the loser would have to serenade the other guy and his buddies as well as buy them the next round. Nick and I hovered close by because we were sure it was going to end in a brawl."

He chuckled as he remembered that night. "Sure enough, Spence lost. No surprise there. Sober, I don't know anyone who could beat him at darts. Two beers, and he was all bluff and blunder. The marine kicked his ass in the game and then ordered Spence to pay up."

Callie looked far happier than she had a short time ago. "So what song did he sing?"

Leif stared up at the roof overhead and lost himself in the moment. "He sang 'Call Me Maybe.' Not only that, he danced around those marines like a lunatic, batting his eyes and holding his hand to his ear as if he really wanted them to call."

Leif pantomimed a few of Spence's better moves. "Then he ended his performance by kissing that marine on the cheek."

"Oh, God, tell me he didn't!"

By now, Callie was holding her sides as she laughed. The story wasn't all that funny, but they both needed the release.

As she wiped her eyes, she asked, "So how bad was the ensuing brawl?"

Ah, now that was another fond memory. The two groups had been evenly matched, so bruises and bloody knuckles all around. He played it down for Callie, although she probably saw through his ruse.

"Oh, not too serious. We ended up closing the place down with those guys. Spence and that marine even kept in touch afterward."

Someone else who had mourned his passing, but Leif didn't let that thought dampen his good spirits. It was time to move on. He realized he'd been hearing the distant sound of a vacuum cleaner in the background. The kid had really taken him seriously about the chores today.

"I'd better go check on Austin. We were going to do some housecleaning today, and I haven't lifted a finger to help him. He's making me look bad."

Callie followed him toward the house. "When you call Nick back, which you will be doing, be sure to tell him how hard Austin is trying. Maybe he won't worry so much."

"I'll tell him, but his talent for mothering those in his charge is part of what helped Nick earn those stripes he wears on his sleeve."

"Yeah, I know. I swear he'd wrap me in bubble wrap and keep me in a box if he could."

She didn't look at all upset about it, either. "You feel the same way about him."

"Yeah, well, that holds true for you, too. And speaking about worrying—"

He'd wondered when she would work the conversation back around to last night. "I'm fine, Callie. The woman in question and I came to an agreement on how to proceed from this point, so we're good. That's all I'm going to say on the matter."

Then there was the other thing. "Uh, just so you know, I have business in town this afternoon. Gage is making me attend a veterans' support group meeting as part of the deal we made the other night when he didn't throw my ass in a cell. It starts at three and lasts about two hours."

It was a relief when Callie didn't follow him up the steps. She stayed down on the ground, shading her eyes from the afternoon sun as she stared up at him.

"You might want to let Nick know what you're doing. Maybe he'd like to go, too, when he gets back, if you find it worthwhile. Either way, neither one of us wants to see you get hurt, Leif. I know you can take care of yourself, but that doesn't stop me from caring about what's going on in your life."

When he didn't immediately respond, she kept talking. "If you ever need to talk, I'm your gal. If you need someone to track this woman down and knock some sense into her, let me know. You don't want to wait until Nick's back to take care of that little chore. He lacks a certain talent for subtlety."

"You think?"

The image of Nick trying to be subtle wouldn't even begin to come into focus, but at least their conversation was ending with a laugh.

"Seriously, I'll keep all of that in mind. Now I think I'd better get to work. Gotta set a good example for the kid, you know."

Callie was already walking away. "Have fun with that."

Then she turned back. "I knew I was forgetting something. With the folks gone, I'm tired of cooking for one, so I'm going to bring over dinner tonight. Say about six?"

Leif countered her offer. "Better yet, let's go out. My treat and your choice of places. I'll pick you up at six."

"See you then."

Chapter 21

He liked that the sign marking the entrance to the church parking lot read ALL ARE WELCOME HERE. He hoped that was true.

As soon as he got out of the truck, he spotted a familiar figure. Damn it, he should've known Gage would be there to make sure he showed up. Leif hadn't called ahead to tell him because he'd been waffling right up to the last minute. He'd spent almost an hour trying to decide what to wear, worrying about his wardrobe decision like a teenage girl about to go on her first date.

A full uniform had seemed over the top, but he hadn't wanted to go completely civilian, either. He'd finally settled on jeans with one of his army T-shirts worn under a short-sleeved sport shirt. His combat boots provided one more connection to his other life, the one he hoped to get back to as soon as possible. The tops of his boots were hidden by his jeans, so there was nothing showing that said "soldier."

In the end, he'd left the shirt unbuttoned with his dog

tags hanging out where they could be seen. When he checked his image one last time, it had still looked wrong, out of focus somehow. Finally, after meeting his own frustrated gaze in the mirror, he decided his unkempt hair had to go. A quick buzz cut fixed the problem, leaving him running late but definitely feeling more like himself.

While it was a relief not to have to walk into the meeting alone, Gage's presence also eliminated any possibility of making a run for it. He slowly walked over to where the other man stood by a set of steps that led down to the basement of the small church. His speed had nothing to do with his injured leg and everything to do with how much he didn't want to do this.

Gage knew it, too. "Glad you came."

Leif shrugged. "It was even money that I wouldn't."

Instead of getting mad, Gage laughed. "Yeah, I felt that same way the first time I dragged my sorry ass down those steps."

Interesting. "So why did you?"

Gage stared past him. "Because my late wife offered me pretty much the same deal I offered you: Either I got help or else. Period. End of discussion."

He shook his head and smiled again. "For such a little thing, my wife sure could sure play hardball, but then she was right. I needed to talk to somebody who'd been there. She offered to listen herself, but she didn't need all that ugliness in her head, too. It was bad enough that I did. Still do, for that matter, but at least it's manageable now. Most of the time, anyway."

That wasn't exactly what Leif wanted to hear, but he should've known there were no easy fixes. His guilt over Spence's death coupled with the ongoing problems with his leg added up to a tangled mess that was bound to take a while to unravel. That is, if it could be done at all.

Three more vehicles pulled into the parking lot. Leif shifted restlessly. He'd have to meet the other members of the group eventually, but standing out here in the parking lot had him feeling exposed.

"Should we go in?"

Gage clapped him on the shoulder. "Yeah, let's. Jack Haliday, the pastor I told you about, prefers to meet with new members in his office before most of the others arrive."

Leif followed Gage down the steps and into a brightly lit room. It resembled one of the rooms at his mom's church, the kind of space that was used for everything from sleepovers for kids to meetings like the one he was heading into. The sense of familiarity helped ease some of his jitters.

Just after they walked through the door, a tall man with salt-and-pepper hair came into the room carrying a large coffee urn. As soon as he spotted Gage, he set it down and headed straight for them.

"Gage! It's been a while since we've had the pleasure of your company at a meeting."

Although he didn't phrase it as a question, Gage answered as if it had been. "I've been doing better lately, Jack. I'm really here to introduce my friend to you and some of the other guys. Reverend Jack Haliday, this is Corporal Leif Brevik."

The older man smiled and held out his hand. "Nice to meet you, Corporal. I'm glad you're here."

What could Leif say to that? He didn't want to lie, but neither was he happy to be there. He shook the man's hand and simply said, "Nice to meet you, sir."

To his surprise, the pastor laughed. "I'm pretty sure you don't really mean that, son, but that's okay."

His smile faded as more men filed into the room. He

lowered his voice. "Few of our members are here because they want to be, Corporal. They are here because they need to be. That's true for me as well. And please call me Jack. I'm not wearing just my pastor hat at these meetings."

Leif found himself warming to the minister. "I'm Leif."

"Well, Leif, let's grab a cup of coffee and then head into my office for a few minutes so I can get just a little information from you. It won't take long."

Gage rejoined the conversation. "I'll save you a seat next to me if you'd like."

Leif nodded, grateful for the lifeline Gage was offering him. "I'd appreciate that."

As he followed Jack down the hall, he couldn't resist one last look back to make sure Gage was still there. The lawman waved before turning away to talk to someone else. Leif hesitated outside the doorway to Jack's office, still not sure he wanted to do this.

The pastor didn't pressure him, but instead took a seat at his desk and gave Leif all the time he needed to decide for himself whether to come in. That little bit of control over the decision was enough to persuade him to move forward instead of retreating. One deep breath and he took that next step.

As Leif pulled out of the church parking lot, he waved back at several of the men who had been at the meeting. It had been a pleasant surprise to find out that he already had at least a nodding acquaintance with several of the members before the meeting.

Running into Clarence Reed had come as a bit of a surprise. Although Clarence's sweater vest, neatly ironed shirt, and bow tie didn't exactly fit the usual image of a marine, that's what he'd been. Then there were the two guys who'd vouched for Leif and Mitch's story after the fight at the bar. Leif had known they were former military but hadn't even considered the possibility that they'd be part of the group.

All in all, the experience wasn't nearly as painful as he'd expected. No one put any pressure on him to talk about his deployments other than to ask where he'd served. He'd gotten quite a kick out of listening to two old codgers who'd served in World War II. Despite some good-natured bickering over which one had seen more action, it was obvious the two shared a strong bond, forged in the hell they'd both lived through. He knew just how they felt. He'd enjoyed the same kind of iron-clad connection with Nick. Well, and with Spence.

There'd been a moment when one of the old warriors had mentioned a friend who'd died in the war. He'd paused to look around at the group with his faded blue eyes and a sad smile. "Damned if I don't miss his laugh even after all these years. Old Will was one helluva marine and a good friend. That's why I come here week after week. No one else understands, not like all of you do."

For a minute, the room had gone silent. Leif had no doubt that every man and woman in the place was thinking about someone in their own lives like Old Will. As sad as thinking about Spence made him feel, sharing that moment with the others had somehow lifted a little of the weight off of Leif's heart and let him smile at the memory of his lost friend.

As he drove down Main Street on his way back to the house, he recognized several people, who waved as he passed by. Bridey was standing outside her shop talking to a couple of older women, and Frannie was changing the list of specials on the chalkboard that hung outside the Creek Café. It occurred to him that, adding in the men at the meeting, somehow he'd started forging the kinds of personal connections that definitely made Snowberry Creek feel a bit like home. It had been years since he'd had any strong sense of belonging to any place or anyone outside of the military. He'd always kept his visits to his parents and their families blessedly brief. Other than them, there was very little that tied him to his hometown.

But when it came time to leave Snowberry Creek, he would miss both the town and the friends he'd made there. Speaking of whom, Callie would be waiting for him. He'd also forgotten all about Austin. He should probably invite the kid to tag along. He made a quick call and told Austin to wait for him at Callie's. He didn't know where Callie was thinking about going, but he'd have to remember to mention to Nick how much fun they'd had the next time he talked to him. Yeah, maybe that would be mean of him, but then what were friends for if not to give each other a hard time?

Past the outskirts of town, he gunned the big engine and hauled ass for the house. He found himself singing along with the song on the radio. As the song wound down, his smile faded a bit. He'd gone into the meeting expecting to hate it. There had definitely been some tough moments, like when a couple of the members had shared memories or the problems they were having coping with civilian life. But there was comfort in knowing there were others like him, especially ones who had made the journey and come out on the other side relatively whole. Hope was a precious gift.

Granted, it would be stupid to think that a single meeting would have a long-term effect on the problems he was having. He glanced at himself in the rearview mirror. Maybe it wouldn't hurt to hit a few more of them as long as he was around.

At least it was worth a shot. Maybe.

Zoe reluctantly followed Brandi into the crowded dining room at the Trillium Creek Lodge Although she had tried hard to come up with a believable reason that she needed to stay home alone on a Saturday night, her brain had fired nothing but blanks.

Clearly Brandi had been confident that she'd be able to coax her into going because she'd issued the invitation from the parking lot of Zoe's apartment complex. At least she'd given Zoe time to change clothes and put on a little makeup. An hour later, here they were, standing in a long line waiting for a table. Obviously, they weren't the only ones who hadn't wanted to cook tonight.

While they waited, Brandi indulged in her favorite hobby of people watching and making snide comments that kept Zoe laughing. They'd been there only a few minutes when Brandi went on point. Zoe looked around to see who had captured her attention. She had her answer when a deep voice said, "Hey, Brandi. How's it going?"

"Much better now that you're here, Corporal Brevik. Don't you think so, Zoe?"

God, she wanted to kill the woman. "Hi, Leif."

Brandi's enthusiasm faded a bit when she realized that he wasn't alone and that his companion was female. It was tempting to let her matchmaking friend think Leif was on a date, but that would be mean. "Hey, Callie, I don't believe you've met Brandi. She and I work together."

The two women shook hands. "It's nice to meet you, Brandi. I've heard a lot of good things about you."

Before her friend could respond, Zoe asked, "So, have you heard from Nick? How is that handsome guy of yours doing?"

Callie's smile faded just a bit. "Fine. The army is keeping him really busy, but at least he'll be back home to stay soon."

"That's really great. I know you're both counting the days."

Zoe hadn't noticed that there was a third member in their party until Callie completed the introductions. "Gosh, where are my manners? Zoe and Brandi, this is Austin Locke. He's recently hired on to work for Nick's new remodeling business."

The younger man nodded in Zoe's direction, but his focus was totally on Brandi. His interest was clearly not one-sided, either; her smile had brightened about two hundred percent. "Hey, why don't we see if we can't get a table big enough for all of us?"

Zoe knew all kinds of reasons why that wouldn't be a good idea, but Brandi didn't wait for anyone to express an opinion. She grabbed Austin's hand and dragged him with her to tell the hostess that they'd be needing a bigger table.

While Zoe chatted with Callie, she could feel Leif watching her every move. When their names were finally called, he followed close on her heels to the large circular booth in the distant corner of the restaurant. He stood back to let her slide in first, but then sat down right next to her, blocking the way for the others.

He gave everyone an apologetic look. "Sorry, but I need to be on this end to have room to stretch my leg out."

Callie had already entered the booth from the other end of the curved bench, effectively trapping Zoe next to Leif. Brandi sat on Callie's other side, and Austin took the other end position. Well, weren't they all one big happy family? With a barrage of conflicting emotions battling in her head, Zoe clutched the menu in her hands like a shield in the hope that no one, especially Leif, sensed how upset she was by this chance encounter.

How badly was he hurting? Had he had any further problems with his leg after last night? This wasn't the time or the place to be asking, but she couldn't help but worry. She certainly hadn't expected to run into him again so soon, especially when she still felt raw over everything that had happened between them.

Finally, she forced herself to concentrate on what to order, knowing the waiter would be back soon. She'd tell him what she wanted. He'd bring it. They'd all eat, and then they'd all go their separate ways. Step by step, she would get through this. Trying to sound more normal than she felt, she announced to no one in particular, "The halibut looks good."

There, one item off her list and closer to escaping this hyperawareness of the man sitting next to her.

Zoe clearly wasn't happy about their seating arrangement, but Leif hadn't lied. Well, not exactly. If she'd scooted to the middle of the booth, he would've followed right after her and not said a word about his leg. They'd agreed to stay away from each other, but it wasn't as if he'd planned this. Did she think he was any happier about this situation than she was? For her sake, he hoped that none of the others picked up on the thick layer of tension thrumming between the two of them. If Callie suspected, she hid it well.

Brandi had blindsided all of them with her suggestion that they share a table. At least right now most of her focus was on Austin. The poor guy probably didn't know what had hit him. Spiky white hair tipped in green wasn't Leif's taste as far as hair colors went, but he had to guess Austin had a different opinion on the subject since the kid kept sneaking peeks at Brandi and smiling. Good for him.

Zoe had finally laid her menu down. He leaned in closer than necessary to ask, "Want to split an appetizer? Callie says the crab cakes are great."

She swallowed hard and nodded. "Sure, why not?"

While everyone else was still studying the menus, he squeezed her hand and said, "I'm sorry. I know this is awkward, but we can handle it."

His mood improved considerably when she squeezed his hand in return. "Yeah, we can. Just wasn't expecting to see you again so soon."

Despite their agreement that right now he needed her medical expertise more than he needed her as a romantic partner, that didn't mean he didn't want more of what they'd shared last night. It took a helluva lot of effort just to look away from her. When he did, Callie was watching them, her expression worried as her gaze bounced back and forth between him and Zoe. So much for nobody noticing. When she realized he was aware of her scrutiny, she arched an eyebrow as if asking if he was all right.

He shrugged his shoulders and forced himself to relax against the back of the booth. In a town the size of Snowberry Creek, he and Zoe were bound to run into each other sooner or later. At least this way, they had the cushion of the others to help smooth over the initial awkwardness.

"Okay, so what's everyone having? Zoe and I are going to split an order of crab cakes, but I'd be glad to order more if anyone else is interested." On impulse, he announced, "Dinner's my treat, so order whatever you want."

As the food courses came and went, conversation became easier. Austin and Brandi discovered they knew some of the same people. Callie and Zoe talked about getting together at Something's Brewing. And then Austin got into a good-natured argument with all three women over the chances of the Seahawks to go all the way. Leif had no particular attachment to any of the local teams, but he added his own opinion to the mix just because.

When the waiter cleared away the last of the dinner plates, he asked about dessert. Predictably, all three women hemmed and hawed over whether they could risk the calories. Leif looked at Austin and rolled his eyes.

"I don't know about you, Austin, but I'm not leaving until I've had a huge helping of strawberry shortcake."

The kid's eyes lit up. "Yeah, I was thinking the same thing."

"We'll have two orders of the shortcake." Then Leif gave the women a hard look before adding, "And to be clear about it, we won't be sharing. Order your own or go without."

Callie looked at Brandi and then Zoe. "Either of you want to split an order?"

Brandi immediately accepted the offer. "I'd love to."

Zoe sighed dramatically. "Fine, I'll have the bread pudding, even if I'll hate myself in the morning."

The idea of two different desserts brought back memories of the night he and Zoe first met. A lot had happened since then, but he couldn't resist reminding her of when they'd shared dessert. When the waiter was gone,

Leif gave her a nudge with his shoulder. "I love bread pudding, too. Want to go halvsies on both?"

Zoe's mouth quirked up in a teasing smile. "But with one condition. This time, the last bites are mine."

He would've agreed to almost anything to see the shadows in her eyes disappear for even a few minutes. "It's a deal."

The waiter came back all too soon with their orders. It wouldn't be long before they ran out of excuses to linger in the restaurant. He and Zoe took turns taking bites from each other's plate, their time together disappearing along with the strawberry shortcake and bread pudding. When the bill came, Leif handed over his credit card despite the protests from both Callie and Zoe that they would pay their fair share.

He smiled at the waiter. "Ignore them."

After signing off on the bill, Leif twisted in the seat so that he could push up out of the booth without putting all his weight on his sore leg. He was uncomfortably aware of Zoe watching his every move, but he managed to stand up and walk without a problem. Out in the parking lot, Austin walked Brandi over to her car while Callie stopped to talk to Zoe. "I'll give you a call about meeting Bridey at her coffee shop. Maybe I can get Melanie Wolfe to join us while she's town to help with her father's estate."

"I'll look forward to it."

After the two women exchanged a quick hug, Callie walked away, leaving Leif alone with Zoe. He tugged her around the corner and out of sight of the others. There should be something he could say, but damned if he could think of a single thing that made sense. He settled for, "I guess I'll see you around."

She flinched as if his words hurt her, but what did she

expect? They'd both agreed that seeing each other outside of her office was a bad idea. "My next appointment is two weeks out."

Zoe nodded. "I know."

And speaking of bad ideas, sometimes you just had to throw the dice and live with the consequences. He gathered her into his arms and kissed her quickly, keeping it short and sweet. As they broke apart, caught between hunger and regret, he brushed a lock of hair back from her face. "Take care, Zoe."

"You, too, Leif."

As she walked away, he had to wonder how a simple kiss could taste so damn sad.

Chapter 22

🦋🦋

After a surprisingly good night's sleep, Leif spent most of the morning lounging on the couch and reading the Sunday paper. After an early lunch, his downtime came to an end. He and Mitch had both gotten a call from the mayor's office inviting them to be part of a work crew assigned to spruce up an elderly woman's yard. It didn't promise to be much fun, but it was better than hanging around the house and moping over Zoe.

He had been spending more time out of his boot lately, but he'd need it to get through the afternoon. After buckling it on, he grabbed his ball cap and sunglasses and headed outside to wait for Mitch. Austin was hanging out with Mooch on the front porch.

"I'll be back for dinner. I put out steaks to thaw, and the makings for a salad are in the fridge. I'll call you before I head back so you can get the coals started."

He half expected the kid to protest Leif's assumption that he would wait around for a call from him. But to his surprise Austin just said, "Okay."

When the roar of an engine signaled Mitch's arrival, Leif started down the steps. "Thanks for taking care of Mooch for me. I hate leaving him locked in the house all day."

"No problem. It's not like I have anything better to do."

Okay, it was nice to know the kid hadn't lost *all* of his attitude. Leif gave him back a little of his own. "Well, if you're that bored, you could always strip more of the wallpaper on the third floor. I just thought you might like an afternoon off."

Austin followed Leif down to the driveway. "Maybe Mooch and I will take a walk into town and grab some ice cream." He shuffled his feet and stared at the ground. "You know, with Brandi."

Good for him. "Have fun. Tell her hi for me."

Mitch pulled up in his convertible with the top down. He didn't look happy. "You could have warned me that your driveway was one gigantic rut!"

"Sorry," Leif said, even if he wasn't. "I thought I'd drive, assuming you wouldn't want a pile of dirty yard tools in the backseat of your car."

"Thanks for that."

"And you're welcome to stay for dinner when we get back. We're going to grill steaks. My man Austin here will have the grill all heated up and the beer chilled."

Mitch waved at the kid as the two of them climbed into the cab of the truck. "Sounds like a deal. Let's go pull these weeds I've been hearing so much about so we can move on to the good stuff."

It didn't take long to find the house where they were going to be working. He and Mitch grabbed the tools out of the truck and joined the cluster of people gathered in the front yard. It was a relief to see Gage was there. As soon as the police chief spotted them, he smiled and waved them over to where he was standing with a woman Leif hadn't seen before.

"Glad you could make it." Turning to his companion, he said, "Mayor McKay, you probably know Mitch Calder, and this is Leif Brevik. He's here in Snowberry Creek helping Callie Redding restore the old Lang place."

The mayor smiled at each of them in turn. "Nice to meet you, Leif. And Mitch, it's been a while. I'd love for you to meet my son if you have the time."

Mitch shook her hand. "Coach asked me to stop by and help out at practice this next week. I've sure heard great things about your son and how well the team is doing this year."

His comments clearly pleased her. "I'll tell Colby you'll be by. He'll be excited."

She looked around. "Looks like everyone is here, so we should get started."

Within minutes, the mayor had everyone organized and working. Leif and Mitch were assigned to prune a row of bushes, a job Leif could do without a lot of bending or lifting. He dropped a handful of cuttings into the five-gallon bucket they'd been given. "That woman would've made a great drill sergeant."

Mitch laughed. "Yeah, although I was thinking offensive line coach."

About thirty minutes in, a woman with white hair and a sweet smile slowly made her way across the yard to where they stood. She had a pair of heavily loaded plastic bags tied to the front of her walker.

"You boys are so nice to be here helping today. You looked like you could use a cold drink." As she held out a bottle of water to each of them, she stared hard at Leif. "I know Mitch here. I had him in my English class back when I was teaching, but I don't think you and I have met. I'm Maggie Shaw."

"No, ma'am, we haven't. I've only been in Snowberry Creek for a few weeks. I'm staying at Spence Lang's house." Leif twisted the top off his bottle. "Thank you for this."

"I heard about Spence. He was always a bit wild, but a good boy at heart. I always enjoyed having him in my class." She glanced down at Leif's left leg. "I'm guessing you got that while serving with him."

It still felt odd to meet all these people who'd known Spence as a kid. "Yeah, I did. We were deployed three times together."

"Thank you for your service to our country, Leif. I bet your folks are proud of you." She lifted up the second bag. "I may not be as good at gardening as I used to be, but there's nothing wrong with my ability to bake. Help yourself."

Leif peeked into the bag and grinned. "Brownies! My favorite."

She beamed with pleasure. "Take two, then. I have plenty more in the house."

Mitch shouldered him aside and cranked up his grin a notch. "Ms. Shaw, it's a pleasure to see you again. You're looking good."

She rolled her faded blue eyes. "Mitch, I didn't fall for your charm back then, and it won't work now. However, since you're being kind enough to help me out, you can have two as well."

Mitch laughed and leaned in close enough to kiss the elderly woman on the cheek. "You always were my favorite teacher, maybe because you didn't put up with any of my sh— uh, my antics."

Maggie chuckled. "Good catch, Mitch. Well, I'd better

keep moving. Let me know if you need anything else, gentlemen."

Leif went back to pruning but kept an eye on her progress as she moved from one volunteer to the next. Mitch glanced in her direction. "She's something, isn't she? I was serious about what I said. No one got away with anything in her class, but she was fair and really taught us a lot. Thanks to her, I still cringe when I hear someone confuse 'less' and 'fewer' when they're talking."

He smiled and went back to work. "If we had to spend our afternoon sweating in the sun, I'm glad it's to help her out."

Leif agreed. Gage had said they only had to show up once to make up for the night they'd gotten into that bar fight, but it was nice to be doing something worthwhile. Part of the reason he'd joined the army was his need to serve. Trimming bushes might not be the same as patrolling the streets of Afghanistan, but it was still satisfying.

Mitch picked up their full bucket. "I'll go dump this, but you keep working. If we don't look like we're doing our fair share, Ms. Shaw won't come by with another bag of those brownies you like so much."

"Yeah, bite me, Calder."

But just in case Mitch was right, Leif kicked it into high gear.

It was a long five hours, but the volunteer crew had made quite a difference in the yard. Maggie made a point of thanking everyone and even hugged Mitch when she got to him. She moved on to the mayor.

"Rosalyn, thank you again for setting this up. I can't believe how nice everything looks out here, and they even finished all the work inside, too. Let me know if there's anything I can do to help next time you set up a work party like this."

"I will, Ms. Shaw. I'm just glad we could help."

Leif nodded at both women as he carried his tools back to the truck. Mitch had stopped to talk to the father of an old friend, so Leif leaned against the side of the truck and waited. The rest of the volunteers waved as they drove away, even calling him by name. His list of connections here in Snowberry Creek was growing by leaps and bounds.

He'd just turned to wave back at Mr. Reed when he realized Maggie was making her way to where he stood. He stepped forward to save her having to come that far. "Was there something you needed, Ms. Shaw?"

She shook her head and held out a bag. "I bundled up a few more of the brownies for you, Leif. "

He accepted the gift with a smile. "I'd say you shouldn't have, but I try not to lie."

She laughed. "Enjoy those and stop by anytime. I'd love to make my special chicken potpie for you sometime."

"I'd enjoy that, although I don't know how long I'll be here in Snowberry Creek. The army might have plans for me."

"Well, if you do get a chance, just give me a call. I put my number in the bag. If you don't, stay safe, soldier."

That was easier said than done, but he settled for saying, "I'll do my best, ma'am."

" And when it comes time to put down some roots, you won't find a better place to live than right here in Snowberry Creek."

"You know, I think you might just be right about that."

"Good. Now go enjoy the rest of your day. I'm sure

you have better things to do with your time than standing around gabbing with me."

Leif winked at her. "That's not true. There's nothing better than hanging around with an attractive, intelligent woman."

She laughed. "You're as bad as that rascal Mitch."

The football player had just walked up beside her. "Did I hear my name being bandied about?"

Maggie turned her smile in his direction. "Yes, you did. It was nice to see you, Mitch. I've been following your career. Even had you on my fantasy team. Now take your friend here and go do something fun."

"Will do. And you take care, Ms. Shaw."

"I always do, Mitch. I always do."

Leif and Mitch got into the truck, but he waited until she safely reached her front door before starting the engine. "Nice lady, but I'm ready for those steaks."

He flipped open his phone and hit Austin's number on speed dial. "Hey, kid, we're on the way. Get those coals burning because we're coming home hungry."

Zoe traced the name on the patient file for her next appointment with her fingertip: Leif Brevik. Her heart lurched in her chest, aching to see him and hating the thought of it in equal measure.

It had been a long two weeks. Except for that chance meeting at the restaurant, they hadn't spoken since That Night. For her, the words were even capitalized in her mind because those precious few hours with Leif in her bed carried so much weight that the words should as well.

What about Leif? Had he emerged unchanged by the experience? It sure appeared so. The few times she'd dared to check on him as he and Mitch Calder had worked out under Isaac's careful eye, Leif had been laughing and joking around with the other two men. If he'd been aware of her watching him, he'd given no sign of it.

Any second now Brandi would announce his arrival. That had her up and moving toward the door, stopping to check her appearance in the small mirror on the wall. The best she could say was that she looked neat and professional. In other words, plain. Maybe she should've left her hair down. When her hand strayed toward the clip, she jerked it back down to her side. This was ridiculous.

Leif didn't care about how she wore her hair. Her looks didn't matter to him now; only her training and skills did. She ran her hands across her hair, making sure it was all tidy. Good enough.

"A bit of lipstick would give you some color. I could loan you mine if you left yours at home."

Great. Brandi had caught her primping. Zoe flinched and turned her back on the woman in the mirror. "No thanks, Brandi. I'm pretty sure black lipstick isn't my color."

Her assistant laughed. "True enough, but I happen to have this other one with me."

She tossed the tube toward Zoe, giving her no choice but to catch it. Not that she was interested in putting any on. Still, her curiosity demanded she at least check out the color. One look and the battle was lost. It was the perfect shade for Zoe's coloring, not to mention how well it went with the blouse she had on.

She gave Brandi a suspicious look. "You went out at lunch and bought this for me, didn't you?"

Brandi didn't bother to deny it. Instead, she shot Zoe an impish grin. "It's no biggie. They were having a two-for-one sale." She giggled. "You should have seen the look on the lady's face when I bought that one and then a tube of green for myself. I told her I had multiple personality disorder and my other half was boring and conservative."

Feeling vaguely insulted, Zoe was tempted to lob the lipstick back at her younger friend. On the other hand, insulting or not, there was a grain of truth in Brandi's assessment. Other than those few fleeting moments with Leif, Zoe's life *was* boring and had been for way too long. Outside of work and household chores, there wasn't much else in it.

She turned back to the mirror and put the lipstick to use. Well, what do you know? The little bit of color did do wonders for her looks and her mood. "There. Are you happy?"

"Happi*er*, but that lipstick is just a start. For sure your blouse is a definite improvement over your usual office attire. Progress is being made, but we have a long way to go, lady."

Brandi stepped out of the room and pointed down the hall with a great flourish. "Next up, I suggest you try out that lipstick on the handsome guy down the hall in room three. Go get him, tiger."

That lurching feeling was back in Zoe's chest, but it was time to face the music—and the man who had haunted both her daylight hours and her midnight dreams for far too long. Putting off the encounter even another few seconds would serve no purpose other than to stir up more acid in her stomach.

She marched down the hall with Leif's chart that contained Isaac's latest report on his progress. A couple of other patients on their way out passed her and smiled. Zoe knew them both and normally would've stopped to chat. Not today. She needed to keep moving; she wasn't sure she could get started again if she stopped now.

After rapping on the door of the examination room, she paused to listen for Leif's response. It wasn't long in coming.

"I'm here."

Taking a deep breath, Zoe stepped into the room. How had she never noticed it was barely bigger than a closet? Of course, maybe that had more to do with the size of the man standing in the center of the floor, taking up far more space than he should have.

"Leif."

"Zoe."

Okay, this shouldn't have to be this awkward. She tried again. Motioning to the bench behind him. "Why don't you have a seat?"

When he got settled, she pulled her stool toward the opposite wall and sat down as well. "So, how are you feeling today? How's the leg?"

"Fine."

Yeah, right. If that was true, why the dark circles under his eyes, not to mention the gray cast to his skin? He'd also phoned in a request a few days ago for a refill on his pain meds. She called him on the lie.

"Leif, we've already established that I can't help you if I don't know what's wrong."

He smiled softly and shook his head. "Yeah, yeah, I know."

Leif leaned forward to rest his elbows on his thighs and pinched his nose as if his head hurt. He stared down at the floor for the longest time. Rather than press him for an immediate answer, Zoe waited him out, giving him all the time he needed. Besides, with Leif, pushing him too hard would likely give her the opposite result of what she wanted.

Finally, he leaned back and stared at her, his eyes

hooded and dull. "Okay, yeah, I hurt. At least a seven on your scale, so why don't we start with you telling me what you think of Isaac's report?"

There was no use in trying to sugarcoat it for him. Straight-up honesty would go a lot further with Leif. "The numbers aren't worse, but certainly not a lot better."

"So I'm screwed."

"How so?"

"Because I've done the exercises until I'm blue in the face. Every morning. Every night. And for all that effort, I get nothing."

Zoe hated seeing him look so defeated. It made her want to hug the man and tell him it would all be okay. But she knew the last thing he wanted right now was to be coddled and told a pack of lies.

"Okay, you've told me what you've been doing right. What have you been doing wrong?"

He jerked back as if she'd hit him with a pitcher of ice water. "What the hell's that supposed to mean?"

"I mean exactly what I said. What else have you been doing that might have aggravated the injury?"

His reaction was immediate and furious. "You mean other than having wild monkey sex with you?"

At least he kept his voice down to an angry growl. She supposed she should be grateful for even that much. She hated the fact that she was blushing, but she would power through this somehow. "Yes, Leif, other than that. Any more episodes like that one? If so, what were you doing that might have triggered it?"

"Yes, I've had several smaller episodes and a couple of bigger ones, but none as bad as what happened that night when I . . . when we were . . . Hell, you know what I mean."

Yeah, she did. Her cheeks were flaming now, but she did her best to sound more in control than she felt. "And what did you do when it happened?"

"I was able to walk it off like you would any other charley horse."

Then he smirked just a little. "And although you didn't ask, I wasn't having wild monkey sex at the time. That only happened with you. The next bad cramp hit when I'd been watching television and went to get up because I needed to take a leak."

Zoe kept writing without looking up. If he'd expected to shock her with his comments, he was bound to be disappointed. She hoped he couldn't tell how relieved she was. They'd agreed not to see each other again. That didn't mean she was ready to hear that he'd already charmed his way into someone else's bed.

"And the second time?"

"I'd been vacuuming the downstairs of the house. I was using one of those lightweight models. I hardly worked up a sweat pushing it around."

She pulled out the physical therapy report and quickly reviewed it again. Isaac's remarks had ended with the comment that he thought maybe Leif would benefit from a consultation with either an orthopedic doctor or a neurologist. She agreed with her friend's assessment. She stared at the paper, wishing like heck she had something more positive to offer Leif.

"Come on, Zoe, tell me. Not knowing is a helluva lot worse than hearing the bad news. Give it to me straight up. I can handle it."

She hoped so. Her decision made, she set his chart aside and rolled her stool closer to him. "Isaac suggested, and I agree, that we should have a couple of specialists evaluate your case."

His eyes flared wide. "Two different doctors? Is it that bad?"

"Not necessarily. One is a bone specialist and the other is a nerve specialist, so they approach this kind of case from different perspectives. I'm hoping the combination of their input will give us a clearer picture of what's going on."

Leif sighed, but nodded. "God, I hate doctors. No offense."

"None taken. Besides, I'm not a doctor, which is another reason I think this is a good idea. I could ask Dr. Tenberg to review your case, but he's a family practitioner."

There was so much more she wanted to ask him. Did he hurt as much as she did? Yet now wasn't the time. "With your permission, I'll have Brandi set you up with someone local."

"What choice do I have? I can't hang out here in Snowberry Creek forever."

Did he have to sound so darn anxious to leave? Not that she'd given him any real reason to stay. She realized he was still talking. "I'm sorry, Leif. I didn't catch that last part."

"I asked if I should keep seeing Isaac until I can get in to see the doctors?"

"It couldn't hurt. Despite the lack of improvement in flexibility, your leg did improve in strength."

"That's something, I guess."

When she reached to open the door, he asked, "What about you? How have you been doing? You know, since we last saw each other?"

What did he want her to say? What good would it do either of them for her to admit how much she hurt, how much she missed him?

"Fine."

Leif actually laughed. When she glanced back at him, there was a devilish twinkle in his dark eyes. "You know, as a wise woman once told me, I can't help you if I don't know what's wrong."

If she was drawn to Leif when he was hurting, he was even more irresistible when he was being charming. "On scale of one to ten, I'm a five."

He called her on it. "Liar. Tell me I'm not the only one with big-time regrets."

"Okay, Leif, I have regrets, but nothing has changed. You want out of Snowberry Creek, and I don't want to be anywhere else. My days of being somebody's good time on R&R are long over. I've got more pride than that."

Oops. Wrong thing to say. Leif was up and heading right for her, his dark eyes blazing with fury. She quickly pushed the door closed and braced herself against it.

Leif crowded close enough that she could feel the heat radiating off his big body even through all the layers of clothing between them. He was breathing as hard as if he'd hiked a mile to reach her.

"Don't you dare insult what we had, Zoe. I've never once acted as if you were just a good time on Saturday night. It meant more to me than that. If it hadn't, I wouldn't be hurting like this."

He was right. "I'm sorry, Leif. You're right. I shouldn't have said that."

"Damn straight." He leaned in closer. "To make up for it, have dinner with me."

God, she wanted to say yes. Maybe even open the door and shout it loud enough for everyone in the clinic to hear. "Leif, we've already agreed—"

He shut her up with a finger across her lips. "You're

turning my case over to the specialists. From there, who knows where they'll send me? They might ship my ass back east to the doctors who did the last surgery on my leg. We both know my time here is limited, and I hated—HATED—the way our last time ended. I wanted another chance with you. Besides, we're both miserable apart. We might as well be miserable together."

Then he replaced his finger with his lips, reminding her even more clearly how much she loved the way he kissed. "Will you have dinner with me tomorrow night?"

"One question."

"One, and then you have to answer mine."

"Is 'Hey, baby, let's be miserable together' the best pickup line you have? Because if that's your best shot, soldier, it's no wonder you're lonely."

He twirled a strand of her hair around a finger. "Maybe over the course of three deployments my flirting skills have gotten rusty. If you let me practice on you, I might come up with something better."

"Well, I guess I have to have dinner with you, then. Not for my own selfish reasons, of course, but for the sake of all the women in the world who deserve better than an offer to get miserable with you."

He kissed her again, keeping it light and easy, but maybe with a promise of more to come.

"To be clear, Leif: No strings. No promises. Just two people enjoying each other for the short term. That's the deal. It has to be."

Because he needed to get his life back on track, and she still carried too much baggage from her past.

His smile faded briefly, but then he slowly nodded. "Deal."

She ignored the niggling feeling that she was letting something precious slip right through her fingers. Rather than dwell on it, she made a determined effort to keep the moment light.

"Now back off, big guy, so I can find Brandi and get her to make those calls for you."

He obliged her. "I'll pick you up at six thirty tomorrow evening. Wear something"—he paused to give her a slow once-over—"slinky, and we'll go someplace special in Seattle. I'm in the mood for a good steak and maybe a little dancing afterward."

Her eyes automatically went to his cane, but for once he didn't get mad. Instead, he gave her a wicked smile and said, "Slow dancing, the kind where we're all tangled up together on the dance floor, moving slow and holding on tight, because I'm definitely up for that."

She suspected he wasn't talking about the effect dancing might have on his leg, but she didn't dare ask or look for herself. Instead, she bolted out the door. Out in the hall, she stumbled to a halt after only a few steps. That damn man had her so twisted up in knots she couldn't remember what she needed to do next.

A movement down by the receptionist's desk caught her attention. Brandi was chatting with one of the other medical assistants. As soon as she spotted Zoe, she headed right for her.

"Did you need something?"

"Yes, I want Corporal Brevik to see these two doctors."

She handed over the chart. "Tell them that we need the appointments as soon as possible. If there's a problem getting him in, let me know. I'll do some serious arm-twisting if I have to."

"Will do. Your next patient is in room one."

"Thanks, Brandi."

"No problem, but before you go in there, you might want to fix your lipstick. It's a bit smeared."

She leaned in close to add, "If I didn't know better, I would think you've been making out with a patient."

Busted. There was no use in denying it. Brandi wouldn't believe her anyway. "Thanks for the advice. Now go make those calls."

Brandi executed a salute and snapped her heels together. "Yes, ma'am. And I promise not to notice if Corporal Brevik is wearing the same shade of red."

"Brat!"

"Yes, ma'am, I am."

Feeling better than she had all day, Zoe only laughed and dutifully headed into the restroom, already reaching for her new lipstick.

Chapter 23

On the drive back home, Leif's mood bounced all over the place. Having to see specialists meant both Isaac and Zoe were concerned about his lack of progress. That made three of them. It was a bitch living in limbo and pretending to both his friends and himself that his leg was improving. He hated the lies and not knowing from one minute to the next if his leg would support him, not to mention the crippling pain.

It was getting worse, too. If Zoe thought the two specialists would be able to give him some definitive answers, he'd drag himself to see them. Maybe Callie would go with him, although he hated to give her something else to worry about.

Brandi had managed to pull some strings and gotten him in to see both specialists on Monday, one in the morning and the other late in the afternoon. It would make for one long, crappy day, but at least it was progress. He'd been afraid that he would have to wait weeks just to get an appointment. As much as he dreaded hearing what they had to say, he still had to find out for certain what was going on with his ankle and leg.

Finally, he tried concentrating on happier thoughts, like his dinner date with Zoe tomorrow night.

When he pulled into the driveway, the first thing he noticed was that Austin's truck was missing. Normally that would be no biggie, but they had plans to meet Mitch for a burger at the Creek Café before heading for the bar and a few games of pool.

Maybe Austin had left him a note. Leif walked into the kitchen and looked around. Nothing. Had he missed a call from him? No, no message. Perhaps Callie knew something. Too restless to sit down, Leif limped the length of the kitchen and back while he waited for her to answer.

"Hey, Callie, I was wondering if you'd seen Austin today."

"No, I haven't." She sounded more puzzled than worried. "Is there a problem?"

Not that he could prove. "No, I just thought he and I were supposed to meet up after my appointment at the clinic. We probably got our wires crossed."

There was a brief silence from the other end of the conversation. "How did it go with your checkup? And don't bother denying you were expecting bad news."

Okay, so he hadn't done as good a job of hiding his worry from her as he'd hoped. "Zoe is sending me to see a couple of specialists on Monday. It's not a big deal. She just wants their opinion on my progress, since this kind of injury isn't her specialty."

That much was true. The bit about it being no big deal, not so much.

"I'm going with you, Leif, and no arguments. Got that?"

He surrendered without a fight. "I'd appreciate the company. I do have to warn you that it will be a long day."

"Not a problem." After giving her the times, he added, "Now I'd better go. Thanks, Callie."

"No so fast, mister. Let me know if there's a problem with Austin."

Damn, the woman was a bloodhound when it came to picking up on potential trouble. "I will. Like I said, it's probably just a misunderstanding."

"Did you try calling him?"

Well, duh, now that would've been a smart idea. "That's next on my list. It should've been first."

There was one more thing. "And, Callie, when you talk to Nick, don't tell him about the appointments on Monday. There's no use in worrying him until I know more. Okay?"

"Yeah, but don't keep him out of the loop for long. I don't like hiding things from him."

"I promise to tell him, but not until I know something definite. Talk to you later."

After he disconnected the call, he immediately hit Austin's number on speed dial. Maybe he was overreacting, but he trusted his gut feeling that something wasn't right. It rang several times before Austin picked up.

"Hey, kid, what's going on? I thought we had plans."

There was a brief silence. When Austin finally spoke, there was an odd note in his voice. "Sorry, Leif. I meant to call. I won't be able to go with you tonight. Something's come up."

His tone was careful, as if he were hoping to sound far calmer than he actually was. What the hell was going on?

"What kind of something? And don't try to bullshit me, Austin. It won't work. Just lay it out plain."

Nothing but silence, which set off major alarms in Leif's head.

"Tell me where you are, kid. I'll come."

"No, don't. You shouldn't get mixed up in this, Leif." His voice wasn't much more than a rough whisper.

Son of a bitch. He needed to find the kid so they could sort out whatever mess he'd gotten himself into.

"Damn it, I said I'm coming, and I meant it, Austin. Don't make me call Gage Logan to hunt you down. If you can't come here, then let me come to you."

More silence but at least he hadn't hung up. That was something. Finally, Austin spoke again.

"I'll try to meet you at that place where I had coffee while you talked to my landlord. If I'm not there in an hour, forget you ever met me. Maybe you should anyway."

When the line went dead, Leif hustled his ass back out to the truck and tore out of the driveway in a spray of gravel. What the hell had that fool kid gotten himself caught up in this time? If there'd been any sign of something worrying him, Leif had clearly missed it. And why hadn't Austin come to him in the first place?

That was easy. Austin had had to scrape and scramble for what little he had, and even then his own father had stolen half of it. Even though Gage, Callie, Leif, and even the judge had reached out to help him, trust wouldn't come easy to the kid.

On the way through town, Leif passed the police department. Should he stop long enough to talk to Gage? No, not until he knew what was going on and how bad it was. Knowing the police chief, he'd insist on riding shotgun. And Austin would probably bolt the second he saw him. He would also see it as a betrayal on Leif's part. If Leif wanted Austin to trust him at all, he had to go alone.

On the other hand, depending on what kind of trouble Austin was in, they might need Gage's help in a hurry. Damn, he hated situations where there was no clear path. All he could do was march forward and hope for the best.

He drove into the parking lot next to the coffee shop, but there was no sign of the kid or his truck. At least if Austin did show, he'd know going in that Leif had made good on his promise to come running. That had to count for something.

Inside, Leif ordered a tall drip for himself and a second one for Austin. He added in three sandwiches in case Austin hadn't eaten, either. After staking out a table in the back corner, Leif ate his sandwich and sipped his coffee. As the time dragged on, he began to seriously regret not calling Gage.

The deadline came and went. He'd give Austin another fifteen minutes and then call in the cavalry. And while he was thinking about it, he also needed to call Mitch to cancel.

Just after he hung up, the door of the coffee shop opened. Leif breathed a sigh of relief when he recognized Austin. He waved to get his attention. It spoke volumes that the kid looked both surprised and relieved to see that Leif was still there.

It had started raining outside, and Austin's clothes were dripping wet. Where had he left his truck? There was no way he'd have gotten that soaked just crossing the parking lot. He looked younger than ever as he shuffled toward the table with his hands shoved in his front pockets and his shoulders slumped. The ragged sweatshirt he was wearing was two sizes too big for his slender frame, and he had the hood up and cinched down around his face. Clearly he didn't want to be recognized.

Who the hell was Austin hiding from? Leif cradled his

coffee with both hands and waited, but right now he wanted to track down whoever put that defeated look in Austin's eyes and put some serious hurt on them.

Austin slid into the other side of the booth. Before he could say a word, Leif shoved the two remaining sandwiches across the table. "Eat. Then we'll talk."

From the way Austin wolfed down the first sandwich, Leif had been right to buy two. At the rate he was working on the second one, maybe he should've given all three to the kid. Austin finally slowed down and washed down one final bite with the last of his coffee. He gave Austin a few seconds for his meal to settle and then launched his opening salvo.

"Okay, lay it all out for me. Start at the beginning and finish with you walking in that door over there. I want details, not excuses. When you're done talking, we'll figure out where to go from here."

He did his best to sound like Nick when he was dealing with raw recruits who'd managed to screw up bigtime. No anger, but at the same time making it clear that no bullshit would be tolerated.

Austin stared out through the window rather than looking Leif in the eye, his body twitching just enough to make Leif think he might bolt at any second. The only thing that was probably keeping him rooted to the spot was that he was more afraid of someone out there than he was of Leif.

"Come on, Austin. It's just the two of us. Talk."

Slowly some of the tension drained out of Austin's body as he sagged against the back of the booth. "It's my dad. He's got himself in big trouble. If I don't do what he wants, they'll come after him."

That figured. The old bastard had his hooks into Austin good and solid. "Tell me more."

"He got in too deep with a local loan shark."

For the first time, Austin looked as disgusted as Leif felt about the situation. "I told him all along that we'd never get rich off of Spence, but my old man has a real talent for spinning a good story. Evidently, he borrowed money from the wrong guy and promised to pay it back when Spence's estate was settled."

He averted his gaze. "I swear, Leif, I never knew anything about this. I just knew my old man kept pressuring me to steal more and more stuff from the house. I thought he wanted money for liquor, but apparently he was using every penny to keep these guys off his back. Now, because that source of money has dried up, he's in big trouble."

"What is it he wants you to do?"

"Dad said they'd back off for a while if I start making regular payments on his debt. But I don't make enough to make a dent in how much he owes. He claims I need to make one big score off the stuff in Spence's house and then the two of us can leave town for good.

"I signed my truck over to him to sell to buy us some time, but it won't hold them off for long." Austin picked up a napkin and began tearing it into little pieces. "Dad put me on the phone with the guy. He said I could make some quick cash running drugs for a friend of his."

Austin gave his old man his truck? How the hell did the kid think he'd get around now? And dollars to dimes, the old man would pocket the cash with no intention of using it for anything other than cheap booze and cigarettes.

Leif already knew the answer to his next question, but he asked it anyway. "Did it occur to you to let your old man take care of his own problems? You almost went to prison once because of this kind of crap. You get caught running drugs, and you won't breathe fresh air until you're old and gray."

Austin's voice cracked as he pounded his fist on the table. "I know that, but at least I'd live long enough to walk out of prison. If my old man got busted for selling drugs, he'd die in there."

There was no denying the truth in that, but there had to be another option. "I want you to call Gage Logan and tell him what's going on. I promise I'll stand beside you every inch of the way, but he's the only one who has a chance in hell of helping you now."

Austin was already shaking his head, but Leif wasn't going to lose this fight. Not now. Not ever. This kid was worth saving.

"One way or another, you know the cops are going to get involved. Better that it's a time of your own choosing."

He pushed his cell phone across the table to Austin. "His number is ten on speed dial."

When Austin picked it up, Leif crossed his fingers and prayed Gage could come through for them one more time.

Three hours later it was all over. Gage had enlisted the help of the police in the town where Vince lived. Together, they'd come down hard on him and rattled his cage but good. It hadn't taken much to have him admitting that he'd made up the whole story about the loan shark. He'd slipped an old drinking buddy of his a twenty to sound threatening on the phone, hoping that would scare Austin into robbing Spence's house one last time.

The old man was currently cooling his heels in the county jail. Leif didn't know what they'd charge the bastard with, and he didn't give a rip. He was worried about

Austin, though. The kid hadn't spoken more than a handful of words since they got back to the house.

Leif poured each of them a shot of whiskey, figuring the occasion called for something stronger than his usual root beer. He handed Austin one and then eased himself down in the chair and propped his leg up on the ottoman. He sipped the whiskey and enjoyed the slow burn as it slid down his throat.

To his surprise, Austin started to take a drink, but then firmly set the small glass on the coffee table. He leaned back and closed his eyes briefly, all the while softly stroking Mooch's fur. "Thanks for the drink, but considering my family history, it's best I stay away from the stuff permanently."

Leif was impressed and said so. Then he added, "I'm sorry about your dad, kid. He's a real piece of work, but that doesn't make it easy to forget he's your father."

Something had changed in the hours since they'd left the coffee shop with Gage. When Austin looked at Leif, he no longer looked like the same kid. There was a new maturity in his gaze that hadn't been there before. Leif had seen the same kind of transformation in young soldiers after their first skirmish with the enemy. It was like the evil in the world finally held real meaning for them.

"He's my father in a biological sense, but that's all. I won't let him pull me down with him. Not again. Unless by some miracle he gets his act straight, he's dead to me."

Leif wasn't sure that was the healthiest attitude to take, but maybe Austin would eventually find some middle ground. However, if it kept him from trusting the old man, it would save the kid a lot of heartache.

"Gage said he'd see what he could to get Vince into a long-term rehab program."

Austin's laugh had nothing to do with humor. "Do you honestly think that will work?"

Leif wasn't about to lie to Austin. The kid had had enough of that in his life. "Maybe not, but you'll feel better knowing that he's being given every chance to change the way he is. That's what counts."

Pointing to the whiskey, Austin whispered, "I don't want to end up like him, but I don't know how to keep that from happening."

He focused on Mooch, as if making sure the dog was listening. "Nobody around here sees me as *me*. At best, they see the high school dropout. At worst, they only see Vince Locke's son. You know, like father, like son, and all that crap."

With few exceptions, that was probably true. "Then set your sights on getting the hell out of Snowberry Creek. Maybe not permanently, but long enough to give people a chance to see you in a new light."

"Got any suggestions on how I do that? My options are pretty limited right now, especially with Gage Logan breathing down my neck."

"Yeah, I do. While you're working for Nick, you can start earning your GED."

Leif reached for his laptop and powered it up. After a quick search, he scanned the information, then shared the basic facts with Austin.

At least Austin didn't immediately reject the idea. From the way he was frowning, he was definitely thinking hard about something. "Or maybe I could enlist in the military and let them train me."

For the first time all night, Leif had a good reason to be smiling. "Maybe you could at that, kid. If you decide that's what you want, both me and Nick will be glad to help you figure out which branch of the service offers what you're looking for, and we'll go from there. Just know we're both prejudiced on the subject."

He raised his fist and shouted, "Go, Army!"

It sounded good to hear Austin laugh. Leif held out the laptop. "There, start reading over what they have to say about the program. Figure out when and where to register, and we'll get you signed up."

Austin acted as if the computer would bite him, but at least he took it. "I already told you that school and I don't get along. What if I can't pass the test?"

How to answer that one? Nothing in Austin's past would convince him that he could succeed at anything, especially not school.

"Austin, you're smart enough to know you want more out of life than what you have right now. Guts and determination go a long way in this world. Besides, you won't be doing this alone. You'll have Callie, Nick, and me helping you. Gage Logan, too, for that matter. So get to reading while I go call in an order for pizza, and I'll invite Callie and Mitch over, too. It's time to turn this evening into a celebration."

Austin didn't look opposed to the idea, just confused. "What are we celebrating?"

Leif laid it all out for him in just a few words. "A future with possibilities."

Feeling better all around, he left the kid grinning and shaking his head and headed for the kitchen to make those phone calls.

Chapter 24

On Saturday morning Zoe had enlisted Brandi's aid in shopping for something to wear on her big date with Leif that night. Although the younger woman's taste ran in a far different direction than Zoe's, she needed her friend's moral support. Besides, if Brandi could pick out the perfect lipstick for Zoe, surely she could assist in the hunt for a dress that would fit Leif's request for "slinky."

But now Zoe stared at herself in the triple mirror and wasn't sure that she'd been right about that. She did a little shimmy and watched the flirty skirt twirl around her legs. The deep blue of the fabric held hints of silver and shifted in color as it moved. She had to admit the color brought out her eyes, but it also accentuated other parts of her anatomy that she wasn't so comfortable having on display. The front was cut low, and the back was almost missing in its entirety.

Brandi stepped back into the fitting room just as Zoe almost succumbed to full-out panic.

"Maybe I should try on something else."

Zoe studied the three dresses hanging on the dressing room wall. When she reached for the sensible black number, Brandi staged a preemptive strike, grabbed the hanger out of Zoe's hand, and tossed it over the door.

"No way you're settling for that. Not when the dress you have on is perfect, Zoe."

She stood with one hand behind her back, no doubt hiding something else she wasn't sure Zoe would like. "Admit it. You look hot in that one. It's even on sale, so you can't complain about the price." Brandi's smile took on a predatory glint. "Which leaves room in your budget for these!"

Her friend finally revealed what she'd been hiding behind her back. Zoe wanted to protest, but she'd always been a sucker for sexy lingerie. She held out her hand to take the garter belt and matching panties in the identical shade of blue as the dress. Oh, yeah, she wanted those.

She surrendered without a fight. "Okay, I'll get these and the dress. I suppose next you'll say I need shoes to match as well."

"Darn straight!" Brandi plopped down on the chair in the corner and gave Zoe another long look. "You know, I almost feel sorry for Corporal Brevik. That poor man won't know what hit him when he sees you in that dress."

Then she wiggled her eyebrows and smirked. "Not to mention out of it."

"Brandi!" Zoe protested, but only halfheartedly. After all, she was right. Why else bother with the sexy underwear?

"Okay, help me out of this, and we can head over to the shoe store next. I want to get home in time for a long bubble bath before I have to get dressed."

After Zoe paid for everything, Brandi asked, "Do you

want me to come over later to help with your hair and makeup?"

It was tempting, but Zoe decided she had to fly solo sometime. "Thanks, but you've already wasted enough of your weekend on me. I might be a bit rusty with mascara and blush, but I promise I'll do the dress proud."

Her friend looked a bit insulted. "Spending time with a friend is never wasted, Zoe. Besides, I love to shop, and it's more fun spending a bunch of your money instead of mine."

Zoe held the door open for Brandi on the way out of the dress shop. "Okay, but try not to have too much fun at my expense at the shoe store."

Brandi linked her arm through Zoe's as they headed down the street together. "I'll try, but no promises. True beauty doesn't come cheap, you know."

Zoe managed to squeeze in a short nap between the shopping expedition and her bubble bath. If she was going to go to all this effort, the last thing she needed was to have dark circles under her eyes from lack of sleep. That didn't mean she wasn't still questioning the wisdom of this whole date thing. The trouble was, she couldn't resist the chance to spend time in Leif's arms, even if it was only on the dance floor.

But their time together wasn't going to end when he brought her back to her apartment door. She glanced toward the bed. They might not have a future together, but they could have tonight. And maybe a few more before he left Snowberry Creek for good.

She stared at herself in the mirror. "Foolish woman. It will be great while it lasts, but you're going to crash and burn big-time when he leaves."

The small voice in her head, the one she rarely let

herself listen to, whispered back, *Yes, maybe that potential pain can't be avoided anyway. He already means too much to you. Perhaps the sweet memories you'll create will help soften the blow.*

Before she could muster a worthy argument, the doorbell rang. The fight was over, and she was down for the count.

Any doubts she had disappeared as soon as she answered the door. If Leif said anything, she didn't hear it. She was too busy drinking in the scrumptious sight of Corporal Leif Brevik in a tux. She didn't know where he'd gotten it, but she hoped they wouldn't mind getting it back in shreds. Right now it was all she could do not to drag him inside and proceed to rip it off him.

"Wow, Corporal, you clean up nice."

He didn't respond at first; he was too busy staring at the neckline of her dress.

"Um, Leif, my eyes are about a foot north of where you're looking."

He blinked and jerked his gaze up, his cheeks flushing hot. "Sorry. Zoe, I can't come up with words that would even come close to telling you how much I like that dress and how you look in it."

She blushed even though she was quite pleased with his response. "I'll let Brandi know you liked it. I took her shopping with me, and she was terrified I'd end up buying something her grandmother might wear."

Stepping back, she opened the door wider. "Would you like to come in for a drink before we go?"

Looking a bit stunned, he stayed right where he was. "I'd better not. If I get you behind closed doors, I'm not sure I'd have the strength of character to leave again. I promised you dinner and dancing, and I try to be a man of my word."

Leif maintained a frustrating distance between them as his smile turned pure rogue. "Unless of course you'd rather stay in and order pizza. You know, afterward. If that's what you want, invite me in again. I won't say no."

She was still trying to bring what he was offering into focus. "After what exactly?"

He quirked one eyebrow and the heat in his eyes kicked it up another notch. "Seriously? You have to ask that?"

Oh, that. She swallowed hard and fought for the strength to refuse the doubly spicy offer of both Leif and pepperoni.

"I'll get my purse."

If he looked disappointed, she didn't care. They both knew they'd end up back here eventually. A few seconds later she joined him outside with the door firmly locked between them and the privacy of her apartment. Before taking a single step, Leif drew her into his arms and kissed her. It was long and hot and a promise of more to come.

When he finally broke it off, she counted herself lucky to still be able to remember her own name, much less where they were supposed to be headed. At least he looked just as rattled by the flash of heat lightning that had just ripped through both of them.

As they started down the stairs, he kept his free hand on her lower back. "You know, I'm pretty sure that the effect that dress has on a poor helpless male is illegal in several states."

"Yes, well, that tux should carry warning signs, too, Corporal. Any woman that sees you in it is going to want to touch. I figure I have a long evening ahead of me having to fend them off."

Looking pleased, Leif laughed. "Then I'm glad I let Callie talk me into renting it. She said you deserved better than a Hawaiian shirt and khakis. Having said that, thank you for stroking my ego. After one look at you in that dress, I wasn't sure I'd measure up."

His ego wasn't the only thing she intended to stroke, and she already knew firsthand that he more than measured up to her expectations. She kept that information to herself, however; otherwise they would never reach his truck.

Maybe it was time to change the subject. "So, big guy, where are we headed?"

Dinner had been good and the dancing even better. He'd convinced the deejay to play a handful of slow songs in a row. Leif hated playing off the guy's sympathy by admitting he was a wounded warrior just back from the front. However, he'd have stooped far lower than that to hold Zoe swaying in his arms out in the middle of a crowded dance floor.

Her hair carried the scent of oranges, or maybe tangerines. Something citrusy. Whatever it was, he liked it. He closed his eyes and breathed it in deep. Yeah, the moment was perfect. The back of her dress plunged down to stop just below her waist. He loved having the palm of his hand resting directly against her silken skin. It was a delicious reminder of what it would be like to touch her all over, which he planned to do as soon as he got her somewhere a lot more private.

This would be their last dance, maybe ever, and he was determined to make the most of it. He leaned down to kiss the side of her neck. There was no mistaking the shiver that coursed through her, so he did it again.

This time she leaned back to look at him directly. Her pretty blue eyes were smoldering. "Soldier, keep that up and I won't be responsible for what happens."

The song was already winding down. "Then maybe we should take this back to your place."

He loved that she didn't hesitate. "Yes, we should."

The drive back from Seattle took a hundred times longer than the same trip had taken going the other way. It didn't help that she'd ridden the entire trip with her hand on his upper thigh. Every so often, she'd given his leg a gentle squeeze, her soft smile making it clear she knew exactly what she was doing to him, and liked it.

He pulled into the first parking spot he could find. He started around the front of the truck to open her door for her to prove his mama had raised him right. However, Zoe had already gotten out on her own. She grabbed his hand and practically dragged him toward the steps.

Okay, so he wasn't the only one in a hurry to get upstairs and get down to it. Mentally, he gave himself a stern lecture about taking his time, going slow, and a whole bunch of shit about savoring the moment.

Yeah, right, like that was going to happen.

Oh, he'd savor the moment all right, but there wasn't going to be anything slow about it. Not the way things were going right now. They made it up to the second floor in record time. If it bothered his leg at all, he didn't notice.

Zoe unlocked the door of her apartment with impressive speed and tugged him inside. This time there was no hesitation, no second guesses.

After tossing her purse and keys on a small table, Zoe backed away from Leif. "Wait there."

He did as she ordered, curious to see what she had in mind. She fiddled with the stereo for several seconds before the slow strains of the same song they'd been dancing to at the club filled the space between them.

"I want to dance."

"So do I," he agreed, although maybe they weren't talking about the same thing. Regardless, he held out his arms, wanting her right back where she belonged.

Zoe kicked off her shoes before slowly starting toward him, her hips swaying softly as she danced her way across the room. She stopped a few feet away and turned her back to him. From this view, her dress covered less than it revealed, yet he wanted it gone. She peeked at him over her shoulder, her lips curved in a siren's smile.

"Thought you wanted to dance, Leif."

She put an extra little shimmy in her next move, slowly raising the hem of her skirt high enough to reveal a hint of silky thigh above her nylons and garter belt. Then she released the fabric and the glimpse was gone.

Enough was enough. This time when she tried to dance back out of reach, he took advantage of his superior arm length and spun her right back toward him. He kept his hold gentle but firm.

"Dancing isn't as much fun if you're doing it alone."

She settled into his embrace. They finished out the song, moving slowly with their bodies pressed together from shoulder to thigh. Zoe laid her head against his chest and rested her hands on his shoulders. He bent down to nuzzle her neck and sought out the pull tab on the zipper of her dress, tugging it down in short bursts.

When the song ended, Zoe stepped back to let the dress slip down and pool on the floor. As sexy as the dress had been, it paled in comparison to the lacy concoctions she wore underneath. The next song started playing, and she moved closer but just out of reach.

"I'm thinking you have on too many clothes for my taste." She paused to lick her lips. "Lose the tie, jacket, and shirt."

If there was one thing the army had taught Leif, it was how to snap to and execute orders. The jacket joined her dress on the floor. He was pretty sure the tie missed the back of the couch and fell behind it.

His shirt took more effort. Too many buttons, and the cuff links were a real pain. Whoever thought cuff links were a good idea? No matter. Once he finally jerked them free, the shirt was history. So were his belt and shoes.

"That's enough for now, Leif. No need to rush things."

The music swirled around them, filling the room. The singer's voice was raspy, low, and sang of two people sharing twisted sheets and a long night of loving. It was Leif's new favorite song.

As the final notes died away, he kissed Zoe, taking his time to do the job right. Their lips and tongues slow-danced just as the two of them had done out on the dance floor. He loved the way she was an equal partner in the process, letting him lead for a while and then taking charge herself. Coaxing and being coaxed in equal measure.

He had thoroughly enjoyed the sweet press of her breasts against his bare chest. Not to be outdone, she upped the ante by unfastening his trousers and then kneeling to pull them down and then off.

Zoe remained on her knees, staring up at him. What was she planning next? Was she going to do what he hoped she was? Oh, hell, yeah, she was. He gently cradled her head as she worked him to a fevered pitch, only to stop as quickly as she'd started.

Leif feared for his sanity.

Zoe thought she had him at her mercy. Fat chance. He outweighed her by sixty pounds of muscle and bone. Desperate men were capable of amazing feats of strength and endurance. She would pay for the torment and love every minute of it.

He stared down into the pure temptation of her midnight blue eyes. "May I remind you that payback is a bitch?"

Before she could respond, he hoisted her to her feet. With no warning, he tossed her over his shoulder fireman-style. Zoe squeaked in protest, but he ignored her. If she was worried about his damn leg, he didn't want to hear it. Luckily, her bedroom was only a few steps away. He'd make it that far or die trying.

They reached her bed with his dignity and determination both intact. After tossing her to the middle of the mattress, he grabbed one of the condoms she'd left on the bedside table and prepared to take this to the next level and well beyond.

Zoe watched his every move. "I have something I want to say. Please let me finish, Leif."

He nodded, not sure where she was going with this. "Okay."

"Carrying me like that might not have been the smartest move you've ever made, and I wouldn't recommend a repeat performance anytime soon—"

She paused long enough to give his left leg a pointed look. "But I've got to say that it was the sexiest thing imaginable."

"Well, honey, if you liked that, I promise you're going to love what comes next."

Then he joined her on the bed and proved himself to be a man of his word. Repeatedly.

Chapter 25

❧ ❧

Zoe hovered at the edge of consciousness, afraid to give in to the growing need to sleep. There was no way she could let down her guard that completely, not with Leif there. What if her nightmares chose tonight to return for a repeat performance? She couldn't risk it.

Besides, the last time they'd been together like this, with their passion on the back burner, it hadn't ended well. She didn't want anything to spoil this night for either of them. In the near future, when she was once again alone, she would need the memory of this night to remain pure and untarnished by anything close to reality.

If only their time together didn't have to end.

The problem wasn't that they were ultimately wrong for each other, not when everything about Leif felt so right. Under other circumstances, she could imagine spending a lifetime's worth of nights just like this one, with him beside her. If she were honest with herself, she knew it wouldn't take much to send her tumbling over the cliff to fall in love with him. Heck, maybe she'd already made that leap.

It didn't matter. It couldn't.

She'd meant what she'd said about tonight. No promises. No strings. No hope.

If she had met him years ago, they might have had a chance of making it together. Back when she still felt whole and ready to take on whatever the world threw at her. But a part of her had been badly broken by her time spent in the war. It was as if she'd absorbed the pain and suffering and death deep inside, where the wound remained unhealed even after all this time.

She'd walked away from her military career and patched herself back up as best she could, but the repair job was shoddy at best. Too much pressure and she would shatter.

Leif stroked her shoulder. "Want to talk about whatever it is that's keeping you awake?"

She'd been so hoping he wouldn't notice, or at least wouldn't ask. Complete honesty would come with too high a price, so she settled for a smaller truth. "I don't want to miss a minute of this."

"As flattering as that is, Zoe, I'm not buying it. You've already seen me at my worst and haven't kicked me out of your bed. I'm a big, tough guy. I can handle whatever you have to throw at me."

It was so tempting to share, but he had enough of a burden to bear without taking on hers as well. Besides, the problems he had stemmed from his time in combat, and he'd come close to dying because of his injuries. He bore the scars to prove it. Even now, despite the pain and everything he'd been through, he was fighting with everything he had to get his life as a combat soldier back.

And her? She'd quit the first chance she'd gotten and come slinking back home to lick her wounds.

"It's nothing, Leif."

Unable to look him in the eye as she lied, she rolled onto her side to face away from him. She expected an explosion, but instead she got cuddling. He curled up along her back and put his arm across her waist to hold her close.

"Whatever it is, babe, I've got you. Go to sleep."

Did he notice her tears? Probably, because he kissed the top of her head and brushed the pad of his thumb across her damp cheek. He didn't yell. He didn't make a single demand. No, he did something far worse: He held her close and warm until blessed sleep finally claimed them both.

Leif awoke to the sound of whimpers quickly escalating into screams and a sharp kick right to his balls.

"What the fuck?" he grunted as he turned onto his back and drew his knees up and tried to breathe through the pain. What the hell was going on? Someone was in pain. Well, besides him.

It was Zoe. She was thrashing around on her side of the bed, her eyes wide open but blank and unseeing. Nobody was home in there, even though words poured out of her mouth in a steady barrage of near gibberish. He made sense of some of it and almost wished he hadn't.

"I can't stop the bleeding! Somebody get over here and help me! God, he's going to bleed out before we can get him into OR."

Leif still hurt from where she'd unwittingly kicked him, but right now he was more worried about Zoe than about the condition of his equipment. And if that wasn't proof of how much she meant to him, he didn't know what was.

He sat up and tried to pin her down to keep her from hurting herself or him. That only made her more frantic. "Let me go to him. I've got to prep him for surgery."

She gasped and shook her head in denial. Whatever response she heard inside her head set off another attack. She pounded on him with her fists. "Bullshit! He can't be dead. David was breathing just a minute ago! I took his pulse myself!"

Despite the difference in their sizes, Zoe had Leif at a disadvantage because he didn't want to hurt her. In the meantime, she did her damnedest to claw her way straight through Leif to reach the man from her past, drawing blood as she sobbed. Leif ignored the scratches. He would cheerfully let her beat the hell out of him if only she would pull out of this nosedive.

"Zoe, honey, wake up! You're having a nightmare. It's not real."

Although for her maybe it was. He repeated a steady litany of soothing nonsense as he fought to remain calm. One of them needed to be, and it sure wasn't Zoe. Despite his best efforts, he suspected he sounded increasingly desperate. She wasn't caught up in an ordinary nightmare, the kind most folks had once in a while.

No, it was the other type, the ones reserved for people who'd lived through hell. The dreams attacked when defenses were down, forcing their victims to relive each horrific moment over and over again in stark detail.

He should know. How many nights had he woken up begging Spence to forgive him for being alive? Every time it happened, he relived the whole fucking tragedy all over again, starting with the panic as the three of them tried to find a way back to their unit, knowing there was greater safety in numbers. The only sound was Spence laughing like a loon as he slammed their vehicle around corners and raced through the narrow streets.

Funny, Leif never heard the explosion, but he remembered the weird realization that their vehicle had gone airborne. The final twist in the dream was him looking down from above to see himself sprawled on the street, his ankle a twisted mess of mincemeat as poor Nick tried to decide which of his friends to save first. He'd blacked out for a short time right after the explosion, but he had no doubt that the images were accurate.

He fought hard against the current of his own memories. Zoe needed him too much right now; he couldn't let himself get sucked back into his past. "Please, Zoe, wake up. You're safe. I'm safe."

And whoever this David was, there wasn't a doubt in Leif's mind that the man was long dead. He'd been special to Zoe, and she'd been there when he died. When her fury slowed a bit, he gathered her in his arms and rocked her. "Come on, Zoe, let it go. I know it's hard, but you can't change what happened. David wouldn't want you to hurt this much."

God knows Leif wouldn't.

Just when he was growing desperate enough to consider calling for help, Zoe quit struggling and went limp in his arms. She stared up at him, her face tear-streaked and her eyes full of panic.

"Leif?"

"It's okay, Zoe. You were having a bad dream."

Zoe snapped her eyes shut to hide from the sympathy in Leif's dark eyes. Oh, God. This was her worst nightmare come true. Literally. When she struggled to get free of his arms, Leif let her go, but only reluctantly. She scrambled to the far corner of the bed and yanked the sheet up to cover her naked body, needing to shore up her defenses any way she could.

Leif didn't move an inch. He remained perfectly still and made no effort to cover himself. "Don't shut me out, Zoe. Tell me what I can do to help."

"Nothing. I'm fine."

Okay, half of that was a lie. There was truly nothing Leif could do to help her right now, but she was far from fine. Right now she could feel all those patched-up cracks inside her head shifting, creaking, and coming apart.

"It was just a bad dream, Leif. Sorry if I worried you."

The smiling lover who'd held her in his arms was long gone. In his place was this implacable warrior.

"Don't bullshit me, Zoe. I know a flashback when I see one. I've had too much personal experience to mistake it for anything else. Whatever was going on in your head right now wasn't a dream. It was a full-blown blast from your past, courtesy of the time you spent in Iraq."

He didn't immediately say more, maybe trying to give her a chance to come clean on her own. That wasn't happening. Not now while her entire being was wounded and scraped raw from the inside out. And maybe not ever.

"All right, we'll do this the hard way." He crossed his arms over his chest and played his trump card. "Who was David, Zoe?"

She flinched, the name alone enough to send her plunging right back down into the hell inside her mind. She didn't want to think about David, didn't want to remember him right now, but Leif wasn't going to let up until he ripped the truth right out of her by the roots.

"He was . . . my lover. We met right after I was deployed. He came in with a minor injury. While he waited until it was his turn to get stitched up, we got to talking."

David's image filled her mind. That fiery red hair, those bright blue eyes, and that wicked, wicked smile. He had the confident swagger all of the recon marines did, but without being a jerk about it. She'd liked him from the moment they'd met. A lot of the guys flirted with her, but he'd been different, and they'd gone from zero to sixty in record time.

"Go on."

She hadn't realized she'd been talking out loud. Most men wouldn't want to know the details about a woman's former lover, but then Leif already knew that David was no competition. Not anymore.

"He spent most of his time out on the front lines, but we'd steal a few minutes together whenever we could. There was a lot of that kind of thing going on."

She made herself look directly at Leif. "You know how it is."

"Yeah, I do."

Sitting still was impossible. Rocking helped, the rhythm soothing. The motion started off slowly, but quickly picked up speed until she was reeling out of control again. She found herself being picked up again, but this time it wasn't sexy. Unable to muster up even a token protest, she gave in and let Leif drag her, blankets and all, onto his lap. He surrounded her with his gentle strength and held her still.

"Take it easy and slow, Zoe. I'll listen, no matter how long it takes."

With her head tucked under his chin, his words were a deep rumble coming straight through his muscular chest. She swallowed hard and forced the words out. "But for us, it was more than just good sex. Our relationship went from flirty fun to serious pretty quickly, although we both knew better than to think much beyond our current deployments. Sometimes what works over there doesn't hold up when you get back home. Even so, neither of us really believed we wouldn't have a future together."

She sighed. "I've only felt that kind of special connection with a man one other time before or since."

To make sure Leif knew she was talking about him, she gave him an awkward hug. "I suspect that's why the nightmares came back. Somehow my mind had connected what I felt for David with how I could feel about you."

"Could or do?"

Damn, he sure had a knack for asking the hard questions. She blinked back a new surge of tears. "Does it matter? We both know . . ."

When she didn't finish the statement, Leif did. "We both know that I've been talking about going back."

Her shakes returned instantly. "And I can't live with that fear again. I did it once, and it damn near killed me."

And if she was going to deny the two of them a future together, then Leif needed to know about her past. "My deployment was almost over, and things between me and David were still going strong. He was due to rotate back to the States about a month after me. Of course, we both knew he'd be sent back eventually. Me, too, if I stayed in.

"About a week before my time was up, his unit got hit hard. I recognized several of his friends when they started bringing in the wounded. Some made it. Others didn't. A typical day at the office."

If she sounded bitter, so be it. She hated seeing so many lives changed forever. "The flow of new cases was slowing down when they brought in one last group. David was one of them."

It all played out in her head. Desperately trying to stop the bleeding. Screaming for them to get him into an operating room even knowing they were all already in use. It wouldn't have mattered. Her medical training knew that much even if her heart and mind didn't want to believe it was true.

"I watched him die. He knew I was there, holding his hand. I couldn't do anything else for him. I was useless."

Once again Leif stubbornly took the opposing view. "Like hell. You weren't useless, Zoe. You were there for him, and that mattered to David just like it mattered to every other patient that's been lucky enough to have you at their side. Never doubt that for a minute."

The dam holding back years' worth of tears shattered, the sobs wracking her body. "There were so many, Leif. Too many to count."

"I know, honey. I know."

He tightened his hold on her. "Let it all out. Don't hold back. They deserve your tears."

She shook her head. There was more truth she needed to share. "Not mine. I was a coward. I got out."

"Don't do that to yourself, Zoe. You weren't a coward for giving and giving until you had no more to give. Your tears honor the wounded and the dead."

She wasn't sure she should, but she very much wanted to believe him. Either way, she let the tears come. When they finally stopped, she fell asleep in Leif's arms.

Chapter 26

Leif stirred the eggs and checked the coffee. There was no telling how Zoe would feel about him making himself at home in her kitchen, but after last night, they both needed to replenish their depleted energy stores.

He'd already been awake for a couple of hours. When the shower finally came on in the next room, he'd made a fresh pot of coffee and started cooking. As he set the table, he imagined various scenarios about how this morning was going to play out. All things considered, there was probably a good chance that Zoe was hoping he'd already be gone.

Since that wasn't happening, what would be her next favorite possibility? That his leg would've given out on him, causing him to fall and hit his head, giving him amnesia and destroying all memory of last night? Maybe that would've been a good thing. He hated knowing how much she hurt, not to mention that he was a bit jealous of a dead guy. But he also knew her nurse's conscience wouldn't allow her to wish further injury on one of her patients.

"You're still here."

Not exactly the greeting he'd been hoping for, but it was the one he'd been expecting. "Yeah, but the good news is that I made breakfast for you."

He divided the pile of eggs between two plates and set them on the table. "I hope you like onions, peppers, and Swiss cheese in your eggs. And although I object to the idea of turkey bacon on general principles, I have to admit it ain't half bad."

She continued to hover in the doorway of her bedroom.

"Come on, Zoe. I'm declaring breakfast as a no-confrontation zone. We can keep conversation light or even nonexistent if you prefer."

Without waiting for her to respond, he poured them each a glass of orange juice and a steaming cup of coffee.

"Please sit. I'm hungry, but my mother would have my head if she caught me digging into a meal while a woman was still standing."

Okay, that won him a little bit of a smile. He pulled a chair out for her and was relieved when she sat down. After taking his own seat, he passed her the plate of bacon. She tried to wave it off.

"I appreciate your going to all this effort, Leif, but I'm really not hungry."

He wasn't buying it, but he had promised to keep it light. "Eat anyway. Dancing that much was bound to take a lot out of you. It did me."

They both knew it wasn't the dancing that had left both of them feeling like roadkill this morning, but she dutifully took two slices of the bacon and a piece of toast. Good. Once she'd actually taken a bite, he turned his attention to his own plate. It took her a couple of minutes to get up to speed, but she finished the bacon, half the toast, and most of her eggs.

He polished off everything on his plate and leaned back to enjoy his third cup of coffee. It was more than he usually drank in the morning, but right now he needed the sharp edge the caffeine would provide.

Zoe picked up her own coffee and left the table to stare out the living room window. She looked so damn alone. He wished he was better with all this touchy-feely stuff, but he had no idea how to offer the comfort she so badly needed right now.

He drifted after her, moving slowly but determined to get close. She let him get within a couple of feet before she finally spoke, not that she bothered to look at him.

"I don't want to talk about it."

"Fine, so you listen while I talk."

Leif set his coffee down to free up his hands. Still moving slowly, he brought them up to rest on her shoulders. Just as he'd expected, her muscles were a mass of knots, and her body thrummed with tension. He began to gently massage her shoulders and neck, drawing comfort from the fact that she tolerated his touch.

"Last night was tough, Zoe. We always seem to end up this way, with the good between us getting all twisted up with the baggage we're each carrying."

He eased closer, still maintaining his steady effort to ease her pain any way he could. "We've both known what my issues are. My leg's screwed up . . . well, actually, it's screwed together. It might get better. It might not, though, so I can't make any kind of decision about my future until I know what my options are."

Which translated into he might get his life as a combat soldier back or he might not. That was his problem, though, and right now he was more concerned about Zoe's.

"I'm going to go out on a limb here and make a guess that you haven't talked to anyone recently about what happened to you in Iraq."

What progress he'd made in loosening up her muscles disappeared immediately. Yeah, he'd guessed right. No surprise there. "Nothing happened to me, Leif. It happened to others, David included."

He wrapped his arms around her shoulders and rested his head next to hers. "Zoe, honey, that's a load of crap, and you know it. You have to have read enough on the subject to know that the patients aren't the only ones affected by their injuries. The people who care for them are, too. Not in the same way, but that doesn't make their problems any less real."

"But—"

"No buts, Zoe. You know it's true. I don't know what's kept you from getting help. Maybe some kind of weird guilt over the fact that you came home physically whole when so many didn't, or maybe it's that you came home at all when David didn't."

"Damn it, Leif, you have no idea how I feel!"

His laugh sounded bitter to his own ears. "Really? You don't think I'm carrying a whole shitload of guilt because I survived and Spence didn't? He was my best friend, Zoe, and if Nick had dragged him to safety instead of me, I would've been the one to die that day. Sometimes I'm scared I really don't want my leg to heal. That the limp is my penance just for living."

God, all of this hurt so damn bad. "Hell, I'm scared to death of what I'll find out from those specialists on Monday. But honestly, Zoe, I don't know if I'm more afraid that they can't fix my leg or that they can."

Leif closed his eyes and fought to stay firmly rooted in the present. "As twisted as that is, my friend Nick has it even worse, because he lives every moment knowing he left a friend behind to die that day. There was no way he could save us both, but that didn't keep the guilt from nearly eating him alive. If it weren't for Callie, I don't know what would've happened to him."

It was time to lay it all out for her. "So here's the deal, Zoe. You're probably hoping I'll simply walk away right now. It's what you want because you think you don't deserve any kind of happiness in your life. I get that. Guilt does screwy things to our minds."

He released his hold on her and moved to face her directly. "I know you don't want any kind of future that involves a soldier on active duty. I guess with all things considered, I don't blame you. At least now I know why."

The need to touch her rode him hard. He settled for brushing a lock of her hair back from her face. "You mean a lot to me, Zoe. If I weren't who I am or maybe if your experience in the army had been different . . . But there's no changing some things. I still want you to have a future with some happiness in it even if that future isn't spent with me. That's not going to happen until you lay the past to rest."

She caught his hand and held it against her cheek. "I've tried, Leif. I really have."

The tears were back. Good, maybe it meant she was finally letting herself grieve over not just David but her own lost innocence.

"Yeah, well, clearly whatever you've tried hasn't worked. It's time to talk to someone."

She was already shaking her head. "I tried counseling right after I first got back. It didn't help."

"If I mean anything to you at all, Zoe, I'm asking you to try one more time."

He drew her close, keeping his embrace gentle, but it was time to play hardball.

"Right after Mitch and I got into that fight at the bar Gage made me promise to attend one meeting of the veterans' support group that meets at the church. I went expecting to hate every minute of it. I won't say it's easy, but I've been going ever since."

His chest hurt, but he kept talking. "Opening up about this stuff and listening to the others leaves me feeling as if I've been on a three-day march without water or food. But it's the honest truth that at least I walk out of there knowing I'm not the only one who's going through this. That alone has made a difference in how I'm sleeping nights."

Silence.

"If the support group can't offer you what you need, I'm betting Pastor Haliday will know someone who can."

Okay, here came the hard part. Leif tipped her chin up to look directly in her eyes. After brushing a soft kiss across her lips, he laid it on the line. "The meeting starts at three next Saturday afternoon. I hope to see you there."

Then he walked out and didn't look back.

Chapter 27

❦ ❦

Deciding to go to the veterans' meeting was one of the hardest things Zoe had ever done. The only thing that kept her driving toward the church was the burning need to see Leif again. She hadn't seen him since he'd walked out of her apartment last Sunday morning. Figuring he'd be at the clinic during the week, she'd let him go without protest, something she now regretted.

He'd had his appointments with the specialists last Monday, so she hadn't expected to see him at his usual physical therapy appointment that day. But then he was a no-show on Wednesday, even though his buddy Mitch was there going through his workout. She'd asked Isaac if Leif had changed his appointment time. He hadn't. No, in fact, he'd canceled all of his upcoming appointments.

She shouldn't have been surprised. The news from the two specialists hadn't been good. Both doctors had agreed on one thing: Leif needed further surgery, the sooner, the better, and even then the prognosis was iffy.

At least he had promised to see her at the church for

the veterans' meeting. Leif was a man of his word, so that's where he'd be. She'd spent the rest of the week with a growing sense of dread. If she wanted to see Leif again, she had to go to the meeting.

If she weren't the one caught up in the neat little trap he'd set, she would've admired his tactics. She wanted to see him. He wanted her to take that first scary step through the church door to meet the members of the veterans' group. To get what she wanted, she had to give him what he wanted in return.

Well, she could get through one meeting. After it was over, she'd drag Leif somewhere private and find out what was going on in that thick skull of his. He would also find that she didn't like being manipulated, not even by the man she—

No, she wouldn't use the L-word. If she admitted that much even to herself, she didn't know how she'd survive him leaving, especially if it was for good.

As soon as she turned into the church parking lot, she spotted him, leaning against the side of his big red truck. He looked way too good to her hungry eyes, which only made her madder than she already was. How dare he look so calm when a stiff breeze was all it would take to shatter her completely?

She parked next to his truck and waited a couple of beats to gather up her purse, keys, and nerve. Gentleman that he was, he was already reaching to open her door for her.

"You came. I wasn't sure you would."

If she'd detected anything but relief in his voice, she might have gotten right back in her car and driven away. Instead, she answered truthfully.

"I almost didn't, but I was worried about you."

Then before she took one step toward the church with

him, she laid it on the line. "I'll go in there, but only if you promise to go somewhere afterward where the two of us can talk. I don't want you to disappear from my life without at least a chance to say good-bye."

He gave her hand a soft squeeze. "That was my plan all along. I promise that if you hadn't come here, I would've come looking for you. There was no way I'd leave town without seeing you again. I couldn't."

So she'd guessed right. He was leaving Snowberry Creek soon. Squeezing his hand was a poor substitute for words, but the lump in her throat made it impossible to speak.

"Can I introduce you to Pastor Haliday? He likes to talk to newcomers for a few minutes alone, but I think he'd let me stay with you if it would be easier for you."

She drew a shaky breath. "I've met him before. I'm sure I can handle talking to him alone."

Hopefully better than she was handling everything else in her life right now. Pride dictated that she take that first step into the building on her own. One way or another, she'd get through the meeting. It was what would come after that had her shaking in her boots.

Three hours later, Zoe found herself parked on top of the same picnic table she and Leif had shared the last time they'd spent time together at the creek. On the way there, they'd dropped her car off at her apartment and then stopped to pick up dinner to go at Frannie's café before heading for the park. The bag Leif had handed her when he got back in the truck felt suspiciously heavy for two burgers and fries, but she was too tired and hungry to ask questions.

As she waited for Leif to divvy up the food, she broke the silence. "Okay, you were right about the meeting leaving me feeling as if I've been on a three-day march with no supplies."

He held out her burger. "Yeah, it can be pretty harsh. Even so, if I were going to stay here, I'd keep going. I like the people, but I also need the support."

That's all he said, maybe waiting for her to respond. Instead, she ate her dinner, telling herself it was a crime to let a Creekburger get cold. When she'd finished off the very last sweet potato fry, Leif gave her an evil grin and held out a single dessert with two forks.

So that's why the bag had been so big. She shot him a dirty look and made a grab for the container. "I already warned you that when it comes to Frannie's banana cream pie, I don't share."

He laughed as he surrendered it to her and then produced a second one. "Then I guess it's a good thing I bought two."

"Well, my hips won't thank you, but I do."

All too soon, their last excuse for putting off the impending talk had disappeared. Once again, she started the conversation. "So, when are you leaving?"

He looked pretty grim. "The middle of next week I'll be flying back east to see the doctor who did my last surgery. The specialists here have already talked to him, and he's got me on his schedule for the week after that, once he confirms their findings. From what the man told me, I'll be back on crutches for a good long while, followed by a lot more physical therapy. They're set up with all the specialized equipment I'll need, so I'll have to hang around there until I'm finished."

She aimed for maintaining a clinical distance. "So they think the surgery can relieve the pressure on the nerves that is causing you such pain."

He nodded. "But he made no promises that it would

improve the mobility in my leg and said it might even make it worse. There's no way to tell. But either way, I can't go on like this, so doing nothing is not an option. I have to roll the dice and see what happens."

Leif scooted closer although he kept his eyes on the flowing water. "All in all, his best guess was that it will be four, maybe five months before I'll know for sure how well it's going to heal. My dad lives close enough that I can stay at his place while I rehab."

He took her hand and tangled his fingers with hers. "I can't make a decision about my future and what I want to do with it until I get through all of this. I'm not holding my breath that I'll be running marathons or marching in formation. Living without pain might have to be enough."

"No pain would be a good thing."

"Yeah, it would be."

Leif finally looked down at her. "So that's my plan for getting better. What's yours?"

Suddenly she understood what he'd found so riveting about watching the water flowing past them. She didn't want to do this. Hated having to do this, but if he could face months of pain with no promise of a cure, she could, too.

"I'm going to attend some meetings. Maybe talk to the counselor that Pastor Haliday recommended. She's had good success with cases like mine."

The effect of throwing those words out there for the cosmos and the rock-solid man sitting next to her to hear was amazing. A strange need to laugh burbled up from deep within her. Leif looked a bit worried by her reaction.

"Sorry, but taking that first step toward hope is a pretty amazing thing."

He smiled down at her. "Yeah, it is."

"So, Corporal Brevik, how do you plan to spend the rest of your time here in Snowberry Creek? If you need suggestions, I might have a few."

The heat in his dark eyes warmed her from the inside out. He released her hand to put his arm around her shoulders for a one-armed hug.

"For starters, I'd love to have you come to the barbecue Callie is throwing on Tuesday evening at her folks' place. Nick gets back on Monday, so it will be a combination welcome home for him and a good-bye party for me. I also thought I'd invite Mitch, Isaac, and Brandi, so you'd know a bunch of people there."

She didn't hesitate. "I'll be glad to come. Tell Callie to let me know if I can bring anything."

"I'll pass along the message, but your being there is all that really matters."

Leif gathered up their trash and got rid of it. When he came back, he held out his hand again. "Now about those other ideas on what we could be doing. Exactly what did you have in mind?"

Nothing she could talk about while they were within hearing of families with small children out for a stroll.

"Some things are easier to demonstrate than describe. Besides, all my best visual aids are back at my place."

Leif's grin was all heat and temptation. After a quick kiss, he tugged her down off the table. "In case I haven't mentioned it, I truly love the way you think."

Monday rolled around too quickly, a reminder that Leif's time in Snowberry Creek was almost at an end. He sat on the front porch and waited for his friend to put in an appearance. Callie had picked Nick up at the airport a couple of hours ago and taken him straight to her parents' house next door.

Boy, he'd have given anything to have been a mouse in the corner when that went down. Sure, Nick was the kind of guy that most parents would be thrilled to have for a son-in-law, but today was the first chance Callie's parents had had to meet the man who had swept into town and claimed their daughter for his own.

From a few things Callie had let slip, they clearly thought the couple was rushing things. Leif figured once they saw how it was between Nick and Callie, they'd come around. That didn't mean the first meeting wasn't going to be pretty damn scary for his former sergeant.

Mooch came charging out of the woods, so Nick probably wasn't far behind. Sure enough, he strolled into sight a few seconds later. The man looked like hell, but then he'd probably been traveling for hours before having to face the inquisition next door.

"It's about time you got here."

Leif stood up to greet his friend. He opened the small cooler and pulled out a couple of beers while Nick tossed his duffel on the porch and collapsed in the other rocker. He accepted the longneck and took a big gulp. Leif waited until Nick was settled before starting his own inquisition.

"So how did it go with the future in-laws?"

Nick leaned back and closed his eyes. "You mean other than Mr. Redding choosing to clean all of his guns right about the time we were due back from the airport? Said they were dusty."

Leif almost choked on his beer. "Yeah, other than that."

"Then it went fine. Well, Mrs. Redding did ask if we planned on a long engagement. Not sure how to take that."

As tempting as it was to give Nick a hard time, Leif took pity on his friend. "She's their only daughter, Nick, and they want the best for her. Just give them a chance to get to know you."

"That's what Callie said, but I don't know. Her mom tried to drag her into the other room, which would've given her dad the perfect time to grill me. And did I mention all the guns?"

Then he gave Leif a suspicious look. "Just what did you tell them about me, anyway?"

"Nothing bad, Sarge." Leif raised his right hand in the air. "I swear. That would've been against the man code."

Maybe it was time to throw Nick a bone.

"Hope you don't mind, but Austin and I made plans to go out to dinner tonight with Mitch Calder. Afterward, we plan to play several hours of pool at BEER. Ordinarily you'd be welcome to come, but my truck's not big enough for four. You'll just have to hang out here with Callie and Mooch without our charming company. We're leaving at five and won't be back until around eleven. If that last part changes, we'll call first."

His friend looked decidedly happier. "Seriously? I might have six whole hours alone with Callie?"

"Well, Mooch will be hanging around, too."

The dog in question had just finished one of his regular patrols around the yard and flopped down on the porch between their two chairs. Nick reached down to pet him.

"You should've seen Mooch when I got out of the car. He was so excited I thought the poor little guy was going to burst apart at the seams."

No surprise there. Mooch worshipped the ground Nick walked on. Leif would've been jealous, but the dog loved him that much, too.

Nick moved on to the next subject. "Speaking of Austin, how is that going?"

Leif shrugged. "He has his ups and downs, but there's hope for him. I'm not making excuses for the piss-poor choices he's made in the past, but at least he's trying. He's been chipping away at stripping the wallpaper on the third floor and helping a lot with the yard work. We also got him enrolled in a GED course that starts in a couple of weeks. I've got to warn you, his experience with school in general really sucked. He's convinced he won't be able to cut it. I volunteered you to help make sure he succeeds, since I won't be here."

Leif felt guilty about that, especially since Nick's response was less than enthusiastic, which came as no surprise. The last time Nick had encountered Austin, the kid had been trying to sneak off with Spence's family silver. Leif had no doubt Nick would come around once he actually got to know the kid.

"I swear Austin is worth saving, Sarge, not to mention he's a hard worker. For sure, he's ready and willing to earn his keep. You'll be glad you have him once you're ready to really get started on remodeling this place."

Nick nodded. "Fine, I'll put his ass to work, but is that your way of telling me that you won't be coming back here to help me?"

Leif had known they'd get around to his situation eventually. He'd asked Callie to let him be the one to fill Nick in on the details. "Not for a while at least. I'm headed back east on Wednesday for another round of surgery on my leg."

Nick let loose with a string of curse words that pretty much summed up Leif's feelings on the subject.

He finished off his beer before continuing. "The damn thing is getting worse, not better. I saw a couple of local specialists, and the news wasn't good. I'll have the surgery they've recommended and then rehab at one of the VA clinics."

Nick reached over to pat Leif on the shoulder. "Son

of a bitch. I'm sorry, Corporal. I figured something was going on when you suddenly got so quiet."

"Yeah, well, I figured you had enough to deal with right now."

They both rocked in silence for a couple of minutes. But there was no way Nick would stop until he learned every last detail. Sure enough, he got his second wind and started up again.

"So what's your plan after the surgery and rehab?"

"It all depends."

This time Nick punched Leif's shoulder. "Quit dancing around and tell me what's going on. And just so you know, after you explain about the surgery, we'll be moving right on to what's up with you and your friend Zoe."

"Callie has a big mouth." Leif held up his empty bottle. "But if we're going to keep talking like this, I'm going to need another one of these or, hell, maybe a six-pack."

Opening his second beer was really only a delaying tactic, and they both knew it. "Okay, the surgery first. If my leg comes back even close to full strength, I'll have to decide whether or not I want to reenlist. I always figured I'd put in my twenty and then move on, but that may not be possible now."

He stared out toward the towering firs that surrounded Spence's house. "Having said that, I really like it here in Snowberry Creek. It already feels more like home to me than my hometown does. Besides, it would make it easier to keep an eye on you if we lived in the same zip code."

In truth, the town did feel comfortable to him. The only drawback was that he wasn't sure he could live here if he didn't have more than a job as an excuse to return.

"Anyway, from what the doctors here said, it's unlikely

that I'll get full mobility back in my ankle. We both know I'm a combat soldier. That's all I've ever wanted to be."

Nick nodded. "Yeah, I get that. Neither of us was ever cut out to sit at a desk all day."

He reached down to scratch Mooch's back. "I'm also guessing that you found something else you want right here in Snowberry Creek. Or actually, I should say someone. So, lay it all out there for me. What's up between you and Zoe?"

She wouldn't appreciate Leif sharing her secrets. But this was Nick, and he knew how to keep his mouth shut. Even so, Leif gave him only enough details to make the situation clear. When he was done, Nick pinned him with one of those looks that promised there would be no bullshitting his way out of answering his next question.

"So, have you told her that you love her?"

Leif spewed his mouthful of beer. "Where the hell did that come from?"

His friend let out a big sigh and shook his head. "It's a damn good thing I got back here when I did if you haven't even figured out that much for yourself."

"Don't be an asshole, Nick. Don't forget it wasn't that long ago that you were walking around all hangdog and pitiful because you couldn't bring yourself to admit that you had some pretty strong feelings for Callie."

"Which is why I know exactly what you're going through. So, if you love her, what's the hang-up?"

"I know how I feel about her, Nick, but she can't handle being married to a soldier. After what she went through, I don't blame her. It's a lot to ask of any woman, but especially one who has her own nightmares from her time downrange."

Nick stopped rocking long enough to stare Leif right in the eye. "So if that's the case, I guess you need to decide which means more to you: another tour of duty or a life with Zoe."

Did he really think Leif didn't already know that? "Damn it, Nick, you know it's not that simple."

Nick pushed himself up out of the rocker. "Yeah, it is, Leif, if you want it to be. I'll support whatever decision you make, but you've already given a lot to the army. Maybe it's time for something different."

His friend shouldered his duffel and took one step toward the door, but then stopped.

Without looking at Leif, Nick said, "Do what's right for you, Leif. Maybe it's selfish of me to want you back here. For sure I'd love to have you for my business partner, but that's not the real reason. I lost Spence. I'm not sure I could survive losing you, too."

Nick disappeared into the house, but his words remained behind, heavy and hard to hear. Granted, he hadn't said anything that hadn't already had Leif spinning in circles for days, but hearing someone else put it so succinctly brought it all into sharp focus.

Maybe Leif's decision was that simple.

He and Zoe had spent Saturday night and most of Sunday together. If he had to describe how that felt, the clearest description he could come up with was that they fit. Yeah, they each had some serious shit to deal with that could very well drive a permanent wedge between them. But maybe, just maybe, it wouldn't.

And he would fight for that chance, no matter how tenuous it was. Tomorrow night after the barbecue, he'd talk to Zoe. Lay it all out there for her even if he couldn't press for any answers because he didn't have any himself.

He just wanted to make sure he wasn't the only one thinking about a future with possibilities.

Chapter 28

Zoe was one stubborn woman. Leif had been trying to get her alone ever since she'd arrived at the bar-becue. So far, she'd managed to make sure they'd had a chaperone all evening long.

It was starting to really piss him off, because they needed to have this big talk. At the rate things were go-ing, he'd have to settle for texting her on his way to the East Coast. In another few seconds, he was going to pull a caveman act and drag her off into the woods.

"You're looking pretty fierce there, buddy."

Leif muttered a curse and gave his full attention to Mitch. He'd been meaning to talk to him, too.

"If I didn't say so earlier, thanks for coming tonight. I really wanted you to meet Nick. Maybe the two of you can shoot some pool and have a couple of cold ones in my honor when I'm gone."

Mitch frowned and shook his head. "While that would be fun, I'm not going to be here either. I've decided that I'm not ready to give up on my career yet. Not like this.

My knee isn't strong enough to play right now, but there's always next year. I want to work with the team trainers to finish getting my knee back in shape. Isaac has done a great job, but hiding here in Snowberry Creek makes it too easy for the entire league to forget about me. I don't want to give them that chance."

Mitch dropped his voice. "And if my career really is over, I want it to be my decision to walk away."

That was an attitude Leif could understand. "I wish you luck with that, Mitch. I'd love to see you back out there on the field. Hell, I might even draft you on my fantasy team again."

"You do that, Corporal." The quarterback's smile faded as he stuck out his hand. "And for what it's worth, it's been a real honor getting to know you. I'd have you as my wingman anytime."

Leif shook Mitch's hand. "Same here, Mitch. It will be interesting to see where each of us ends up. For sure, though, if we're ever in the same time zone again, the first round is on you."

Mitch laughed. "Sounds good. Now quit wasting your time talking to me. You keep staring at that woman as if she's the only oasis in the desert. Go get her."

"I was on my way to do that exact thing. Wish me luck."

"I'm guessing you'll need it. In my experience, when a woman acts that skittish, she's more afraid of herself than she is of the man who's after her."

Leif wasn't so sure of that, but he was running out of time and options. He cut straight through the crowded backyard to where Zoe stood talking to Isaac. If she thought hiding behind the huge trainer would save her, she definitely had another think coming.

"Isaac, would you excuse us for a little while? I have something I want to show Zoe next door."

The big man looked from Leif to Zoe before backing away, holding up his hands in surrender. "I, uh, I was just about to take a walk anyway. Go somewhere. Maybe talk to someone."

He was gone before Zoe could get a word out. Leif immediately took her hand in his. "Please come with me."

"All right." She didn't sound all that enthusiastic, but she let him lead her down the path through the woods that separated the yard from Spence's.

Once they were out of sight, she dragged her feet long enough to ask, "Where are we going?"

"Someplace where we can talk without two dozen people jockeying around to listen in while pretending they aren't."

At least she didn't argue. When they reached the other house, he led her around back to the gazebo. Once they were inside, he released her hand. As usual his eyes were immediately drawn to the dedication on the back wall. Every time he looked at it, his heart hurt.

"I'm glad we built this place in Spence's memory."

He wasn't sure why it was important for her to know that, but it was all part of why he'd brought Zoe to this particular spot. "I'm leaving tomorrow."

"I know."

"I wish I could tell you how this is all going to play out, Zoe, but I can't."

Her voice was small, but her words were clear. "I know that, too."

His leg was hurting again, so he sat down. Or maybe it was just his excuse to tug her down onto his lap. At least she didn't resist.

"So here's my thoughts on the subject. My leg might be better after the surgery, but it might not be. Either way, I'm finding I might not be quite so eager to reenlist as I thought. Maybe if I had a compelling reason, when it's all said and done, I might prefer to come back here to Snowberry Creek."

When she started to speak, he stopped her with a brief kiss. "I'm not asking you for anything you're not ready to give me, Zoe. We both know I need time to get my own head straight, so I'm going to take the next few months and do exactly that. It will be the new year before I know anything definitive anyway."

He kissed her again, hoping that would tell her everything he couldn't find the words for right now. This time she wrapped her arms around his neck and kissed him back.

She closed her eyes and rested her head on his shoulder. "So, Corporal, here's my thinking on the subject. If you're going to work on fixing you, it's only fair that I work on fixing me. You were right. It needs to be done. Once you've found your answers, promise you'll come find me. We'll see where we go from there."

"I promise, Zoe."

And then, with the same hot surge of adrenaline he got riding out on patrol, he gave her one last truth. "I love you, Zoe. I just thought you should know."

"I love you, too, Corporal Leif Brevik." Her arms tightened around him like a vise. "No matter how this turns out, I really do love you."

Chapter 29

✣ ✣

Zoe dug another hole and stuck in another primrose. After patting the dirt around the roots, she rocked back on her heels to survey her work. Yeah, the line of bright color snaking its way along the edge of the flower bed went a long way toward brightening her mood. It had been a long, gray winter, even for the Pacific Northwest. These hardy little flowers were a promise that spring was on its way.

Ever year about this time, the people in town turned out to clean up the park and other common areas. The empty planters that were scattered along the sidewalks in town would be filled with crocuses, daffodils, and tulips. The flower beds in the park would be raked, edged, and then planted with primroses.

Until the last few months, Zoe had been too caught up in her own problems to want to get involved. However, the veterans' group always participated, so she'd agreed to pitch in. She was glad she had. It felt good being out in the sunshine with friends. As much as she loved her job, it was nice to spend time with people outside of work.

She looked up when a shadow fell across the freshly planted flowers. Callie Redding admired Zoe's handiwork with a bright smile.

"It's looking good, Zoe. Do you need another tray of plants or do you have enough to finish this area?"

She smiled up at her friend. "I have plenty. I thought I'd finish up here and then take a break."

"Sounds good. Don't wait too long, though. Those goodies Bridey just set out won't last around this crowd. She and Seth also brought urns of hot coffee, tea, and hot chocolate. I'm embarrassed to say that Nick and Austin are already on seconds."

She glanced toward the tables that had been set up for refreshments and frowned. "Okay, now they're on thirds, the greedy idiots. I'm going to run them off so other people can get some."

Zoe didn't blame the two men for making sure they got their fair share. Heck, Bridey's pastries were definite motivation to pick up speed getting the last few flowers planted. A muffin—or maybe two—with a tall hot chocolate sounded good right about now. She dug the last two holes and settled the plants into their new homes.

Another shadow let her know she was no longer alone. "Did you need something else, Callie?"

Except it wasn't Callie. Her heart did a slow somersault in her chest when she recognized the man standing almost within touching distance. Considering they'd been on opposite coasts for months, she should have been thrilled to have Leif right there where she could see him.

She wasn't. She struggled to find the words to say something—anything—as her hungry eyes drank in the sight of him. He was bigger than she'd remembered, his muscles more sharply defined. He'd definitely been spending a lot of time in the gym.

One thing was missing, though.

It took everything she had to push herself up from the ground to face him directly. Her knees were wobbly, but not from kneeling so long. She pointed at his left hand.

"No cane. Good for you."

Okay, that wasn't the best opening line. Blushing, she busied herself wiping some of the dirt off her knees and pulling off her gardening gloves. Just like a man to give a woman no warning. Here she was, dressed in her oldest jeans and a ratty sweatshirt.

Her attire was perfect for working in the dirt, but not for seeing him for the first time in months. It didn't help that he looked as if he'd just stepped right off the army's latest recruitment poster, his uniform crisp and clean.

Nevertheless, she tried again. "What I meant to say is that you look good, Leif. I was just talking to Callie, but she didn't mention you were back in town."

For which Callie would get an earful the first chance Zoe got. A heads-up would've been appreciated.

Leif grinned as if he read her mind. "She didn't know. Neither did Nick. The last they knew I was still visiting my mom and her family."

Okay, their friends could live another day. So why did he arrive with no warning? At first they'd kept up a steady correspondence after he left town, but for the past couple of weeks he'd been pretty much missing in action. After several of her e-mails had gone unanswered, she'd stopped sending them, hoping he'd get back in touch when he was ready.

Although he hadn't said so, his rehab had to be winding down, which meant the man had some major decisions to make. Good news or bad, once the final tally was in on his progress, he needed time to think it all through on his own. If he'd been in contact with Nick or Callie, neither of them had said so.

"Look, I was just going to get a cup of hot chocolate and one of Bridey's muffins before your buddies Nick and Austin eat them all. Want to join me?"

"I'd love to, especially after the glimpse I got of all the stuff on her table, not to mention they didn't feed us on the plane. Let's grab some and then head over to our usual table."

As they made their way through the line, several people stopped to greet Leif, including Tim and Kevin from the veterans' group. As much as she wanted to have Leif to herself, the interruptions gave her some much-needed time to pull herself together.

Muffins and hot chocolate in hand, they headed for the table and sat facing the creek, which at least allowed them the illusion of privacy. Poor Bridey's muffins might as well have been made from sawdust for all Zoe could tell, and her best mocha hot chocolate tasted like sludge.

Zoe gave up and set everything aside. Leif hadn't come all this distance just to sample the local baked goods. He'd done a more credible job of consuming his own muffin, but right now he was sitting with his hands wrapped around his drink as if more intent on absorbing its warmth than drinking it.

"Sorry I've been off-line and out of touch the past two weeks. There's been a lot going on, although that's no excuse."

"It's all right." Although it really wasn't. "I figured you had something going on."

He took a deep breath and then another one, which only increased Zoe's growing sense of dread. "The doctors released me. No more surgery. No more rehab. When it was all said and done, I got back about eighty percent of the mobility in my leg and ankle. If I continue the exercises on my own, I might even get back a little more, but they made no promises. The pain is gone, though. Mostly, anyway."

She was happy for him. She really was, but did that mean he could get assigned to another combat unit, even if just in a support capacity? There was only one way to find out.

"So are you going to be deployed again?"

There. She'd given voice to the one question she'd never wanted to have to ask him. Despite all her claims that she couldn't stand being involved with an active-duty soldier again, her heart knew that was no longer true. She would learn to live with the fear if that was the only way to keep Leif in her life.

He set his drink aside and reached for her hand. "That all depends. How are things going for you?"

One of the conclusions she'd come to through the long months of meetings and therapy was that she had no right to force the man she loved to choose between her and the life he wanted. If Leif's sense of duty drove him to head back into danger, she would somehow find the strength to support his decision and live with the risks. He was that important to her.

She needed to tell him that.

"I haven't had a nightmare in a couple of months. Joining the support group and talking things out with people who've been there, done that, has really helped. So has seeing the therapist Pastor Haliday recommended. I only have to see her once a month now."

She offered him a teasing smile. "I figure I've got about eighty percent of my calmness back. If I keep working at it, I might get back a little more, but no promises."

Leif's laughter had her joining in. "Good for you! So I guess it was time well spent for both of us."

His arm snaked around her shoulders to pull her closer. It felt so good, so sweetly familiar. She leaned against him, taking simple pleasure in the moment.

He drew a long breath. "Damn, I've missed you, Zoe. Missed this."

His words were a gift. She'd hate to be the only one who'd had a gaping hole in her life the past five months. "Yeah, e-mails and phone calls are okay for a while, but they don't come close to actually having you right here beside me."

He looked around them and frowned. "I'd really hoped to have you more to myself when I got here."

She jabbed his ribs with her elbow. "Well, if you had called to let me know you were coming, that could have been arranged."

"Yeah, I know, but I wanted to surprise you. I've been on the run for the past two weeks taking care of a bunch of stuff so I don't have to go back there for a while. I'd been staying with my father and his family during rehab, but I needed to spend a little time with my mom's side, too."

His expression grew more serious. "I wanted to let them know that I would be moving to the West Coast."

"How did they take the news?"

"They weren't thrilled that I won't be living on the same side of the country as they are."

Her pulse was picking up speed. Did that mean what she hoped it did? That he'd been transferred to the local army base?

And was he going to make her pry it out of him with

a crowbar? Or better yet, his combat knife if he didn't start talking a whole lot faster.

"You still haven't answered my question, Leif. When are you being deployed?"

"That's the thing. I'm not." He looked down at her with a sad smile. "Going back, that is. Yeah, maybe they could have reassigned me, but it wouldn't be to a combat unit. Things over there are dangerous enough without having someone who isn't one hundred percent. What if something triggered the nerve pain again?"

She shuddered at the thought. "I'm sorry, Leif. I know that's what you wanted."

He stared out at the mountains in the distance. "You know, as it turned out, it wasn't. That last night, at the barbecue before I left, Mitch told me that he wanted it to be his decision whether or not to walk away from his career. I think that's what I really wanted all along.

"And when it came right down to it, I couldn't picture me back over there, going through all of that again, especially without Nick and Spence. It wouldn't be the same."

She still owed him the truth. "I guess it's a bit late to be telling you this, but I would've supported your decision to go if that's what you wanted, Leif."

"Thank you for that."

He stood up and looked around. "Listen, can we walk for a little while? I've been cooped up in a plane most of the day, and I need to work out some of the kinks."

They strolled along the river for quite some distance, until they'd left the rest of the work party behind.

Finally, Leif coasted to a stop to stare up at the sky. "So I have one more decision to make, but I needed to talk to you first. Nick still wants me to go into business with him. To be honest, I don't know much about construction, but he says he'll teach me. Seems if he had to choose, he'd rather have someone he trusts with his life over someone he can trust with a power saw. I think there's a compliment in there somewhere, but with Nick you never know."

"That sounds like him."

"Yeah, it does, but he's right. Besides, I still plan to finish my degree in business, so I can handle that part of things for our company."

"It sounds like a perfect plan for both of you."

"There's still one piece missing."

He gathered her into his arms. "When I left, I told you I loved you, and that hasn't changed. I'm really hoping you still feel the same way about me, because Snowberry Creek is the perfect place for an ex-soldier like me to build a new life. I want to live here, but only if I can have it all: the house, the picket fence, the dog, a couple of kids, and a wife. I'm thinking the first boy should be named David. So, what do you think, Zoe? Any part of that sound good to you?"

It was a good thing Leif was strong. Right now, without his support, she would've been in a boneless heap on the ground. This wonderful man was offering her everything she'd ever wanted.

"Not just part of it, Leif. All of it."

Through a sheen of tears, she glared up at him with an anger she didn't feel. "But don't think this is going to count as an official proposal, Corporal."

"Why not?"

"Look at me and then look at you. I look like I've been playing in the dirt all morning, which I have, while you're all spit-and-polished handsome. It's so not fair. I want a romantic dinner, flowers, some of that special slow dancing you're so good at, to be followed by an official proposal. Have I made myself clear?"

He released her long enough to snap to attention, salute and all.

"Yes, ma'am! Perfectly clear. May I have permission to kiss you, ma'am?"

Happier than she'd been in years, she stepped back into Leif's waiting arms. "Permission granted, Corporal."

See what happens next in the
Snowberry Creek series in

A Reason to Love

Available in May 2014 wherever books and
e-books are sold.
Turn the page for a special preview. . . .

A last name shouldn't be a burden, but Melanie's sat squarely on her shoulders as she strolled through the cemetery. The pressure increased dramatically as she passed the neat rows of nearly identical markers, all bearing the same inscription: Wolfe.

The library in town had the same name carved in the arch over the front door, as did the local high school. There was no escaping her family heritage here in Snowberry Creek, so Melanie moved on down the hillside, taking her time to enjoy the fresh air and warm sunshine. Rushing wouldn't change a thing.

Her great-great-grandfather, Josiah Wolfe, had parked his covered wagon next to a small stream tumbling down through the foothills of the Cascades and shoved the family's roots down deep into the rocky soil. He'd been an ambitious man, one determined to make his mark in the world, and the town of Snowberry Creek was his creation.

There, under his firm hand, the family had proudly

flourished in both number and wealth for two generations. Even the stock market crash and the Great Depression had been mere setbacks. Since that time, the size of the family had dwindled dramatically in number until there were only two Wolfes left in town: Melanie and her mother, Sandra. But the money had slowly found its way back into the family coffers, and the Wolfe fortune was rock solid.

Or at least that was the fairy tale Melanie had always been told.

She reluctantly started down the slope to where a brand new granite headstone had been set in place. Her mother had instructed Melanie to ensure that everything had been done properly. Melanie had bitten back the suggestion that if her mother was worried about it, she could always come back to check it out for herself. Lord knows there were more important things on Melanie's to-do list screaming for her attention right now.

Instead, here she was playing the part of a dutiful daughter again. It was a role she'd never been well-suited for, but right now she had no other choice. Not since something inside her mother had shattered the day her husband's heart stop beating. Three weeks after the funeral, the reality of their changed circumstances had come crashing down. Sandra had immediately left town on an extended visit to her older sister, Marcia, down in Oregon, abandoning Melanie to deal with the fallout from her father's death alone.

It would take a better person than Melanie to not resent having her whole life uprooted, especially when she'd worked so hard to escape Snowberry Creek in the first place. But unfortunately, according to Melanie's aunt, Sandra Wolfe had become little more than a shadow of herself and rarely left the house at all. Figuring out what to do about that was also on Melanie's to-do list.

She coasted to a stop a short distance from her father's grave. From a distance, the gray granite marker blended in seamlessly with all the others. It was only on closer inspection that she could see the polished stone was a little shinier than those on either side of it.

Edmond Wolfe would've approved. Even in life, he'd preferred to maintain a quiet, dignified lifestyle. The only anomaly had been that bright red pickup truck he'd loved so much. Looking back, Melanie should've known something was wrong when he'd sold it days before he'd died. What other signs had she missed that all was not as it should have been? She'd grown up believing her parents were financially secure and that her father had inherited her great-great-grandfather's head for business.

As it turned out, she'd been wrong on both counts.

The silence in the cemetery was oppressive, but what could she say to a slab of granite? She settled for the obvious. "Well, Dad, looks like they got everything on your headstone right. It suits you."

Considering all it contained was his full name and the years that spanned his life, there wasn't much that could've gone wrong. The Wolfe family didn't go in for inspirational sayings or emotional displays, private or public. Melanie snapped a picture with her phone to text to her mother after she got home. For now, she set down the small bouquet of lilies she'd brought for her father's grave.

Staring down at the headstone, she whispered, "Dad, the business is on the brink of disaster. I'm doing my best to figure things out, but I've got so many questions I wish I could ask you right now."

Not that he would've liked answering them. He'd

never discussed finances with his wife, much less his only daughter. No, like his father and grandfather before him, her father had preferred to shelter women from the hard realities of the business world. Well, that train had left the station. Melanie now knew all too much about the precarious state of the family's finances.

It was time to get moving. She had other, happier places to be this evening. Turning to leave, she realized she was no longer alone on the hillside. A man dressed in a camouflage uniform stood by a grave on the far side of the cemetery. He had his back to her as he stared down at one of the markers. From the slump in his shoulders, the name on the headstone had to be causing him great pain.

She knew why because she knew who was buried there: Spence Lang. Last summer, the whole town had turned out for his funeral to pay homage to one of their own. The war was being waged on the other side of the world, but that day it had come home to Snowberry Creek.

Although she'd been living in Spokane at the time, Melanie had taken the day off work and had driven down to attend the service. She'd owed Spence that much. The solemn ceremony had been excruciatingly painful in its intensity. As the final strands of "Taps" faded away, the army honor guard had carefully folded the flag that had covered the coffin and presented it to Vince Locke, Spence's uncle.

Melanie bet she hadn't been the only one who had wanted to snatch it right back out of that bastard's hands. Considering the despicable way that man treated his nephew in life, Vince didn't deserve the honor of claiming that last reminder of Spence's service to their country. It had been a relief to see Callie, Spence's best friend, take it from him before he left the cemetery.

Even now, months later, the memory still made Melanie's heart ache. He'd been such a force of nature, always a bit wild but with an easy smile for everyone.

Even the shy daughter of the first family of Snowberry Creek.

God, she'd had such a crush on Spence back in their senior year, not that she'd ever admitted how she felt about him. If anyone had found out, it would've only embarrassed Melanie in front of the whole school. Not to mention her parents would've been horrified to learn their daughter was attracted to the town bad boy.

Enough about the past.

No doubt the soldier had come to town for the wedding, the same one Melanie would be attending. Callie was marrying Nick Jenkins, who had served in Afghanistan with Spence. The couple had met when Nick had driven across the country to bring Callie the dog their unit had adopted over there. The couple might have bonded first over their shared loss, but there was no doubt about how much they loved each other. In truth, Melanie was a little jealous.

It was time to get moving if she was going to arrive at the church on time. But before heading for her car, the least she could do was introduce herself to the soldier and maybe nudge him along, too, since he hadn't moved since she'd first spotted him. Visiting Spence's grave was no doubt hard for the guy, and who could blame him? How many of his other friends had been wounded or killed over there?

As she made her way across the cemetery, she decided to do more than simply exchange names with the man. For Spence's sake, she would offer to show him the way to the church. If he was in town by himself, maybe she would even invite him to sit with her. That way he would meet at least one other person in the crowd of locals besides the groom and his best man, Leif, another member of Spence's unit.

If the soldier was aware of Melanie's approach, he gave no sign of it. He remained frozen in that one spot even though Melanie made no effort to be especially quiet as she approached. She stopped a few steps away, pausing right in front of the double headstone that marked the grave of Spence's parents.

"Excuse me? I don't mean to intrude, but I was wondering if you were in town for the Jenkins-Redding wedding. If so, I'm headed there myself and thought you might like to follow me to the church."

The soldier's shoulders snapped back as if coming to attention. He didn't turn to face her, but something about his rigid stance and clenched fists bothered her. Melanie backed up a step, keenly aware that she was a woman alone with a strange man on an isolated hillside.

Suddenly, she didn't want him to turn around even if she couldn't pinpoint the reason for her misgivings. When he finally glanced back over his shoulder, her pulse went into overdrive as she tried to make sense of what she was seeing. That jawline. That profile. They were all too familiar even as her head tried to convince her heart that what she was seeing—no, make that *who* she was seeing—just wasn't possible.

"Melanie?"

With that single word, her lungs quit working altogether as her knees buckled and the ground came rushing up to meet her. She heard a muttered curse as a pair of strong arms caught her right before she hit the ground. She stared up at the man's face, blinking hard as if that would clear her vision. When that didn't change the new reality of her world, she pointed out the obvious.

"Spence?"